AF069752

THE CATALIN CONNECTION

TREVOR DOUGLAS

BOOKS

Vinci Books

vinci-books.com

Published by Vinci Books Ltd in 2026

1

Copyright © Trevor Douglas 2023

The author has asserted their moral right to be identified as the author of this work in accordance with the Copyright, Designs and Patents Act 1988. This work is a work of fiction. Names, characters, places and incidents are the product of the author's imagination or are used fictitiously. Any resemblance to actual persons, living or dead, places and incidents is entirely coincidental.
All rights reserved. No part of this publication may be copied, reproduced, distributed, stored in any retrieval system, or transmitted in any form or by any means, including photocopying, recording, or other electronic or mechanical methods, nor used as a source for any form of machine learning including AI datasets, without the prior written permission of the publisher.
The publisher and the author have made every effort to obtain permissions for any third party material used in this book and to comply with copyright law. Any queries in this respect should be brought to the attention of the publisher and any omissions will be corrected in future editions.
A CIP catalogue record for this book is available from the British Library.
Paperback ISBN: 9781036704032
The EU GPSR authorised representative is Logos Europe, 9 rue Nicolas Poussion, 17000 La Rochelle, France contact@logoseurope.eu

By Trevor Douglas

The Catalin Series
The Catalin Connection
The Catalin Code
The Catalin Crossing

The Bridgette Cash Mystery Thriller Series
Cold Comfort
Cold Trail
Cold Hard Cash
The Cold Light of Day
Out in the Cold
Hot and Cold

Rowan Whitecross Murder Mystery Series
Murder on Stark Street

Standalone Novel
The Final Proposition

Throughout the development of this book I undertook research into people with disabilities, particularly those who are confined to wheelchairs. I read many inspiring stories of people who have refused to let their condition get in the way of them living their best life and achieving their goals.

If you fit into this category in any way, this book is dedicated to you.

Chapter One

Bucharest, Romania

The black S-Class Mercedes crawled up the laneway before coming to a stop next to a large hole in a chain-link fence. From his position on the upper level at the back of the warehouse, Petru watched through a broken window as the driver casually got out of the vehicle. He felt his gut tighten as the driver walked around to the back of the vehicle and popped the trunk. Petru kept his focus on the driver as he glanced up at a gray sky. He guessed the driver was about thirty years of age. Dressed in denim jeans and a black leather jacket, the driver looked like a bodybuilder—not the typical guy who drove a limousine worth two hundred thousand euros.

From his vantage point in the abandoned building, Petru focused on the windows of the Mercedes, narrowing his eyes to see if he could see anyone else inside. But the fading afternoon sun and dark window tint on the vehicle made the task impossible. The driver scratched his shaved head while looking up and down the laneway. Satisfied that he was alone, he removed a long metal object from the trunk. At first, Petru thought it was a rifle, but then quickly realized the man was holding a large pair of bolt cutters. After closing the trunk, the driver rapped once on the roof. Immediately, both rear doors of the vehicle opened and two men got out. They walked to the front of the vehicle and stood in a huddle with the driver, staring up at the factory.

Petru eased his wheelchair back from the window just a fraction. This area of the building was naturally dark and he was confident he wouldn't be spotted in the shadows. He grimaced as he watched the three men engage in conversation as they looked up at the building. The other two men were not as tall as the driver, but they were dressed similarly. Petru swore under his breath. These were guys you didn't want to mess with; not in a bar, not on the street, not anywhere. They seemed in no hurry. The shortest of the three lit a cigarette while the middle guy took a call on his cell phone.

Petru felt a shiver run down his spine as the man with the cigarette withdrew a pistol from his pocket. It was a brazen move during daylight hours, even in a secluded area of an industrial estate in Sector 4. The man seemed to have no fear of reprisals as he continued to smoke while he studied the building. Petru grimaced—he was in no doubt they had come for him.

The man who had been on his cell phone disconnected and put the device back in his jacket pocket. As if by magic, the phone became a pistol as he withdrew his hand. He made pointing gestures with his other hand as he studied the building. It was clear to Petru that he was the leader, as he issued instructions to the other men. He knew they were planning their entry as the man pointed toward the building's rear loading dock.

Petru had been hiding out in the warehouse for days. Despite being confined to a wheelchair, he had scouted the building for entry and exit points before considering it for shelter. The two doors at the front of the building had been welded shut. A set of metal stairs at the side of the building led up to a fire exit for the upper level. Even though he couldn't get up the stairs, the sizable padlock on the fire door was clearly visible and he hadn't investigated the entrance any further. After wheeling around to the back of the building, he had discovered a rear door that had also been secured by another heavy padlock. Despite being rusted with age, it still appeared secure. The roller door for the loading dock was another matter. After maneuvering his wheelchair up the dock's ramp, he discovered the lugs that had welded the roller door to its frame had been broken off. Even with his disability, it had only taken him a couple of minutes to get inside what would become his temporary home.

As he watched the men pick their way through a hole in the fence, Petru let out a long breath. They would be inside in minutes, and it would be impossible for him to hide. He had hoped his hideout would have kept him safe until he was ready to leave Bucharest. All his plans were in place. Another few hours was all he needed, and he had been very careful to cover his tracks on the few occasions he had left the building. He wondered how the men had tracked him down. Was it just guesswork? He doubted it. Luca Razvan, the man who wanted him dead, had deep pockets and would have spared no expense in finding him. Ultimately, the question didn't matter anymore as Petru watched the three men screw silencers to their pistols as they waded through the weeds and rubbish toward the rear of the building.

Petru considered his options as the men paused about halfway across the open area between the laneway and the warehouse. He knew he probably only had minutes to live, but he wasn't about to give up without a fight. If he could take out one or two of them along the way, he would consider that a victory. Petru cocked his head slightly to try and hear their conversation, but he wasn't close enough to make out what they were saying. He assumed they were planning how they would enter and conduct their search.

The warehouse was a concrete and metal construction. Petru had guessed it was about seventy years old when he had first entered the building and started exploring. The lower level had rows of empty industrial shelving that were covered in dust and rat droppings. He figured the building had originally been a textile factory after coming across old plans and documents in one of the two upstairs rooms while looking for a place to sleep. He wasn't sure how long the building had been abandoned, but its most recent tenants had used the ground floor as a meth lab and the upper rooms on the mezzanine as sleeping quarters until they were arrested in a drug raid a few weeks earlier.

Far from the center of the city, and with most of its windows broken, the building was cold, damp, and drafty and had little appeal even to homeless people. The meth people had rigged up power via an illegal line they had run out of an adjacent building. To Petru's surprise, the power had not been disconnected and he had been thankful it gave him a chance to keep his laptop and cell phone charged.

Petru had hoped, even prayed, that this day would never come. He was now richer than he ever dared dream. That part of his plan had paid off and he could now start a new life free from the crime and violence that had marked out most of his life in Bucharest. At first, he had been stunned when the message had finally come through from his contact in Vancouver that the money was now in his bank account. Now a millionaire, he was tempted to spend his last two days in Bucharest in a five-star hotel, sleeping in a king-size bed rather than on a soiled mattress in an abandoned warehouse. The temptation to eat gourmet meals rather than beans and stale crackers had also been tempting. But he decided it wasn't worth the risk. Here, he was out of the way, in an abandoned part of the city, and far from prying eyes. At a five-star hotel, he would have been surrounded by people and he knew that as a young man who was paralyzed from the waist down, he would attract attention. Razvan had his people everywhere, and there would be a bounty on his head. He realized now that staying here as long as he had was a huge mistake as he watched the three men below strategize their entry. He gritted his teeth. He should have shifted around—perhaps staying overnight in cheap hotels before moving on would have kept him safe. He cursed under his breath as he realized his strategy had been flawed and would now cost him his life.

He had made his defense plans as best he could. There was little he could do to protect himself. Without a gun, he was an easy target in a wheelchair. The three men moved forward again. He frowned as the driver veered to the left, while the other two headed directly to the rear of the building. Petru swore again as he realized the driver was going to head up the side stairs with the bolt cutters. The flimsy preparations he had made to protect himself had relied on people entering via the rear roller door only.

He let out a long sigh and murmured, "This is it," as he rolled away from the window.

Petru peered over the mezzanine's wooden balustrade at the ground floor below. As an added precaution, he had wedged a rod into the frame of the roller door on the inside to prevent the door from being lifted. He only ever removed it when he left the building and figured it would buy him a minute or two while the men jiggled it loose. He looked down at the crowbar in his lap. It would be useless against two men, but it might prove effective against someone coming up the stairs if he could surprise them. Now adept at using his wheelchair, Petru spun his transport in a one-hundred-and-eighty degree arc and headed for the fire door at the other end of the mezzanine. Petru tried to focus on the job at hand as he wheeled himself at full pace along the seventy-foot corridor. Just three months ago, he had been an able-bodied twenty-three-year-old with a bright future. But that future had been ripped away. Now, just a shell of the man he once was, he resigned himself to what was ahead.

He heard a metallic snap just as he reached the end of the corridor and knew the driver had already used the bolt cutters to cut through the door's external lock. The driver tried to push the door open but was thwarted by an internal latch that prevented his entry. He watched as the driver briefly peered in through a narrow security window next to the door before attempting to bust the door open with two huge shoulder charges. Petru hoped the driver would give up and retreat downstairs when the door held firm, but the driver wasn't easily dissuaded. He felt helpless as the driver cut away three metal security bars for the window with his bolt cutters. He gasped as the glass in the window exploded just a few seconds later as the driver rammed the bolt cutters through to make an opening.

The Catalin Connection

High on adrenaline, Petru wheeled forward as the driver reached his right hand through the narrow opening to unlatch the door. His first impulse was to swing the crowbar at the man's arm, but as Petru caught sight of the broken glass embedded in the bottom of the window frame, he changed tack and grabbed the driver's arm with both hands.

He pulled down for all he was worth, savoring the small win as the driver roared in pain as the broken glass embedded itself deep into the flesh of the man's bicep. The driver tried to withdraw his arm, but despite his disability, Petru's grip held firm. The driver grunted, but still managed to unlatch the door with his free hand and push it open. Petru felt his chair being pushed backward as the door opened about two feet. Before he could adjust, the driver reached around with his free hand, swinging the bolt cutters wildly at Petru's head. Petru ducked under the blow and raised the man's right arm again and slammed it down a second time onto the broken glass. The man bellowed in pain and dropped the cutters. Pressing his face up against the window opening to get a better look at his quarry, the driver shoved back hard against the door. They locked eyes for a moment as the driver swore at him in Russian before he reached around the door with his free arm to grab at Petru's shirt. In response, Petru yanked down hard on the man's right arm a third time, further embedding the broken glass into his arm.

The driver, now a ball of sweat, seemed oblivious to the pain. Gripping the door with his free hand, he attempted to pull his injured arm back through the window opening. Despite spending many hours in the gym before losing the use of his legs, Petru realized he was no match for the strength of the larger man. Keeping his grip as firm as he could with one hand, Petru picked up the crowbar and swung it at the man's right forearm. He heard a snapping sound above the bellow of pain the driver made and knew the crowbar had broken a bone as the driver's head momentarily slumped forward. Any thought of victory was short-lived as the man regrouped and hooked his foot around the door for purchase as he re-positioned his body. Before Petru could react, the man swung a clenched left fist around the edge of the door at his head. The fist struck a glancing blow but did no actual damage. Spurred on, the driver attempted to pull his right arm back through the opening again. Petru could feel the momentum shifting as the blood from the driver's wounds dripped down onto his hands, making his grip slippery. He knew he could only hold on for a few seconds more as they continued to wrestle.

The driver re-positioned his body again and peered around the door at Petru. With his head covered in sweat and his complexion now red, the driver's face turned into a macabre grin as he reared back for a second punch. Petru knew he only had two options and a fraction of a second to make a decision. The first was to duck and hopefully avoid the man's punch. But that would only buy him a few more seconds before he swung again. The second option was to swing the crowbar at the man's head. Despite the driver rearing back a long way, he knew the math for speed and distance didn't work in his favor and he wouldn't be able to avoid the man's punch. The survival instinct made the decision for him, and he chose option two.

Petru swung the crowbar as the man's fist connected with his head. His vision exploded into a sea of colors. First, all he saw was vivid yellow, and then purple, before the palette settled on a cool white. He wasn't sure if the driver's blow caused him to momentarily pass out, but when his vision cleared, he saw the driver's arm was still hooked in the broken window frame, but the rest of his body was hidden below the window sill. Still gripping the crowbar, Petru cautiously wheeled forward and peered out onto the landing. The driver's head was slumped at an odd angle and his eyes remained closed as blood gushed from a large gash the crowbar had inflicted on his skull. The ringing sound in Petru's head seemed to grow louder as he stared down at the pool of blood forming beneath the man. Petru wasn't sure if he was dead or just unconscious. Before he could investigate, the ringing sound changed pitch and turned into a metal-on-metal sound as it reached a crescendo. Petru whipped around as he realized the source of the sound was external. He swore softly as he stared down through the banister rails at the rear roller door as it slowly began to rise.

Chapter Two

Petru gritted his teeth. When the roller door had risen about three feet, the guy who had been smoking a cigarette scurried underneath and was quickly followed by his partner. He watched as the two men disappeared amongst the rows of storage racks on the ground level in search of him. Unsure what to do, he knew they would complete their search in minutes and then turn their attention to the upper level.

He contemplated trying to escape by the external side stairs, but realized that would be impossible. Even if he got out of his wheelchair and dragged himself down the steps, he doubted he would get anywhere near the bottom before he was discovered. He thought about trying to barricade himself in one of the two rooms upstairs, but the meager furniture wouldn't hold them at bay for long. Petru looked to the other end of the mezzanine. His only hope of survival was the ramp that lead up from the ground floor.

When he had first explored the building, he had discovered the elevator to the upper level didn't work and the only other internal access was by a wooden ramp. The ramp was attached to the rear wall of the building, but years of exposure to the elements through the broken upper windows had left it in serious disrepair. The top section had almost rotted away completely and had been replaced with a flimsy plywood span. The structure, he presumed built by the meth people, creaked and flexed under his weight as he attempted to roll across it. After finding used mattresses in both upstairs offices, he decided this was the best place to sleep. But the ramp bothered him and he knew he was tempting fate if he continued to use it. If it broke, the twenty-five-foot drop to the concrete below would either kill him or leave him even worse off than he already was.

Petru had needed a solution and found an old chain pulley, along with some ropes, in a locker on the ground floor. With some trial and error, he had managed to lob a rope over one of the building's roof beams and then used it to secure the pulley system. He needed a landing area and had knocked out a section of the mezzanine's balustrade near the ramp to give him a landing platform. With practice, and the aid of a sling he had fashioned from some old straps, he was able to raise and lower himself in in under ten minutes.

Petru could hear the two men crashing around downstairs as they searched for him. The noise made him recall his second night in the warehouse. The sound of someone trying to break in through the rear door had woken him. Petru wasn't sure if it was homeless people or Razvan's team looking for him, but he knew he needed more of a defense. The plywood span on the ramp was the weak link and he used an old saw he'd found to cut almost completely through the upper support beams that connected the ramp to the mezzanine. He figured the weight of anyone larger than a small child would cause the ramp to collapse. Petru let out a breath as the two men moved back through the shelving racks. He knew it would only be seconds now before they headed up the ramp to continue their search.

In unison, both men looked up. Cigarette guy pointed towards him and shouted, "There he is!"

Petru felt his blood run cold as the two men sprinted up the ramp. Phone guy was about fours steps in front of cigarette guy and there was every chance the ramp would only take out one of them.

Petru held his breath as phone guy sprinted across the plywood span. He managed three steps before it collapsed under his weight. His momentum carried him forward towards the mezzanine's platform edge. In one smooth maneuver, phone guy let go of his gun and grabbed hold of the edge of the platform with both hands as he fell. As he held on like a trapeze artist, Petru glanced back at cigarette guy who was not so lucky. By the time phone guy had hit the temporary span, cigarette guy was only a step behind and had no time to react as the span collapsed beneath him.

Petru watched as the concrete below brought him to an abrupt halt. While the man lay motionless in a crumpled heap, phone guy was now pulling himself up onto the platform. Petru gripped the rims of his rear wheels and rolled forward at speed.

Using all the strength he could muster, Petru closed the gap quickly, but not quickly enough. Ten feet still separated them when phone guy scrambled up onto the mezzanine. As phone guy withdrew a second gun from his jacket, Petru powered forward crashing his chair into him. The man grunted as the force knocked him backward and off his feet. Petru watched as the gun dislodged from his grip and skidded across the floor.

The Catalin Connection

Petru grabbed the crowbar from his lap and swung it at phone guy's back as he went to stand. Phone guy groaned and collapsed again, giving Petru time to wheel around behind him towards the gun.

As he reached down to pick up the weapon, Petru heard scrambling behind him and knew phone guy was getting to his feet again. Petru spun his chair in a one-hundred-and-eighty degree arc and re-gripped the crowbar.

Phone guy looked down at the gun beneath the wheelchair and grinned. "Looks like we have a stalemate."

Petru held his position. Steering his chair with only his right hand while he held the crowbar with his left was going to be difficult. The man circled to his right, testing out how adept Petru was at moving his chair to protect his position. Petru eased his chair around so that he was still facing the man head on. The man stepped forward, stopping about eight feet in front of him as Petru raised the crowbar. Phone guy focused on the gun which was still beneath the wheelchair as he kept circling right.

Petru cursed under his breath as phone guy stepped on a piece of wood. The man looked down and said, "Well, well, what do we have here?" as he picked up an old broom handle.

Petru silently admonished himself, *'Let him make the first move,'* as phone guy examined the object.

The man looked at a wire hook Petru had wrapped around one end of the pole before glancing up at the pulley system he had rigged up next to the ramp.

"This is how you get up and down, isn't it?" he said. "You use the hook to bring the sling in and then—"

Phone guy never finished the sentence. Petru saw a blur

to his left as the man lunged forward and swung the broom handle at his head. The weapon smashed into his neck, but the handle was old and brittle and snapped on impact. Phone guy propped and then rushed forward bringing the broken handle down like a club.

Petru raised his crowbar to deflect the blow. The handle glanced off the crowbar and barely clipped Petru's shoulder on the way through. Phone guy's momentum caused him to overbalance and crash into the frame of Petru's chair.

The man tried to pull back as Petru swung the crowbar again, but he wasn't quick enough and let out a groan as the bar crashed into his shoulder. Petru swung the bar again and phone guy's eyes rolled back into his head as the bar struck his temple. The man went limp and slumped into his lap as blood streamed from the wound.

Petru tried to push him off, but he was too weak from fighting and instead rolled his wheelchair backward until the man slid off. He looked down to see if he was still alive and cursed as he realized the man had collapsed on top of the gun.

Too exhausted to retrieve the weapon just yet, Petru put his hand up to massage the welt left on his neck by the broom handle. Staring back along the corridor, he noticed the driver's arm was still caught in the fire exit window and it didn't look like he had moved since their encounter. Petru wheeled his chair to the edge of the mezzanine and peered down at the concrete below. Cigarette guy still lay motionless in a pool of blood. He was positive the man was dead and then looked up through one of the broken glass windows as the last remnants of daylight streamed in. It would be dark soon, and he knew Razvan would be eager for an update from his thugs. He figured he had half an hour at most before the reinforcements would arrive to finish him off. He needed to get out of the warehouse as soon as possible, but he wasn't leaving without the gun.

Petru wheeled back over to phone guy who lay motionless on his side. As he studied the man's sizable frame, he realized there was no way he could move the man's body while he was sitting in his wheelchair. With a practiced move, he locked the rear wheels and slid out of his chair. Using his hands and arms, Petru dragged himself across the floor toward phone guy's body.

After a deep breath, Petru gripped the man's clothing and pushed him over onto his back. He stared down with relief at the sight of the gun and almost allowed himself a smile. As he reached forward to pick it up, a voice called out from the other end of the corridor. He knew without looking up that it wasn't the driver suddenly back from the dead who was advancing along the corridor. It was a voice he was familiar with. A voice that had come to represent pure evil to him.

A shiver went down his spine as he slowly raised his head. Even before the man emerged from shadows, he knew it was Luca Razvan who had a gun pointed at his chest.

Chapter Three

12 Weeks Earlier

Petru removed his headset and pushed back from the computer screen. He did his best to shut out the battery of noises being made by his colleagues in their neighboring cubicles as he stared up at the stained ceiling tiles. Above the babble of his colleagues urging 'clients' to follow their advice and the clatter of keyboards entering information into databases at eighty words per minute, he murmured, "What the hell am I doing here?"

Petru stood up and stared out across the sea of tiny office pods. Each was occupied by someone with a similar profile to his; young, intelligent, ambitious, and willing to do almost anything to get ahead. He glanced up at the clock on the wall. It was still ten minutes until his scheduled break, but he needed time out. Time to collect his thoughts and regroup. Time to rationalize what he was doing so that he could pick up the phone again to contact the next victim.

He glanced across at Andrei, who sat in his small glass

office in the far corner of the second floor office. From his fishbowl, Andrei Pellea supervised a team of sixty 'security analysts.' His job was little more than monitoring each worker to make sure they were working the phones diligently during their ten-hour shifts, and ensuring they were bringing in the required revenue each week.

Some of his colleagues feared Andrei; he had a hot temper and wasn't afraid to publicly berate anyone who was under performing. But Petru had worked him out in his first week on the job and wasn't scared of him. He knew if you brought in your quota each week, you were left alone. Andrei wasn't any different from the rest of them, even though he was ten years older. He was just another guy who did what he was told. He'd made it as far as his goldfish bowl in the corner, but Petru doubted he had the talent to go any further.

Petru studied him for a moment. Andrei had his head down, staring at his desk with his cell phone glued to one ear. He would occasionally get up and walk around, checking that everyone was hard at work for LEU Security.

Petru watched as Andrei swiveled in his chair to face the back wall of his office. As he continued his call, he gestured wildly with one hand. He had noticed Andrei did this a lot when he got animated. He wondered if he turned his back on the team because they distracted him, or if he was afraid someone was going to lip read what he was saying. Petru didn't care. This was an opportune moment to walk out, and he didn't need a second invitation. He strode through the office to the rear metal fire door and out onto the balcony.

In truth, it was a stretch to call the landing area at the back of the office a balcony. The 'balcony' was about eight feet long and two feet wide and littered with cigarette butts. He'd given up smoking at sixteen and normally found the stench of cigarettes nauseating. But today, as he looked down over the rusting balcony rail at the small parking lot at the back of his office block, he barely noticed the smell.

He watched as a mangy black cat prowled around beside an open dumpster looking for food scraps. The animal looked up in his direction before turning and sauntering off down the narrow delivery laneway at the side of the building. Petru closed his eyes and breathed in the last rays of the morning sun as it beamed down on him. The high-rise buildings in this part of Bucharest hid the sun for most of the day. Petru knew that at roughly 11:35 AM each day, there was a small fifteen minute window where the sun reached the balcony. Petru used it as therapy. A chance to remind himself that there was more to life than the job he was currently stuck doing.

He tried to block out the last call. The woman was as gullible as she was vulnerable. This was not what he had signed up for. But who was he kidding? He'd been here five months and knew before the end of his second day that what they had hired him for bore no resemblance to the work he was doing each day.

A voice behind him asked, "What are you doing out here, Petru? It's still ten minutes until your break."

He knew without turning it was Andrei who had come to check on him.

Petru opened his eyes. As he stared down at the black cat who continued to saunter down the laneway, he said over his shoulder, "I needed a break, Andrei... I need to clear my head."

"I want you to come inside now! You're setting a poor example for the rest of the team."

"My numbers are good. I've got a day and a half to go and I've already hit my target for the week."

Andrei appeared beside him. "I don't want to make an example of you, Petru… but if I have to—"

"She has liver cancer!" roared Petru! "I found all the medical records on her computer. She's got less than six months to live. She needs the money for painkillers. It's not right—"

Andrei grabbed Petru by the shoulder and hissed, "You don't get to decide what's right. That's not your call or my call to make." Andrei let go and added, "You get paid to make revenue for LEU and now is not the time to be developing a conscience."

Petru shot back, "This is not what I signed up for. I'm a good hacker. When am I going to get my opportunity? I didn't sign up to be fleecing money from vulnerable people. I signed up to go after corporations—companies in the west who have plenty of money—"

Andrei soothed, "Your time will come."

"But taking money from people who are sick, or lonely? It's not right!

"You have to prove yourself with small things first," said Andrei as he glanced up at the third floor. "Luca allows no one into his inner circle until he's sure he can trust them."

"And how long does that take?"

"It depends," said Andrei. "Sometimes six months, sometimes longer. He knows who you are, and he knows that you're good, but he doesn't know if he can trust you yet."

"But he knows what I'm capable of or he wouldn't have hired me," said Petru with a frown. "On my own time I've been working on a college in Seattle. I've only been at it a few nights, but I've already got through two firewalls and as far as one of their Unix servers. As soon as I get in I'm going to have access to credit cards and—"

Andrea hissed, "Are you crazy? It's an unwritten rule here that you never, ever, do any hacking on your own now. That's tantamount to stealing from Luca, and he won't tolerate it."

"I want to show him what I can do."

Andrei shook his head. "Do you remember Yuri Lebedev?"

Petru nodded. "He was here when I joined, but he left at the end of my second week."

"Do you know what happened to him?"

Petru shook his head. "I assume he went back to Russia."

Andrei grimaced. "They found him in the river four days after he disappeared."

"He drowned?"

Andrew murmured, "Not exactly. He'd been shot in the back of the head three times. The river was just a convenient means of disposal."

Petru's eyes widened. "He was murdered?"

"That's not a question you need to ask, Petru. The question is why?"

"Okay, *why* was he murdered?"

"He was running a side scam using information he'd found out working here."

"How do you know this?"

"I was called up to the third floor with Yuri to talk about it. When Yuri confessed, they asked me to leave Lucas' office... I never saw Yuri again."

Petru frowned. "We all know LEU is not exactly legal, but—"

"Everybody knows LEU is a front for organized crime—that's why the pay is so good."

"But murder?" said Petru with a frown.

"You need to listen to me," said Andrei as he grabbed Petru by the shoulders. "Three bullets to the back of the head is Luca Razvan's signature. Everyone knows this, even the police."

"How does he get away with it?"

Andrei sighed. "Luca is a lot more than just the CEO of LEU Enterprises. He has many business interests and the right contacts in all the right places. High-ranking police officers, politicians and government officials are all at his beck and call. He pays them well and he can do what he likes. He's untouchable."

Andrei paused and studied Petru for a moment before adding softly, "You need to keep this in mind if you want to live to see your next birthday." Before Petru could respond, Andrei glanced at the fire door. "We need to get back inside. I don't want anyone catching me out here talking to you. Too many questions will be asked."

Chapter Four

It was almost eight PM when Petru arrived home. He usually took the subway—a trip of less than fifteen minutes. But tonight he needed to think. The walk took him over an hour, but it was what he needed to process everything he had learned from Andrei earlier that day.

He paused out front of the drab five-storey concrete apartment block that had been home for most of his life. The walk had resolved little, but it had cemented a few things in his mind. Knowing his Russian colleague had been murdered terrified him. While he worked for LEU Enterprises, he knew he was vulnerable, but how could he get out?

Petru grimaced. After his mother's stroke, eight months earlier, his world had come crashing down. Only halfway through his university studies in computer science, his part-time job as a computer repair technician wasn't enough to pay the rent and medical bills that were piling up now that his mother could no longer work. The prospect of homelessness forced him to look for full-time work to become the family's main breadwinner.

As he became more and more desperate to find a job that paid enough, a colleague at university suggested he try an IT security company called LEU. Petru did his own research and found out the company paid well, but didn't always operate completely inside the law. But he couldn't afford to be choosy and applied anyway.

During the interview, they had asked him point-blank if had ever done any hacking. When he admitted he had dabbled in it as a teenager, more for the thrill of using his skills to break into computer systems than to make money, they hired him on the spot.

The job solved some of his immediate problems. Petru now had money to pay the rent, put food on the table, and take care of his mother. But the nagging doubts about LEU grew the more he learned about what they were prepared to do to make money.

At first, he'd been able to justify it. *'I need to look after my family. I need to take care of my mother.'*

But as Luca Razvan's company began forcing him to steal money from people who were worse off than his own mother, he knew he had to look for a way out.

Petru let out a long breath as he walked in through the grimy glass doors at the front of his apartment block. The Romanian economy was going backwards at present and jobs, even in IT, were in short supply. He had been making discrete inquiries for about a month, but, so far, he hadn't found a job that paid enough to cover all the family expenses.

Andrei Pellea's warning that he may not make his next birthday echoed through his head. He didn't want to be the next employee found in the river with three bullet holes in the back of his head.

No job was worth his life. He'd always planned to go back to university to finish his degree and then get a legitimate job. But that seemed like a pipe dream. He knew enough about Luca Razvan's operation now to know that trying to leave was risky.

As he climbed the stairs to the third floor, he let out a sigh. He would need to be careful. He considered his options. Perhaps he could talk to Andrei and tactfully find out whether anyone had successfully left the business without ending up floating in the river. Petru grimaced. He wasn't sure he could trust Andrei, and asking questions might get him reported straight back to Razvan—something he needed to avoid.

He was friendly with a few of the other analysts in his team. Some of them had been there longer and perhaps knew more about how people 'left' the organization. He could always look for ways to work the question into a conversation without appearing to be overly interested. It was all he could think of at present. As he walked down the hallway on the third floor, he figured he might need to walk home more often to give him more serious thinking time—his very life could depend upon it.

After inserting the key into his apartment door, he paused a moment. This was not something he could share with his mother or his sister. He would pretend everything was normal until he had an exit strategy figured out. "Business as usual," he murmured before opening the door.

Petru stood in the doorway and glared at his sister, who was lounging on the couch in the living room watching TV in the semidarkness.

The Catalin Connection

Elena Janco was Petru's sister. She was eighteen years old, but he often felt her maturity level was closer to a twelve-year-old. She was tall, with long dark hair, high cheekbones, and an olive complexion. Elena was pretty enough to be a model and had dreamed of a career in fashion, but her mother had insisted she needed a degree first.

After some protestation, Elena had finally agreed to go to university. Her approach to her studies was hap-hazard and Petru suspected she was cutting classes. He could feel the anger welling inside him as he asked, "Where's Mamma?"

Without taking her eyes off the screen, his sister replied, "She's in bed."

"But it's not even eight o'clock."

"She was tired," said Elena with a shrug. "I gave her dinner and put her into bed."

"Did you bathe her today?"

"I didn't have time."

Petru raised an eyebrow. "Did you go to the university today?"

Elena glared at him. "What are you? My mother?"

Petru slammed the door behind him and stood with his hands on his hips. "Did you go to university today?"

"No," she answered with a smoldering look. "I studied with a friend instead."

"Which friend?"

Elena rolled her eyes. "None of your business."

"You're not doing drugs again, are you?"

Elena pointed the remote at the TV to switch it off and then snarled, "I'm going out and I don't answer to you."

"Where are you going? You need to be careful. If you get in with the wrong crowd—"

"Are you deaf?" she spat. "I don't answer to you."

Elena pushed past him and put on her coat. Without looking back, she stormed out their apartment. Petru swore under his breath. He knew he needed to be more tactful, but tact wasn't his strong suit, particularly with his sister.

After closing and locking the apartment door, he tiptoed down the tiny corridor and opened the door to check in on his mother. She had the slightly larger of the two tiny bedrooms and was snoring softly. Petru was relieved she appeared to have slept through the row he had just had with his sister.

Petru stared across the hallway at his sister's bedroom. The door was closed, and he was tempted to go in and search for drugs. He grimaced as he realized it wouldn't change anything, and he needed Elena to trust him before he could help her.

He sighed and trudged back across the threadbare carpet to the couch in the living room, which doubled as his bed. He had lost his appetite and wasn't in the mood for TV. After stripping down to his underwear, he lay down and pulled a blanket over himself. He did not know when Elena would be home or even if she would return tonight.

As he lay in the semi-darkness, he knew he wouldn't be able to sleep. He felt his stomach turn as he first thought about Elena and then about Andrei's words earlier in the day. Petru frowned. Life throwing him curve balls was nothing new. Normally, he figured out a way forward quickly. But what he'd learned today worried him. He bit down on his lip and shook his head as he realized he was in a hole and had no idea how he was going to dig himself out of it. He would need to be careful—very careful.

He reached up a hand and switched off the lamp next

to the couch and then did something he hadn't done in a long time and prayed for his sister. When he had finished, he opened his eyes and stared up into the darkness. He needed to hold it together. His family needed him now more than ever now, and he couldn't let them down.

Chapter Five

Petru tossed and turned all night. It was just after six AM when he gave up on any further sleep and opened his eyes and stretched. He needed coffee, but first he needed to pee and trudged off to the bathroom. After returning to the kitchen, he fixed himself a strong black coffee as he thought about his sister.

He hadn't bothered to check her room on the way back from the bathroom—he was a light sleeper and he knew she hadn't come home. He sighed and walked through the living room to an old set of French doors that led out onto a tiny balcony. The balcony was about eight feet wide and four feet deep. It was just big enough for two adults to stand side by side while they admired the view of the city. Unlike his sister, he rarely came out here because it was too cold for most of the year.

Elena spent hours on the balcony—and in all kinds of weather. As a pack-a-day smoker, she regularly needed to feed her nicotine habit and their mother had forbid her smoking inside the apartment. He stared down at the ashtray that seemed to live permanently on a small wrought iron cafe table. It was full of Elena's cigarette butts. Perhaps this was why he had come outside, he thought. To be closer to her.

Petru picked up the black metal ashtray. It was heavy and, according to his mother, had been crafted from metal by his father and painted black to keep it from rusting. Petru liked having it around as a reminder. Apart from a few photos, this was the only thing his mother had kept that provided a connection back to his father who had died suddenly when Petru was still a boy. She had promised Petru that he could have it when she passed, even though he didn't smoke. He liked the idea of having a permanent memento of his father—something he had made and used. Petru gagged as he caught a whiff of the cigarette butts. He put the ashtray down and leaned back against the rusted iron railing of the balcony, staring across at the Bucharest city skyline as he thought about Elena. He checked his phone to see if she had left him any messages and grimaced as he stared down at a blank screen.

Staying out all night was unlike her. Most of her friends lived in cramped apartments like she did, and staying over with anyone meant sleeping on a lumpy couch or the floor. He debated calling her, but decided against it. He wasn't sure what he would say, even if she answered. Accusing her of taking drugs had been stupid. He knew it would only get her back up and that wasn't the way to help her. He needed her to be open and honest if she was experimenting with drugs again and he would need a softer approach.

Petru turned and looked out across the city. A thick fog had settled overnight making his visibility poor. He looked down and could barely make out a truck on the street below as it tried to maneuver out of a tight parking spot to begin its daily delivery run.

As he sipped on his coffee, he tried to focus on his own problems as he thought back to yesterday's conversation with Andrei.

He had turned over each word of their discussion as he lay on the couch last night. It occurred to him that he might be the only one outside Razvan's inner circle who actually knew what had happened to Yuri Lebedev. He felt his gut tighten as he thought about Andrei's warning. Making the wrong move could be fatal, and he needed to plan his next steps carefully. He needed to get a new job—that much was certain. But would Razvan allow him to walk away from LEU? That was the question.

Petru pulled out his phone and composed a text message to his boss. He needed more time to think before he went back to LEU and decided he would call in sick. Biting down on his lower lip, he thought about some excuses. He decided not to say he had a cold or flu just in case Andrei called and he had to fake symptoms. After settling on a message, he keyed it into his phone.

Hi Andrei, Sorry, but I've been up most of the night vomiting (food poisoning, I think) and I won't be in today. Hopefully back tomorrow. Call if you need anything. Petru

Petru read the message and decided it was appropriate and pressed send. The day would not be wasted. He would look for another job, while he tried to figure out how to get out of the mess at LEU. His thoughts were interrupted by his mother as she called his name.

Petru went inside and knocked once on his mother's

door before opening it. In the dim light, her tousled gray hair covered most of her face as she tried to lift her head from the pillow.

"Good morning, Mamma. Let me open the curtain for you."

Petru did his best to make sure his smile was as natural as possible as he attended to the task. He moved back to the bed and added, "Do you need to pee, Mamma?"

She nodded and then added, "Help me up. We need to talk first."

After Petru had lifted her up into a sitting position and got her settled, she thanked him before asking, "Where's your sister?"

"She's not home at present."

"I heard you two arguing last night."

Petru grimaced. While his mother could barely walk and the paralysis had slurred her speech, her mind was still sharp. "Sorry, I thought you might have slept through that."

"Our apartment is small. I hear everything."

Petru tried to change the subject. "Should I take you to the bathroom now?"

His mother ignored the question. "About last night. Your sister..."

Petru nodded, but said nothing.

"Elena is not like you. She never has been and never will be. You got your father's drive, but that's not in her makeup."

Petru wasn't sure where his mother was going with the conversation. But she was honest, sometimes brutally direct, and he appreciated that about her.

After a moment's silence, she continued. "What is wrong, Petru?"

"Do you mean with me or Elena?" said Petru with a frown.

His mother held his gaze. "I mean with you. You have been more irritable recently. And distant…"

Petru looked away. "I guess I'm worried about Elena. She is skipping classes, and—"

"Dealing with your sister has never been easy. Unlike you, she never really got over the death of your father… She is not strong like you."

"I worry about her."

"So do I," said his mother. Reaching up with her good hand, she gently grabbed his chin and made him look at her. "But right now, I'm more worried about you?"

Petru's eyes widened. "Why?"

"Something is troubling you. I can see it in your eyes."

Petru gave his mother a tired smile. His mother had been beautiful before her stroke. But the numbness in the left side of her face made her look lopsided and she now looked twenty years older. "Work is very busy, that's all."

"You used to be so happy. You were the life of the party—the positive one."

"I guess I have more responsibility. Since your illness…"

"This is true. And I am sorry."

"It's not your fault. We are making the best of it. We are getting by."

"This responsibility… for me and your sister… it is too much."

"No, you're wrong, Mamma. I am happy looking after you."

His mother managed a weak smile with half her face. "You know, I pray for you and your sister every night. I sometimes think your sister is a lost cause, but I know you will never let me down. That is not your way."

"Thank you," managed Petru with half a smile.

They were silent for a moment before his mother said, "So, are you going to tell me what is troubling you? Or are you going to keep hiding things from me?"

"There is nothing to tell."

His mother raised the index finger of her right hand and pointed at Petru. "You are not being honest with me."

"I don't want to burden you with my problems."

"I have handled a lot in my life, Petru. The death of your father and my stroke. We have never had much money and I'm not sure why God is doing this, but I am strong. I can handle whatever troubles you."

Petru looked away as his mother added, "What are you not telling me?"

Petru let out a long sigh. "I found out some things at work... things that are very disturbing."

"What kind of things?"

"The company that I work for is engaged in some illegal activities... I am involved."

Petru shared his story with his mother. He focused on how the company was swindling people out of their life savings. He left out the details about Yuri Lebedev and played down the danger he was facing. He finished by saying it wasn't the kind of company he wanted to work for.

The room was silent for a moment. His mother looked at him with knowing eyes as if to say, 'I know you're not telling me everything.' Finally, she said, "I know nothing about computers, Petru, but I'm not surprised."

"Why are you not surprised, Mamma?" asked Petru with a frown.

"The money. It seemed to be too good to be true—how much you were earning—but being just out of hospital, I was very grateful for your help." She held his gaze and added, "So, what do you plan on doing?"

Petru shrugged. "I've called in sick today—I'm going to look for another job."

"The economy is hard at present. Are there jobs out there that pay as much?"

"It will be hard," conceded Petru. "Until I finish my university studies…"

"Can you get your old job back?"

Petru frowned. "Repairing computers at the computer store?"

His mother nodded.

"Possibly. I'm still on friendly terms with my old boss, but it doesn't pay enough. Even if I was full time, it wouldn't pay enough."

"Would it be enough for you to rent a room somewhere here in Bucharest and feed and clothe yourself until you finish your studies?"

"It would be enough," said Petru with a frown. "But I need to look after you and Elena and pay our rent."

His mother sighed. "I've been giving this a lot of thought. Elena's heart is not in her studies. She is still very much a child, and my situation is not going to get any better. I've been speaking with my sister on the telephone."

"Okay."

"Ingrid has retired and is returning to the village where we grew up. She is lonely since Uncle Emil died and would like to have me return home, too."

"Would she be able to care for you?"

His mother managed a weak smile. "We have had some

long talks about it. Ingrid used to be a nurse before she married Emil and knows what is involved. She's lonely and would like to have some of her family back home again."

A thousand thoughts raced through Petru's mind. "What about Elena?"

"She is failing in her studies," grumbled his mother. "I will insist she come with me. She can work in your uncle Joseph's bakery until she figures out what she wants to do with her life."

"She will not like it."

"I don't want her staying in the city. It is not a good influence on her. This way, she has no choice."

His mother reached out a hand and rested it on Petru's arm. "You are a good boy at heart. That is why your work is troubling you. We have done our best, but the time has come to accept that we cannot go on living like this."

Petru nodded. "But what about the apartment?"

"I will arrange for Joseph to come with the bakery truck. He will take what we need and the rest we leave behind."

They were quiet for a moment before his mother said, "There is just one more question I have for you."

"Yes?"

"Are you in danger, Petru?"

Petru answered honestly. "I'm not sure, Mamma. The man who runs the company is unpredictable."

"See if you can get your old job back. We are two weeks ahead on the rent. That will give you time to find somewhere else to live… and it will give me time to organize things with my sister."

His mother held his gaze for a while and said, "You have a good heart, my son. And I know God will look after you. Now help me up, I need to pee."

Petru helped his mother into her wheelchair. The prospect of both his mother and sister leaving Bucharest lifted a weight from his shoulders. But the gnawing feeling in the pit of his stomach remained. It didn't make leaving LEU any easier, but if he needed to hide out for a while, being on his own would increase his chances of survival.

Chapter Six

After the talk with his mother, Petru went for a long walk. His walk had included him calling in on his old boss's computer store. Petru had casually mentioned he might be going back to university and his old boss had offered him his job back on the spot. After thanking him, Petru told him he would take a day or two to think about it.

Having a job to fall back on and his mother's impending move to the country had lifted one weight from his shoulders, but he still had Luca Razvan to contend with. Andrei had called him twice during his walk and then sent a text message demanding he call him immediately. This was out of character for his boss as he had taken sick leave before without incident. He would go back to work tomorrow and pretend everything was normal for now. As much as he hated the thought of having to continue scamming money from unsuspecting victims, he didn't think he had any choice. He would wait until his mother and sister were safely out of the city before he made his move. He would find somewhere else to live—a room somewhere that didn't require a formal rental agreement and then he would leave.

After returning home late in the day, he was concerned that his sister was still not home or responding to calls. He slept fitfully that night and had awoken early the following day and tried to call her just after seven AM. He disconnected after leaving another message, pleading for her to get in touch with him, and then dropped his phone on the small kitchen table in disgust.

His mother looked at him from over a steaming cup of coffee and said, "This is so unlike her."

Petru nodded. "I'm not sure what to do, Mamma. I've called her at least ten times and left her almost as many text messages, but she won't call back."

"Should we be reporting her missing to the police?"

Petru tried to downplay the situation. "There could be many reasons why she hasn't called."

"And what are they?"

"Her phone might be flat," he mused. "Or she might have lost it. Or she might be staying with a friend and is still angry with me. Things might get worse if the police are involved."

Petru could see the worry on his mother's face. He secretly shared her concern, but tried to play it down as he announced, "I will go out and look for her. I've already messaged a couple of her girlfriends that I know through social media. Hopefully, one of them knows where she is."

"And what about your job?"

Petru grimaced. He had already told his mother he was going to pretend everything was okay at LEU until they were safely out of the city. "I promised Andrei I would be back today, but I'll call him and tell him the truth. Elena is missing and I have to find her."

His mother nodded. "And what if you don't find her?"

"If we haven't found her by five PM this evening... I will go to the police."

"I'm worried Petru. Elena might be in—"

Petru held up a finger as his phone buzzed. He looked down at the screen and murmured, "This is one of Elena's friends calling me back," as he picked up the phone.

Petru pressed the answer button and then said, "Hello."

He listened intently for a few moments. "It's not a lot to go on. Can you show me?"

After listening for a few more seconds, he said, "I'll meet you in an hour."

His mother said, "Who was that?" as he disconnected.

"One of Elena's friends from the university. She saw her briefly yesterday, but she didn't want to talk on the phone, so I'm going to meet her."

"Why couldn't she tell you over the phone?" said his mother sharply.

"I'm not sure, Mamma, but hopefully I'm about to find out."

Petru was about ten minutes early for his meeting with Elena's friend. They had agreed to meet out front of the main entrance to the university complex near a massive bronze statue of the first King of Romania riding a horse. Petru sat on the steps leading up to the monument so that he would be easy to spot. Despite the sun being out, it was cold, and he blew on his hands for warmth while he looked up at the statue of Carol I.

He had met Sofia Rizea only once at a party two years earlier after an introduction by Elena. His sister had been keen on seeing Petru and Sofia go on a date, but that never eventuated. They got as far as becoming friends on social media, but she rarely posted and it occurred to Petru that he may not recognize her now. He pulled out his phone and quickly scrolled through his social media contacts until he came across her name. Sofia's photo had not changed. He recalled she had a slim build, shoulder-length brown hair, and was quite shy when he had tried to engage her in conversation. A voice called out, "Petru?" just as he started scrolling through some of her posts.

Petru looked up at Sofia Rizea. She was about twenty years of age and dressed in a slim fit pair of jeans and a black puffer jacket that almost reached down to her knees. Her hair was longer now, and even though she was wearing glasses, he would have recognized her anywhere.

Petru stood up. "Hi, Sofia. Thanks for agreeing to meet me."

"It's been a while, Petru," said Sofia with a smile. "I don't think I've seen you since that party."

Petru nodded. "Almost two years. But I would recognize you anywhere—you haven't changed."

"My hair is longer," said Sofia with a laugh, "But I'm still me..." Sofia frowned and added, "So Elena is missing?"

Petru frowned. "I'm not sure, but that's what I'm trying to find out. We had a fight two nights ago, and she hasn't come home. I've tried calling and texting her, but she's not responding. I can understand her being mad at me, but she is close to our mother, and she has never gone this long without contacting her."

Sofia nodded.

Petru continued, "So you saw her yesterday?"

"Yes," said Sofia and pointed to a parking lot on the opposite side of the quadrangle. "She looked to be waiting for someone. I waved at her, but she didn't see me. We haven't spoken in a month, so I thought I'd say hello. But as I approached, a man in a black BMW pulled up. They spoke for about ten seconds and then she got in and they drove away."

"Did you recognize the man?"

"No, but I didn't really get a good look at him either—he stayed in the car."

"What did he look like?"

Sofia chewed on her bottom lip. "Hard to say. He was older—about forty. I think he was wearing a suit, but I couldn't be sure."

"And you've never seen him before?"

"Not that I recall."

Petru decided on a different tack. "So, prior to yesterday, you said you hadn't seen Elena for about a month? Don't you take the same classes?"

"We do, but she hasn't been attending." Sofia grimaced and added, "To be honest, I actually thought she had dropped out."

"So she wasn't part of your friendship group here on campus anymore?"

"Not really. She's been running with a different group of girls who... Let's just say they aren't as focused on their studies."

"Parties?"

Sofia nodded.

"Drugs?"

Sofia held up her hands. "I'm not sure, and that's none of my business."

"Sofia, don't hold anything back," urged Petru. "I know she was experimenting with drugs. That's one reason I'm so worried about her."

"Can you let me make a phone call?"

"Sure."

Sofia pulled out her phone and dialed a number. A moment later, she said, "Hi, Cella, it's Sofia—how are you?" There was a moment's pause before she continued, "I've just had Elena's brother contact me. Apparently, she hasn't been home in a couple of days and the family is quite worried. Have you seen her?"

Petru studied Sofia's face as she listened intently. He wasn't close enough to hear any of the conversation, but he didn't like the frown that spread across Sofia's face when she finally responded, "Okay, thanks for that. I'll let him know."

Sofia let out a long breath as she disconnected. "I hang out with Cella occasionally, and I know she sees Elena sometimes…"

Sofia looked away and then added, "Cella thinks Elena's back on drugs. She's been hanging out at the Babylon Club quite a lot. She thinks that maybe that's where she's getting the drugs… and is probably working there, too."

Petru frowned, "The Babylon Club is a bar in the Old Center."

Sofia nodded.

"And Elena works there as a barmaid?"

Sofia grimaced. "Not necessarily… she may have been doing something else…"

Petru shook his head as he realized what Sofia was inferring. He had seen similar things happen to several girls he knew in high school who had drug habits that were out of control. The prospect of his sister turning to prostitution had never crossed his mind.

He recovered and said, "Is there anything else you can think of?"

"Not right now," she said with a shake of the head. "I'm

sorry, Petru. I hope it's just a misunderstanding, and she calls you soon."

"Me too..." Petru managed half a smile and added, "You've been very helpful, Sofia. I really appreciate it."

"I have to get to class," said Sofia as she looked at her watch. "If I think of anything else, I'll message you, okay?"

Petru nodded and thought about his sister as Sofia walked away to class. He had learned that Elena was still alive yesterday and maybe working at the Babylon Club. It wasn't a lot to go on, but it was more than he had a few minutes earlier.

Chapter Seven

The Babylon Club was a ten-minute walk from the university. Petru knew he would arrive well before opening time and debated stopping for a coffee along the way. But with all the worry he had about Elena, he knew he wouldn't enjoy the experience and kept walking. The revelation that Elena might be taking drugs again hadn't surprised him, but descending into prostitution to pay for her habit rocked him. He was no prude, but prostitution was a dangerous business in any city. Clients could be violent, and the pimps you worked for were even worse.

He wondered how he would break the news to his mother if he didn't find his sister. Telling his mother that Elena was doing drugs and perhaps involved in prostitution was not a conversation he looked forward to. Her stroke may have affected her physically, but her mind was still as sharp as ever and she would know if he was lying to her. He decided he would need to be honest.

Petru rounded a corner and stepped into Bucharest's Old Town. Located near the center of the city, the district

The Catalin Connection

was all that remained of Bucharest at the end of the second world war. It was an eclectic mix of ancient stone buildings and apartment blocks, some of which dated back to the nineteenth century. The streets were narrow and some of the buildings were boarded up and covered in graffiti.

He felt safe enough cutting through a back alley during the day to get to Brătianu Boulevard, but it wasn't a trip he would have liked to make at night. Petru thought about how he would make his inquiries as he weaved his way between parked cars, dumpsters, and rubbish bins. He couldn't imagine anyone who worked there would be very forthcoming with information if the club was a front for prostitution and drug trafficking. He would need to be subtle and pick his targets. Owners and managers would be off limits. He figured he would get more information from the wait staff and perhaps even some of the prostitutes if he could find them.

Petru checked his watch as he emerged onto Brătianu Boulevard. It was just after ten AM. He was sure the club wouldn't be open yet, but he decided he would check it anyway and come back later when it was trading. He walked two blocks and slowed his step as the red neon sign for the club came into view. The front of the building was painted a blue-gray and had a large double brass door. On each side of the door were two columns of animals. The animals were gold and alternated between llamas and horses with horns. Petru had studied a little history at school and recalled seeing animals like these inside Egyptian tombs. On the far side of each column was a narrow floor to ceiling fixed glass window. The windows were tinted dark, making it impossible to see inside. Petru debated going up and pressing his face to the glass to see inside, but he didn't want to draw attention to himself. He gently pushed on the brass door, but it was locked.

He walked to the side of the building and peered down an alleyway. There were several vans parked near the Boulevard entrance, but it was a delivery truck parked further down the alleyway that caught his eye. Its rear doors were open, and he watched as a man stacked two boxes on a trolley before wheeling them in through a side door to the club.

Deciding he had nothing to lose, Petru walk down the laneway and stopped when he got to the rear of the truck. The cargo area was stacked with boxes of wine, beer and other spirits.

A voice behind him barked, "Hey! What do you think you're doing?"

Petru spun around and looked into the face of the driver he had seen a minute ago. The driver had a stocky build and was barely five-foot-six. He was in his early twenties and wearing work boots and overalls.

He didn't look like he belonged to the club, but Petru asked anyway. "Do you work here at the club?"

The driver snarled, "I asked you first. What the hell were you doing looking in my truck?"

Petru soothed, "I'm looking for my sister. She's missing, and I've been told by a friend she might work here." He added, "I'm just trying to find her," as he pulled out his phone. He showed the driver a picture of him standing next to Elena at a party. "This was taken about eighteen months ago. Her hair is a little longer now and her name is Elena."

The driver shook his head. "I don't work here. I'm just a driver." He gestured with a thumb toward the side door. "Carl might be able to help you," and then pushed past him with his trolley to return to his truck.

Petru turned and looked in through the side door. He could see a lean man in his early forties with graying hair counting boxes that were stacked on the wooden shelves. He was wearing black pants and a black shirt and held a clipboard in one hand and a pen in the other. Petru walked in and stopped about eight feet short of him.

Carl turned and said, "We're not open for another two hours. You'll need to come back—"

Petru held up his phone again. "I'm trying to find my sister. Her name is Elena. She's been missing for two days. I understand she works here."

Carl looked at the picture. Petru noticed his eyes widen just a fraction before he said, "Never seen her."

"Are you sure about that?"

Petru took a step forward. "Please, have a closer look. I'm just trying to figure out if she's okay or not. That's all…"

The man looked closer at the picture. "Maybe I've seen her around here once or twice. But she doesn't work here… At least not as a barmaid."

Petru nodded. "Thanks, that helps. Can you remember when you last saw her?"

The man went back to counting. "Maybe a week ago. I'm not exactly sure."

"Was she on her own? Or with friends?"

The man stopped counting. "Sometimes she comes in with a group, but mostly she's on her own. She uses this as a meeting place for her clients, if you know what I mean."

Petru grimaced as he realized what the man's innuendo behind the word 'clients'.

The man added, "Look, if she's your sister, I'm sorry, but that's how it is."

"You have no idea where she lives?"

"I never ask, and I don't get involved."

Petru nodded. "Is there someone else I could talk to? Perhaps one of her friends."

The man put his clipboard down on the shelf and stepped forward. In a low voice, he warned, "I wouldn't call the group she hangs with friends and this is not the kind of place where you ask questions."

Petru held his hands up. "I'm just trying to make sure she's safe."

The man picked up his clipboard to resume counting. "The group she hangs with deal drugs. They're lowlife and the owner here moves them on pretty quick."

Petru went to ask another question, but the man held up his hand. "Look, I gotta get back to work or you'll get me in trouble. All I can tell you is they operate out of a warehouse in Sector 4. But if you want my advice, stay away. Let her contact you when she's ready—"

"What's going on out here? Carl, who is this?"

Petru turned to see a man standing in the doorway that separated the storeroom from the main bar area. He had a full head of dark hair cropped short and wore a black leather jacket over dark pants. He had the build of a wrestler and filled out most of the doorway.

Carl answered, "Just a guy looking for his sister, Boss."

The man walked forward and stopped two feet in front of Petru. "What's your name?" he demanded.

"Petru."

"Your sister isn't here." The man pointed towards the door and added, "And you're trespassing."

Petru held his hands up. "I'm just trying to find my sister."

The man jabbed a finger into Petru's chest. "Are you

stupid? I said she's not here. Now get out of here while you can still walk."

Petru kept his hands up. "Okay. I'm going."

He could feel the stares of both men on the back of his neck as he stepped out onto the laneway.

As he walked past the driver, who was loading more boxes onto his trolley, the man murmured, "I wouldn't come back here if I were you."

Petru gave him a slight nod and kept walking. As he made his way out onto the boulevard, he reflected on his encounter with the two men from the Babylon Club. He hadn't expected the owner to be that aggressive and knew he would need to be careful in the future.

He stopped about fifty yards further down the boulevard at a small coffee shop. After ordering an espresso, he found a cafe table just inside the front door next to a window that gave him an uninterrupted view of the Babylon Club. There were only two patrons at tables, so he figured he could sit for a while and replay in his mind what had just happened.

The heated exchanged with the club's boss troubled him. Petru was six-foot-one and spent hours in the gym each week. He had a well-developed upper body, but he knew if things had turned ugly at the club, he would have been no match for the owner, who was at least four inches taller and probably sixty pounds heavier. He had avoided fights at school and had no idea how to throw a punch or defend himself. As he emptied a sachet of sugar into his coffee, he murmured, "You need to be careful."

Petru played back the conversation with the barman in his mind while he sipped his coffee. He had learned that Elena was a semi regular at the venue, was sadly working as a prostitute, and seemed to mix with a group who were making drugs in a warehouse in Sector 4. It wasn't a lot to go on and he needed to find out more.

Petru scratched his chin as thought about the club again. He didn't fancy his chances of being able to walk in and start asking questions when it opened. The owner had made it clear he wasn't welcome, and he figured a stay in hospital would be a lucky outcome if they caught him. He would need a different tack. The barman had seemed friendly enough. Maybe he could talk to him on his way home from work. Maybe he knew more and would talk when he was away from his boss?

His phone interrupted his thoughts as it buzzed on the table. He looked down and saw the call was from Andrei. He debated letting it go to voicemail, but decided it was better to take the call.

After pressing the answer button, he said, "Hi, Andrei."

Petru pulled the phone away from his ear slightly as Andrei barked, "What the hell do you think you're playing at, Petru? I know you know you're not sick. You need to get back here now. I'm warning you—"

"Like I said in my text this morning, I'm not coming in to work today, Andrei," said Petru firmly. "In fact, it may be a few days before I'm back. My sister is—"

"Don't you understand? You don't get to decide when you do or don't work. Luca is really pissed, and I've promised him you'll be back in today."

"My sister is missing. I need to find her. My family has to be my priority, Andre. Surely you understand that."

"You don't understand…"

Petru rolled his eyes. "What don't I understand?"

"Petru, I'm going to level with you. Luca is very upset and I don't know what's happening. He specifically asked about you this morning. He wants you back. And he even wants a meeting with you. You'll have to search for your sister on your own time."

"What does he want to talk about?"

"I don't ask those kinds of questions."

Petru frowned. Apart from skipping work yesterday, he had done nothing to draw Razvan's attention. "I'm not coming in today, Andrei. This needs to be my priority until I know Elena is okay."

There was silence for a moment before Andrei responded, "Then I'll let Luca know…"

Petru swore under his breath as Andrei disconnected. He had visions of Yuri Lebedev floating in the river as he mused about his six months with LEU. Until two days ago, he had always hit his targets and worked without complaint. Petru knew he was a talented hacker who had not come close to reaching his potential for the organization yet.

'Why does Razvan want to meet with me?' he thought. Apart from one incident in the server room shortly after joining LEU, he had been a model employee. He replayed the key moments of the event over in his mind. There were no security cameras in the room, and he had been on his own. He was sure nobody saw him. He wondered if he'd left a digital trace of his visit, but he had used local admin credentials on the server and he was positive nothing had made it to the log files.

"That can't be it," he mumbled as he took another sip of coffee. Petru's thought process was interrupted as he saw the front door to the Babylon Club open. He leaned forward in his chair and watched as two young women emerged from the club. They were both in their early twenties and dressed in skimpy dresses. One wore a short fur coat and the other a glossy black jacket. Both were wearing heavy makeup as if they were about to head out for a night out on the town, only it was about ten hours too early. He noticed one of them was wearing a wig. He immediately knew who they were as they walked down the boulevard towards him.

Petru sat back in his chair. He had never been with a prostitute, but knew they worked all hours of the day and night. He studied the women as they continued to walk towards him. The skimpy dresses and heavy makeup were almost like a uniforms advertising their profession. Petru downed the rest of his coffee and paid the bill. He waited inside the door and watched them as they continued their slow walk. They were engaged in deep conversation as they passed by the coffee shop and were oblivious to his presence inside. He waited until they had gone about another ten yards down the street before he stepped outside to follow them. He was comfortable with the distance between them. Close enough that he wouldn't lose them, but hopefully far enough that he wouldn't raise their suspicions. They walked to the end of the block and stood on the corner while the girl with a wig lit a cigarette. Petru paused and pretended to look into the window of a pastry shop while keeping one eye on them. A moment later, the two girls hugged and then separated. The girl with the wig took off down a side street while the other continued down the boulevard. Petru had to decide who to follow. He thought it would to be harder to follow on the side street without being noticed and stuck with the girl in front of him.

Chapter Eight

Petru followed the girl for another block before stopping just short of an intersection when she turned to head down a side street. As he contemplated his options, he grimaced. He feared she might realize someone was following her, but he had not come this far to quit now. He waited five seconds to allow a little more distance between them before he continued around the corner. To his surprise, the girl was standing in the middle of the laneway with her arms crossed.

"Are you following me?"

Petru stopped dead in his tracks. "Are... well, kind of..."

The girl took two steps towards him and then snarled, "What do you want? I've got people who look after me. And they could make a real mess of you—"

"How much?"

The girl's eyes widened. "What do you take me for? Some common street whore?"

"How much?" said Petru, a little more firmly. "I know who you are and..."

The girl crossed her arms. "It's a little early, isn't it?"

Petru shrugged. "I don't think so."

The girl looked him up and down. Petru noticed the lines around her eyes and the wrinkles on her face. She had looked younger at a distance, but up close he realized she was in her late thirties if not older.

"Forty for oral and seventy if you want full sex. And it's cash upfront."

Petru knew he only had about forty-five euros in his wallet. "Oral it is then."

"What's your name?"

Petru didn't see any point in lying and answered, "Petru."

The woman held out her hand. "Money now."

Petru pulled out his wallet and withdrew the cash. After handing it over, the woman added, "I supply condoms and they're compulsory. Follow me—it's about half a block down."

Petru nodded and followed. He felt his gut tighten and hoped he wasn't walking into a trap. He had heard of guys at the university who had handed over cash to prostitutes, only to be robbed of all their money later.

The woman was silent until they got to the front of a rundown three-storey stone apartment block. The ground level was covered with graffiti and heavy metal bars protected all the windows. The structure appeared to be ready to be condemned.

The woman said, "I'm up on the second floor."

"Okay," said Petru as he followed her inside and into a dimly lit hallway that smelt of urine.

Petru felt his heart race as they walked up the stairs which creaked with each footfall. He thought better of holding the railing for stability.

When they got to the second floor, Petru saw an overweight, balding man sitting on a wooden chair just beyond the landing. He looked up from a newspaper he was reading. "You're early today, Sasha."

Sasha laughed. "I have a keen one..." and kept walking.

The man called out. "Number two is free."

Sasha gave him a thumbs up without looking back. The man made eye contact with Petru as he walked past, but said nothing.

When they got to a door about halfway down the hallway, Sasha pulled out a key. Petru waited while she unlocked the door and then followed her inside. The room was furnished like a waiting room at a doctor or dentist surgery. There were four chairs arranged in an L shape around a coffee table that had two stacks of pornographic magazines on it. Two lava lamps provided the only lighting for the room.

Sasha said, "Have a seat. I need a minute to set up."

Petru watched as she disappeared down a short hallway. He muttered, "Sure," as he sat down. He felt his palms grow sweaty as he looked around the room. Was this a setup? Had the man in the chair called thugs who would burst through the door at any moment to take the rest of his money?

He murmured to himself, "You're a sitting duck," as he tried to relax.

A moment later, Sasha reappeared, but only came as far as the end of the hallway. She had stripped down to a skimpy bra and panties, but still had her high heels and fishnet stockings on.

"Okay, I'm ready. Come on through."

Petru got to his feet, not sure what he would say. He decided he would wait until they were in the room with the door closed before he asked her any questions. He wasn't sure who else was around and figured Sasha might tell him more in private.

Sasha held the door open for him as he walked in. The room was sparsely furnished, with a double bed covered in a pink sheet, a wooden chair, and a small wardrobe with a full-length mirror.

Sasha pointed to the chair. "Take your pants off and anything else that you want to, and then I'll put the condom on."

Petru held up a hand. "Actually, I don't want sex, Sasha. I just want to ask you a few questions."

Sasha fumed, "What are you, a cop? Get out!"

Petru held up a hand and soothed, "I'm just trying to find my sister. She's been missing for two days, and it's unlike her. I was told she worked out of the Babylon Club, just like you."

Before Sasha could reply, Petru pulled out his phone and showed her the same picture he had shown the bartender earlier. "This photo was taken about eighteen months ago. Have you seen her?"

Sasha didn't look at the phone. "I told you to get out. One scream and the man in the hallway will come running. He'll be carrying an axe handle and he knows how to use it."

Petru sat on the bed. "I don't want any trouble. I just want to pay for your time so you can answer some questions. That's all, I swear."

Petru held up his phone again. "Please, just take a quick look. If you haven't seen her, I promise I'll leave you alone and you can keep the money."

Sasha sighed and grabbed the phone. She studied the photo for a moment and then said, "What's her name?"

"Elena."

"I've seen her around a few times," said Sasha, "But she's new. I don't talk to any of the other girls unless they've been around for a while and I trust them."

She handed the phone back and added, "Her working name is Tina."

"When was the last time you saw her?"

"Maybe a week ago, but that means nothing. In this business, we do different shifts and sometimes I don't see girls for a couple of weeks."

Petru nodded. "Do you know where she's living?"

"No idea. Obviously, this is where we work, but not where we live."

Sasha opened the cupboard and began putting on her dress.

"Can I ask you just two more questions?"

Without turning, Sasha responded, "Depends what they are."

"She was seen getting into a black BMW yesterday. The guy was about forty. Do you know who he is?"

"Lots of guys have BMW's and lots of guys are forty…"

Petru wished Sasha was facing him. With her back turned, it was hard to tell if she was lying or not.

"One last question—I'm told she might hang with a group that makes drugs in an old warehouse in Sector 4. Do you know who they might be? Or how I can get in touch with them?"

Sasha turned to face him. "Trust me, you don't want to get mixed up with them. They're bad news."

"Do you have any idea where the warehouse is?"

Sasha shook her head. "You're not listening. These are not the kind of people you just go visit."

"I'm prepared to take my chances. I've got to find Elena."

Sasha sighed as she smoothed out her dress. "I've never been out there, but I've heard a couple of the girls talking. If it's the same group I'm thinking about, it's near the rail depot, but that's all I know."

After putting on her coat, she added, "Like I said, Petru, they're bad people. If they're cooking meth, you're not likely to get out of there alive if they catch you."

Petru grimaced. "Thanks for the tip." He added, "I appreciate your help, Sasha."

Sasha gave a weak smile as she checked her face in the mirror. "I hope you find your sister."

"I'd best be going. Thanks for your time."

As he walked into the hallway, Sasha called out, "Hey Petru, I give my regulars a twenty-per-cent discount. Remember that for next time."

Without breaking stride, Petru said, "Thanks. I'll keep it in mind."

Petru breathed a sigh of relief when he was back out on the street. He looked back over his shoulder several times as he walked back onto the boulevard to make sure he wasn't being followed. Engaging Sasha might have been risky, but it had yielded some valuable information. It saddened him that Elena was working as a prostitute. He realized she was deeper into the drug scene than he had originally thought.

He stopped as the Babylon Club came into view and pondered his next move. There was no reason for Sasha to lie to him about the warehouse's location and it was worth exploring. Although she hadn't given him an exact address, he figured the rail depot she was referring to was most likely the METROREX in Berceni. This was the main depot for commuters on the southern line in Sector 4 and next to a major industrial area of the city.

He remembered taking a trip out to there when he was about twelve to help his uncle pick up some equipment for his bakery. The sketchy recollections of the drive through a sprawling mass of warehouses and storage facilities soured his mood. He recalled many of the buildings were run down and some even boarded up. He knew it wouldn't be easy finding the right location.

Sashas' words, 'Near the rail depot,' echoed in his mind. What did that mean? Was it one or two streets from the depot? Or one or two blocks? Or further still? And in which direction?

Petru grimaced, oblivious to the people on the street who walked around him. He believed Sasha had told him all she could. It left him with the choice of either going back to the club to get more information, or heading out to Berceni to start a street-by-street search. It was still an hour before the club opened. He thought back to his encounter with the club's owner and decided trying to find out any more details was too risky. And the fewer people that knew what he was doing, the better. Petru checked his wallet. He had seven euros left—more than enough for the train fare. He would catch a train out to Berceni and start his search. Petru turned and headed east for the train station. The trip would take him around half an hour. He figured he would be searching for Elena before midday.

Chapter Nine

Petru used the train trip to plan his search. He picked a seat at the back of the last carriage away from other passengers to prevent distractions and then pulled out his phone. He opened the Google Maps application and studied the area immediately around the rail depot. On the western side of the rail line, the majority of the properties were zoned for housing, while on the eastern side, the zoning was all industrial. Petru knew this should be his area of focus.

He was familiar with Google's street view feature, which the company had produced by having vehicles drive down each accessible road, street, or laneway on the planet taking photographs in a 360° arc. The photographs were then assembled by Google on its servers in an array that made it possible for users to take a virtual 'walk' down any road or street on its maps application.

After experimenting with the street view feature and being able to stop and turn on a 360° arc with just the gesture of your finger. He realized the app might be a valuable way of short listing properties he needed to check and would potentially save him hours of physical walking.

Starting with the street that ran parallel to the rail depot, Petru used the app to start his virtual walk. He noticed the timestamp on the photos showed the images had been captured eighteen months earlier. Even though they weren't as current as he would have liked, it still gave him a good feel for the area and hopefully highlighted the older buildings he should be checking first. Petru used finger gestures to stop every thirty yards or so and do a 360° scan. He could see cars and trucks parked out front of buildings as well as people loading and unloading goods in delivery docks. By the time the train pulled into the Berceni station, he had managed to scan six streets and associated laneways that ran next to the railway line. Any warehouses that were new, or obviously open and operating he dismissed immediately. There were a few that he would need to investigate further because the Google photographs were obscured by trucks being parked out front of the buildings. But it was his virtual tour of the south-west corner of the estate that piqued his interest. The area was well away from the rail depot and looked rundown. A number of buildings had already been demolished and it looked to Petru as if the entire area was being prepared for redevelopment.

Petru had focused most of his time on this sector. Some of the warehouses had weeds growing up through the concrete driveways and others were boarded up or closed off by locked gates and six-feet-high chain link fences. He decided this was the area he would investigate first. He figured anyone cooking meth would want to be as far away from prying eyes as possible and this was the ideal location. There were nine buildings on his list that he would focus on first, but he knew the search might take him all day. He had debated calling some of his friends to come and help but he decided he didn't want to put anyone else in danger.

He recalled Sasha's words as he stepped off the train; 'You don't want to get mixed up with them, they're bad news…' As he pushed his way through the throng of people and headed for the exit, he knew he would need to be careful.

Petru zipped up his jacket to keep out the wind as he crossed an intersection that led onto the last road in the industrial park. He had been searching for close to fours hours without success. He had checked all nine warehouses on his list. They were all abandoned just as he had expected, but there was no obvious sign of anyone living in them or using them to cook meth. One building had a notice affixed to its locked gates, showing it was due for demolition next week, and he assumed the rest of the buildings, which were now just stripped out empty shells, would be next.

Petru walked past three trucks laden with shipping containers to better examine the road beyond. The road was lined with spindly black Locust trees that restricted his view. He moved out to the center of the road to get a better look. The black tarmac was potholed and badly cut up in places through overuse by heavy vehicles. From his vantage point, Petru could see that all the buildings, save for two at the far end of the road, had been torn down. The area looked more like a war-zone than an industrial estate, with only concrete slabs and piles of twisted metal and rubble remaining as remnants to a once thriving business area.

Petru checked his watch as he set off at a brisk pace. It

was well after three PM and if he didn't turn up any clues to Elena's location in his search of the last two buildings, he would honor the commitment he made to his mother and report his sister as missing to the police.

It took Petru less than two minutes to walk to the end of the road. The two remaining buildings were on the right-hand side behind six-foot-high chain-link fences. He stopped in front of the first building and checked the metal gates. They were secured with a heavy steel chain and padlock and barely moved an inch when he pushed against them. Petru gripped the fence and stared through the mesh at the structure. The building was set back from the road and constructed from concrete and steel. He didn't know how old it was, but guessed it had been built back in the sixties or seventies. The place looked deserted. There were weeds growing out of cracks in the concrete and rubbish littered the compound. The front doors were covered in bars that looked to have been welded in place for additional security when the building had been closed. Petru glanced up at the upper level. Most of the windows were broken, and some boarded up.

He knew little about drug dens, but this looked like the kind of place a dealer would use to manufacture product.

Petru felt uneasy as he studied the windows. It would be easy enough to clamber up and over the gates, but he worried about how much noise he would make. He could be a sitting duck if he wasn't careful, and decided to check around the back to see if there was a better entry point. He glanced to his left at the other building at the end of the road. It, too, was in a similar state of disrepair and was also locked up with chains and a heavy padlock. Petru retraced his steps back up the road about fifty yards to a vacant lot next to the building. The building, along with the front and rear fences had long since been removed. All that was left were a few piles of rubble hidden among the weeds. He figured if would be easy enough to cut across the vacant lot and in under a minute Petru found himself in the rear laneway. He stood for a moment with his hand on his hips. The laneway wasn't much more than a potholed dirt track —wide enough for a car or small truck, but not wide enough for two vehicles to pass in opposite directions.

Petru walked along the laneway towards the first of the two warehouses. He frowned as he studied the chain-link fence. It surrounded the entire property and still looked to be intact. He noticed the building had two main rear entrances, one of which was a loading dock with a large roller door, and the other, a double wide metal door. Both doors looked locked and the windows on the ground floor were covered in metal bars to prevent break-ins. Petru glanced up at the broken windows on the upper level. Nobody appeared to be watching him, but he wasn't about to be complacent.

Petru walked along the rear fence line, looking for any holes in the chain link. He got to about the halfway point and noticed the weeds had been trampled down. He followed the path to the fence and noticed a small gap in the mesh next to one of the support posts. Petru pulled the mesh back and slipped through the gap and stood for a moment, examining the rear of the warehouse. He could see a small path through the weeds leading to the rear loading dock. Petru crept forward, keeping his focus on the windows and rear doors of the building for any sign that he wasn't alone. When he got to the main rear door, he stood and listened. He heard nothing and peered in through a grimy barred window. He could see a large wooden table with some overturned chairs surrounding it. As his eyes adjusted to the darkness, he could see rows and rows of empty shelving, but no sign of anybody living there or using it to make drugs.

Petru studied the rear metal door to the building. A heavy paddock secured it. He pushed against it, but it didn't budge. He moved across the to the rear roller door at the loading dock. Unlike the rear door, the roller door had not been padlocked. Instead, the owners had welded the roller door to its frame with two metal lugs on each side of the door. Petru's interest piqued as he noticed scratch marks and indentations in the door around each lug. He moved in closer and noticed the welds had been broken. He felt his heart race as he gripped the base of the door and lifted it.

Despite the door creaking and grating in protest, Petru raised it about four feet with no real effort. He held his breath as he bent down and peered in underneath. The warehouse looked empty. No one was waiting with a crowbar or worse to attack him with and, apart from two small scuffling sounds he put down to mice or rats, the warehouse remained quiet.

Petru lifted the roller to head height and then stepped inside. The warehouse smelt of oil, mold, and urine. There were rat droppings on the concrete floor, but he ignored them as he walked inside. It was clear the building hadn't been used for any commercial purposes for a long time, but he could see the telltale sign of footprints on the dusty floor. The footprints looked recent and were of different shapes and sizes. He figured multiple people had been here, and recently. Petru walked between two rows of shelving towards the front of the building.

He only got about halfway down before a voice behind him shouted, "Stop! Put your hands in the air!"

Petru cursed under his breath and stopped walking. The

gruff tenor voice behind him demanded a second time, "Put your hands in the air."

Petru came to a halt. As he raised his hands, the man added, "Now, turn around slowly."

Petru complied and turned around. He tried to swallow as he and stared into the barrel of a sawn-off shotgun. The man who held the weapon was in his early forties and had a stocky build. He wore a greasy pair of overalls and didn't look as if he had shaved in a week.

He kept the gun pointed at Petru's chest as he stepped forward. "What the hell are you doing in here?"

Chapter Ten

Petru kept his gaze fixed on the shotgun as he stammered, "I'm not looking for any trouble here."

Stocky guy sneered, "Who are you? You don't look like a user, so you must be a dealer."

Petru shook his head as he met the man's gaze. "I'm neither. I'm just looking for my sister."

The man frowned. "Sister? What the hell are you talking about?"

Conscious that the man still has the gun pointed at him, Petru blurted out the story of Elena's disappearance and how he thought she had become part of a drug gang that was operating in the area. He finished by adding, "I came to find her and bring her home. I don't want any trouble."

Stocky guy considered him for a moment as Petru added, "Elena and my mother are all that's left of my family. I've got to find her."

The man took a step back and lowered the weapon. "What's your name?"

"Petru."

"Well, Petru, I'm afraid you're out of luck. The cops raided this warehouse at dawn yesterday. They arrested nine people who've apparently been using this place to cook meth. They spent the whole day dismantling and removing all the drug cooking equipment. It was almost dark when they finished."

Petru nodded.

Stocky man added, "If your sister was mixed up with them, she'll be in jail now, and that's where I'd start looking."

"Okay, thanks. I was going to report her as a missing person anyway, so…"

As stocky man unloaded his weapon he said, "You shouldn't be hanging around here. If the cops came back and found you here, they'd shoot you before they asked any questions."

"Thanks, that's good advice. Do you mind if I ask you how you know all this?"

Stocky man grinned as he stuck out his hand. "My name is Oberon. I'm a truck driver. I was here at dawn yesterday, picking up a load one street over. When we heard all the commotion, we came down here and found the warehouse surrounded by cops. It wasn't long before they started hauling people out."

Petru let go the man's grip and pulled out his phone. "I've got a photo of my sister here."

Oberon shook his head as he said, "I didn't get that close. As soon as I knew it was the cops and what they were up to, I got back to work." Oberon rested the shotgun on his shoulder and raised his eyebrows. "I was grabbing a couple of hours sleep in my truck before I start my next run, when I saw you walking down this road. I watched you in my rear-view mirror. You had no idea I was there, did you?"

Petru grimaced and shook his head.

"Look, it's great that you're trying to find your sister, but you need to be more careful. These people all carry weapons and they're not afraid to use them."

"Is that why you carry a gun?"

"I often sleep in my truck," said Oberon as he pointed to his gun. "And this is a useful deterrent for anyone trying to rob me. I've never had to actually use it and I hope I never do."

Oberon studied Petru for a moment. "Look, I'm sorry about your sister. I'm sure it must be awful for your family, but you're not going to find her here. I'm just about to head out on my next run, so I can give you a lift to the police station if you like? It's on my way."

Petru nodded. "I'd appreciate that. I think the sooner I report Elena missing, the better."

Petru glanced up at the clock on the wall in the police interview room as he sipped his coffee. It was close to six PM, and it had been almost twenty minutes since the missing persons detective had finished taking his statement. As each minute passed, he became more uneasy. What was the holdup? Why were they taking so long? Petru wondered if the police had somehow made a connection to where he worked. He frowned. Andrei had been clear right from the day he had started with LEU; "Stay away from the police. If you have any issues, come to us and we'll sort them out."

He had been truthful with all the information he had provided when he had filed the Missing Person report for

Elena. He had willingly handed over their home address and phone number. The only thing he had been vague about was his occupation, which he listed on the form as 'computer technician.'

When he had shown the detective several photos of Elena on his phone, he hadn't expected the detective would want to borrow his phone to take copies. "I'll be back in ten minutes," he had said, as he explained how they had an IT Team who would download the photos from his phone into their missing person's database.

Petru had casually suggested he could email or SMS the photos through to the detective, but he had insisted a direct download would be quicker.

Petru didn't want to make a scene and reluctantly handed over his phone. Andrei had drilled into him that no information connected with Luca Razvan's organization was ever to be stored on personal phones. Petru had always been careful with the information he stored on the device. Apart from Andrei's phone number and one general office number that were both listed with code names, his phone was clean. He wondered again why they were taking so long. Were they going over it in the hope they would discover something?

Petru tried not to appear anxious while he waited. He'd hardly ever been in a police station and had never been interviewed. The ten by twelve room he sat in had one table and four chairs. It was painted an off white and looked similar to police interview rooms he had seen on TV. He glanced around—there wasn't a two-way mirror on the wall, or any cameras or recording equipment that he could see. He took another sip of his coffee, which was now cold, as he stared up at the panel tiles on the ceiling.

Petru took a couple of deep breaths and tried to relax as

he murmured, "Don't get paranoid." He thought back over the day. He'd never had a gun pointed at his chest and reflected on the warning Oberon had given him about getting in over his head. He was an amateur and had a lot to learn about being a detective.

Petru gritted his teeth as the image of the shotgun pointed at his chest flooded back into his mind. He was glad Oberon hadn't panicked. He figured it much better to end the day on a chair in a police station than on a slab in the mortuary. He had appreciated Oberon dropping him at Bucharest's central police station. Petru had expected just a ride to a local police station in Sector 4. But Oberon had insisted the central precinct was on his way and it was always better to file a report with the officers who did the actual investigations.

Petru looked up at the clock again. It had just ticked past six pm. He felt his palms sweat as he thought again about what they might be doing.

It crossed his mind that Luca Razvan might have the police on his payroll. If that were the case, could they be conferring with him while he waited? Petru shook his head and muttered, "Keep it together," just as the door to the interview room opened.

The same detective who had taken his statement burst in. "Sorry that took so long," he said, as he handed Petru back his phone. The detective explained there had been a problem with the download and he had needed to wait for a technician to help. Petru wasn't sure if he believed him or not, but said, "No problem," anyway.

The detective was a slim man in his early thirties with short brown hair that had been stylishly cut. He wore a two-piece gray suit to complement the professional look. As he sat down, he said, "While I was waiting for the computer guy, I went through the file on the nine people we arrested in that warehouse in Sector 4."

Petru leaned forward. "Was Elena one of them?"

The detective shook his head. "No. The two females who were part of the group are both in their early thirties and well known to police for drug possession and prostitution. I did a quick search on our database of females under thirty who have been arrested in Bucharest in the past forty-eight hours. Unfortunately, none of them looks like a close match for your sister."

Petru grimaced. The detective added, "It's early days yet. She'll probably turn up shortly. Most missing persons' reports are resolved within seventy-two hours. They typically go off the grid after having too much alcohol, or they're high on drugs, and need to sleep it off on somebody's couch. When they come to and make their way home, they often have no idea the grief they've put their loved ones through."

"I hope you're right."

The detective leaned back in his chair. "I can't give you any guarantees, of course, but that's my experience."

Petru nodded as he stared at the table. He wondered how he would break the news to his mother when he got home. The room was silent for a moment before the detective said, "I think we have everything we need for now. By all means, keep checking in with her friends and acquaintances, but other than that, you just need to be patient."

Petru looked up at the detective and nodded once. He felt helpless and hated the thought that there was nothing more he could do. The detective slid a business card across the table. "Here's my number. It goes without saying that this is now an active case, and we'll it work as hard as any other we have on file."

"Thanks, Detective, I appreciate it."

The detective responded, "If you think of anything else that might help, please call my number," as he rose from his chair.

They shook hands before the detective escorted Petru back to the station's main reception area. Petru pushed through the main glass doors and emerged onto Calea Avenue. The street lights cast a purple hue on the pavement in the drizzling rain. He was relieved to be out of the police building and strode away from the main entrance just in case someone from his work saw him out front and started asking questions. He took a deep breath. There was nothing more he could do here and he decided to head for the subway. He wasn't sure how he would break the news to his mother when he got home. Outwardly, she would remain stoic, but he knew on the inside her heart would be breaking as she worried about her daughter.

Petru ducked under an awning as the rain intensified. He decided he would wait a few minutes before he continued in the hope the rain would ease. He stared at nothing as his mind churned over today's events. He was happy enough the police were now trying to find Elena, but he wasn't about to leave the work just to them. He would take the night to think over his next move. There had to be other lines of investigation he could take. He thought back to his conversation with Elena's friend Sofia at the university and the guy in the black BMW. He had mentioned the man to the detective, but he hadn't seemed overly interested without a number plate or a better description of the man. Petru decided this would be where he would start tomorrow. Somebody must have seen something, and if not, there were security cameras everywhere these days and the license plate had to be recorded by a camera somewhere nearby.

Petru nodded to himself as the rain eased. It wasn't a lot to go on, but it was a start.

The train trip home gave Petru some valuable thinking time. His only lead was the man in the black BMW. He tried to speculate about who he was. Was he Elena's pimp or sugar daddy? Did she owe him money? Was he her drug supplier? Could he have been all of those things or something else entirely? He didn't know, but answering those questions would be his focus tomorrow. He decided any information he found he would pass on to the police. After having a shotgun pointed at his chest earlier that day, he knew he was pushing his luck if he tried to do this all on his own.

His thoughts returned to his mother as he checked his phone for messages. His mother had promised to call him if Elena returned during the day or got in touch. He grimaced. No messages meant his sister was still missing. He decided he would play down Elena's disappearance for a little longer. He would reassure his mother with the advice from the detective about most missing persons turning up alive within seventy-two hours. They weren't there yet. It had been just over forty-eight hours since she had walked out of the apartment. His phone buzzed. He looked down at the number—it was Andrei. He ignored the call and put his phone back in his pocket as he trudged up the three flights of stairs in his apartment block. Cold, tired, wet and hungry, he realized he hadn't eaten since breakfast that morning, and he was now starving. He was looking forward to a hot meal and a shower. His mother would want to talk, and he resigned himself to an hour or more of conversation with her before he could go to bed.

Petru let out a sigh of relief as he reach the third floor landing. It was good to finally be home. As he walked along the corridor towards his apartment door, he wondered where Elena was and what she was doing. He hoped he was overreacting, and that she was just taking a little longer than normal to cool off after their fight.

Petru froze when he got to his front door. The door was open about six inches. They lived in a high crime neighborhood where nobody ever left their door open. He wondered if Elena had come home and not closed the door properly, but that wasn't like her. Petru's heart raced as he moved forward and pushed the door open a fraction. The main living area of the apartment was in darkness. He switched the light on and stepped inside. Petru gasped as he looked around the room. Most of the furniture had been upended, the coffee table was on its side, and all the books in the bookcase were strewn across the floor. He wondered what had happened. Was it a robbery? The color TV was still in its cabinet, as was his personal stereo system.

A moaning sound in the hallway interrupted his thoughts. Petru immediately thought of his mother as he rushed through the living room. He paused when he got to the hallway and found her lying on the floor, face down, and groaning.

Petru shouted, "Mamma!" and dropped to his knees. He gently rolled her onto her back. She had two black eyes, a large gash across her forehead, and a cut lip. She opened her eyes briefly, and whispered, "Petru."

Petru moved around to cradle his mother's head in his lap, and said, "Mamma, what happened?"

His mother went to speak, but her voice was hoarse and

weak. She managed, "Water…" before closing her eyes again.

Petru gently laid her head down and said, "I'll get you a glass of water," and then rushed to the kitchen. He returned a moment later with a glass of tap water and a cushion from the sofa. When he got to his mother's side, he dropped to his knees again and carefully placed the cushion under her head.

"Here, drink this," he soothed, as he lifted his mother's head and offered her the water.

Petru was relieved when his mother began to sip. He added, "Just try to relax. You're safe now."

After a few minutes, the color returned to his mother's face. She said, "Help me up onto the sofa."

Petru responded, "And then I'll call a doctor."

His mother shook her head. "No, just help me up. You should hear what I have to say first."

Chapter Eleven

Petru picked up his mother and gently carried her through to the living room. After he had her settled on the sofa, he said, "I'm really sorry, Mamma."

His mother reached out a hand. "I will be alright, Petru."

"I would like to call the doctor now," said Petru with a frown. "We can talk about what happened later."

"No, Petru, we need to talk first. I insist."

"Can you remember what happened?"

"They came not long after you left. I heard them outside. I thought it was you, and you had forgotten something. Then they started banging on the door, and shouting..." Tears welled in his mother's swollen eyes as she continued, "That's when I realized..."

Petru put his arm around his mother. "It's okay, Mamma. I'm not going to leave you. You're safe now."

"I thought they would go away if I pretended nobody was home."

"And then what happened?"

"They stopped pounding and the door burst open. I think they must have picked the lock."

"How many were there?"

"Two. Both were big like you, but maybe older. One of them had a beard, and they both had guns. I was terrified. They began rummaging around the apartment as if they were looking for something specific."

Petru had heard of home invasions in Bucharest. They were usually limited to richer districts of the city where people had more valuable possessions. But they lived in a poor neighborhood and home invasions were rare unless large quantities of cash or drugs were the target. "Did they say what they wanted?"

"No," said his mother, shaking her head. "I tried asking them what they wanted, but…" His mother closed her eyes as tears ran down her puffy cheeks. "The bearded man punched me and told me to keep quiet."

"Oh, Mamma, I'm so sorry…"

"They found your laptop and Elena's too. They put them near the front door, but kept on searching. I'm not sure what for. I was still in my wheelchair and I had my phone hidden. I tried to send you a text message, but the bearded man saw me…" She sobbed for a moment while Petru rubbed her back. "He hit me again and then pushed me out of my wheelchair. He told me not to do anything stupid, otherwise he would shoot me. I was so frightened, I thought he was going to kill me."

Petru waited for his mother to regain her composure. "And then what happened?"

"I don't know how long they stayed. Perhaps fifteen minutes, perhaps a little longer. They went through every room… As they were leaving, the bearded man pointed his gun at me and told me not to call the police. He said he would come back if I did."

Petru frowned. "I'm sorry this happened to you, Mamma. You have had enough trouble. You don't deserve this."

"We don't deserve many things that happen to us, Petru, but it is God's way."

"I wonder what they were they were looking for?"

His mother leaned back and closed her eyes. "Maybe something to do with your work? But it could also be Elena."

Petru said, "Let's not worry about that now. We need a doctor to examine you."

His mother sat up straight. "No doctor! They will ask questions and may want to report it to the police."

"But you need a doctor. You could have been—"

"No! I'm cut and bruised, but I will heal." Petru's mother squeezed his hand. "I am very afraid they may come back... and reporting it could make it worse for all of us."

Petru spent half an hour cleaning and dressing his mother's wounds. She appeared quite lucid, and he took some comfort from the fact she didn't appear to have any broken bones or concussion.

As he was finishing up, his mother said, "Petru, I have something to tell you." She motioned him to put down the iodine and continued, "A few weeks before your father died, he came home late one night from work. His clothes were ripped, and he had bruises on his face and body. It was clear he had been in a fight. I didn't say anything to him, I just cleaned and bandaged his wounds…"

Petru nodded, unsure where the conversation was going.

"Two days later, he told me he had taken a bribe."

Petru frowned. "What kind of bribe? From where he worked?"

"I think so," said his mother with a nod. "As you know, he worked on the wharves. There was always money to be made avoiding customs. Your father was a very honest man. He always resisted this temptation… but he wanted to give us a house. A place where we could live and be happy together. He promised me that this was the only time he had ever done such a thing."

"How much money are we talking about?"

"He wouldn't tell me exactly, but it was enough for a house deposit."

"Wow. So what happened?"

His mother's shoulders sagged. "Initially, I was very excited. Naturally, he told me not to tell anyone. But he reassured me that whatever it was, it was safe for now in the apartment."

Petru frowned. "So, it wasn't cash?"

"I don't think so."

"And he hid whatever it was in the apartment?"

"Yes. I tried asking him again what it was and where it was hidden, but he wouldn't tell me. He said it was better that I didn't know anything more until he had converted it to cash and put the money in the bank."

"You never knew what it was?"

His mother grimaced. "Your father died shortly after in that work accident."

Petru shook his head. "Did you search the apartment?"

His mother rolled her eyes. "I searched for years. I've

been over every square inch of this apartment and everything in it multiple times. I've even looked in the pipes and ventilation shafts. I thought it might be something small, like jewelry or diamonds. I searched all your father's clothes, the linings of his pockets, his work bag—everything. And I would never throw anything out without triple checking it. When we got the new refrigerator, I went over every inch of the old one. Everything from the motor to the seals to the door liner. I even defrosted all the ice cube trays. But I never found anything that was valuable."

His mother shook her head. "It drove me crazy. I concluded that whatever it was, it was no longer here. He must have taken it with him or hidden it some place else. Perhaps he felt it was unsafe to leave it here. I don't know, but I think that is why he was killed in the accident."

Petru's eyes widened. "You think he was murdered?"

"Yes. It is the only thing I can think of."

Petru was only eleven when his father died. He remembered his mother telling him how he had been crushed under scaffolding while working on the wharves. He realized how easy a murder could be made to look like an accident in that setting.

His mother touched his arm. "It was a long time ago, Petru. I don't expect the men came looking for something that vanished so many years ago, but I thought you should know."

Petru nodded. "Why didn't you tell me this before, Mamma?"

"Because I didn't want to give you false hope. I only say this to you now because of what happened tonight. And... I didn't want to tarnish your memory of your father."

Petru thought for a moment—it was a lot to process. "None of us are perfect, and... I have wonderful memories of Papa." He managed a weak smile and added, "This doesn't change how I think of him."

"I'm glad."

"You look tired, Mamma. Let me fix you something to eat. Then I'll straighten your room and put you to bed."

His mother shook her head. "We have much to do. It's not safe for us to stay here any more. I am almost certain they will be back and we need to make arrangements tonight."

Chapter Twelve

Petru sat on the rickety chair on the balcony of his family apartment staring at the heavy smog that covered the city skyline. He checked his watch. It was late morning and his mother would now be safely out of the city.

After cleaning and dressing her wounds the previous evening, they had talked well into the night. The story about his father accepting a bribe was still something he was coming to terms with. But he had agreed with his mother, it was unlikely to be the reason for the home invasion. They talked about the possibility of the attack being linked to his work or to Elena's disappearance. They both agreed it was not safe for her to stay in the apartment any longer. A call was made to her sister and brother, who lived in the village of Băleni. The conversation had been intense, but everyone agreed his mother should move to the village immediately for her safety. Knowing that his aunt was a retired nurse and could care for her properly brought him comfort.

Băleni was only an hour's drive from Bucharest, and his aunt and uncle arrived just after seven that morning in the bakery truck. It took less than half an hour to pack up his mother's meager belongings, but a lot longer to say goodbye. His mother had no qualms about leaving so many possessions behind. She had taken a few photos and other items that had sentimental value, but was happy to leave the rest. She struggled with the idea of leaving Bucharest while Elena was still missing. Petru had stayed quiet during the discussion between the siblings and was relieved when his mother had finally agreed that moving to Băleni was in her best interests.

The final goodbye to his mother had been difficult. They both wept and held each other tightly. Few words were spoken, but Petru promised to call her each day with an update on Elena. They had agreed that the moment she was found, he would call and his uncle would return to collect her. Petru waved goodbye as the truck drove away and then returned to the apartment. He needed time to think and wedged the sofa in behind the front door. Confident the apartment was now reasonably secure, he went out onto the balcony.

His initial plan had been to look for security cameras near the university in the hope of finding one that captured the number plate of the car Elena had driven away in. But his mother's assault changed everything. He had found his expensive Jabra earbuds and his portable Sony speaker on the floor amongst the scattered pile of books during the cleanup. He figured the men weren't there simply to steal things if they left valuables like that behind.

After straightening up Elena's room the night before, he searched her room for clues. But he wasn't sure what he was looking for. Apart from a wardrobe of clothes and a pile of makeup, the only thing of significance he found was a small quantity of marijuana in one plastic bag and three dubious looking pink pills in another. He figured the intruders probably weren't there for drugs unless she had a large stash somewhere that he was unaware of.

It was one AM on Thursday morning before he collapsed on the sofa. He had wedged it up against the front door and made himself as comfortable as he could, but sleep eluded him. He had continued to mull over the reasons for the break in. Was this connected to Elena? Or was it connected to his work at LEU Security? It had to be one of those things. Nothing else made sense.

So far, the laptops were the only items that had been stolen. After his mother's departure that morning, he had re-searched the apartment again and discovered only one other item that had been taken. A portable external hard-drive that he used as a backup for his laptop. There was nothing on it worth stealing, save for a couple of hacking programs he was developing, but they were incomplete and still of no use to anyone.

Petru pulled his overcoat tight to keep out the cold. He wondered why the intruders would have stolen a second hand hard-drive that was barely worth fifty euros. His mind swirled with a dozen possibilities, but he kept returning to one. If he was right, the break-in had nothing to do with Elena. He shivered as he thought back to the event in the server room at LEU. It had been a stupid stunt that he thought no one knew about. No harm had been done, but if Razvan had found out about it, it would account for the visit by the two thugs.

Petru felt his gut tighten. If he was right, Razvan wouldn't stop until he got back what he rightfully believed was his. He got to his feet as an icy breeze whipped up. There was a lot more to think about, but not here. He needed to leave, just in case they came back. The city skyline momentarily distracted him as the smog cleared. He thought about some of the happy memories he and his family had made in this apartment. Birthdays and some Christmas celebrations came to mind. He sighed as he took one last look around the balcony and then walked inside to pack.

Petru's backpack wasn't particularly large, and packing it didn't take him long. He stuck to the basics; socks, underwear, a fresh pair of chinos, a couple of shirts, plus some soap, a razor, and a toothbrush from the bathroom. There were several other items he packed as well, including his Jabra earbuds and portable Sony speaker. He was unsure if he would ever return and grabbed two small family photographs off the sideboard as well. He lifted the backpack to test its weight. It still wasn't full, but he didn't fancy carrying any additional load and was satisfied with what he had.

A sense of emptiness settled over him as he looked around the living room. His family had been happy here as he thought back to when his father had been alive. Although his father had worked long hours, he still found time for his family. He managed a sad smile as he recalled the times his father would play football with him at the back of the apartment block and how he would read bedtime stories to Elena.

He looked at the vacant spot in the TV cabinet. The TV had sat there until about an hour ago. Petru had taken it, along with a wall clock, to the local pawnshop about a block away. It wasn't the money he was after and he had traded the goods for something that he hoped would prove

The Catalin Connection

far more valuable than cash—a security camera. He stared up at the device which he had fitted above the cabinets in the kitchen. The camera had a direct line of sight to the front door. Although the camera wasn't new, it was reasonably modern. He had hooked it up to his home's Wi-Fi system and configured it so that it would send any images it captured directly to a file server in the Cloud.

He wasn't sure if the two men would come back. But if they did, he wanted video footage to help identify them. Petru opened up an app on his phone that was connected to the camera. The camera was movement sensitive and recorded his every move as he walked around the apartment. Satisfied that it was working correctly, he picked up his backpack and moved to the front door. He had tried fixing the lock earlier, but the mechanism was broken beyond repair when the door had been kicked in.

Despite all the furniture in the apartment being old and worth little, Petru hated the thought of people ransacking his home once he left. He wanted to give the appearance at least that the apartment was locked and had devised a way he hoped would work. After placing his backpack in the hallway, Petru stepped back inside the apartment and gripped hold of a thin piece of rope he had fastened to one leg of the sofa. The sofa was close to the front door, but just back far enough to allow the door to open. Petru slid the rope under the door and then pulled the door closed behind him.

Petru re-gripped the rope and backed away. He was able to pull the sofa forward about three feet before it wedged hard up against the door on the inside of the apartment. Petru knelt down and pushed the rope back under the doorway. He stood up and took a couple of steps back and examined his work. He nodded once—he couldn't see the rope and the door looked closed. It was the best he could do.

Petru checked his watch. It was just after three PM. He wasn't sure where he would sleep tonight, but he would worry about that later. For now, he needed to get away as quickly as possible.

Petru looked up at the clock in the central bus transit station. It was nearly eleven PM, and the place was almost empty. Without the bustle of travelers heading in and out of Bucharest, the depot had a cavernous feel to it. He sat on a bench at the far end of the complex away from the vending machines for coffee, drinks, and snacks. He counted off eight people. They all had luggage and kept a watchful eye on the departures and arrivals board at the other end of the facility.

He looked down at a ticket stub he still held in his right hand that he'd picked off the floor in the men's room. It had come in handy earlier when one of the station crew had come around, checking tickets to make sure everyone was a genuine traveler and not a homeless person seeking shelter. He smiled at the employee before he got too close and the held up the stub. The young attendant had nodded at him and then left him in peace.

Petru knew he couldn't stay here for more than one night. He was positive the staff knew who the homeless people were and moved them on quickly. He felt his back spasm and leaned forward to stretch his muscles. Although physically tired, he knew sleep would be almost impossible as he shifted on the bench. The bar in the middle discouraged him from lying down and he had never been any good at sleeping in an upright position.

He sighed as he thought back over the day. It was one of those watershed moments in life, he mused. Like when you left school on the last day, never to return. He remembered feeling both dread and excitement as he walked out of his school for the last time. There was excitement about going to university. But there was also dread as he realized his life would never be the same. But Petru liked routine and he had quickly adapted to the new routine of university life. It had almost been just like changing from one school to another. But leaving the apartment and saying goodbye to his mother all in the one day would take a lot more adjusting to.

He reflected on a call he had made to his mother earlier in the evening. She had sounded a little brighter as she told him they had arrived safely in the village of Băleni. He was relieved she hadn't asked where he was staying. Lying to his mother was something he never wanted to do. Petru bit his bottom lip as he recalled breaking the news to his mother that there was still no progress on Elena's disappearance. He explained how he had called the detective in charge of the case earlier in the afternoon to check in. His mother had tried to hide her sadness, but he knew she was hurting.

After shifting on the bench again, Petru debated getting up and going for a walk. But he had spent most of the afternoon walking. Walking and thinking. He had wondered how different the outcome might have been, had he been home when the men had called. Would he still be alive? Would they have taken him with them? He frowned as he thought about his missing hard drive. It's removal made it increasingly likely they were after him and not Elena.

Petru pulled a Mars bar from his coat pocket and removed the rapper. He wasn't particularly hungry even though he hadn't eaten all day. But it was going to be a long night. And there was a lot more to think about and a sugar hit would be good for his brain. After putting the wrapper back in his bag and taking a bite of the confectionery, he brushed his hand across his stomach to check his money belt was secure. He decided it would be safer to live off the grid; at least until he'd found Elena. He had withdrawn seven hundred euros from his savings, but was paranoid about carrying that much cash, particularly while he was sleeping rough. He figured a money belt was his best option and he had bought a cheap one earlier that day to carry most of it. Knowing he didn't have to worry about people picking his pockets while he slept made spending the night in the bus station a little easier.

He relaxed a little after finishing the last morsel of his snack. It would keep him going until he found a place to eat a proper breakfast in the morning. Petru was half-way through a stretch when his phone buzzed in his coat pocket. He pulled it out, expecting to see a text message, but it was his security app showing movement inside his apartment. Petru held his breath as he opened the app. He stared at a live video feed as a man with a beard pushed aside the sofa in his apartment and walked inside. He stood holding a gun out in front of him while he scanned the living room. There was no sound, but he thought he saw the guy's lips move. A second man appeared in the doorway of the apartment. He too, was holding a gun in his hand.

Both men were tall and well built—like they spent a lot of time in a gym. He had no doubt he was staring at the men who had attacked his mother. The second guy pointed towards the camera. The bearded man's face turned to anger as he strode forward. Petru could see him reaching up for the camera just before the screen went black.

Chapter Thirteen

Petru stared at the black screen on his phone for a moment. He cursed under his breath for not doing more to hide the security camera. It was clear the intruders had smashed the camera to prevent it from recording any further.

He quickly switched to another app that showed a list of camera recordings that were automatically uploaded to the Cloud as it captured them. He held his breath as he looked at the list. The recording at the top had been added less than a minute ago. It was only seven seconds long.

"Maybe long enough," he murmured as he pressed play.

A grainy shadowy image of his apartment came into view. By the time the camera motion sensor started recording, the bearded man was already inside the apartment. The video quality was poor in the dim light. He cursed as he realized he should have left a light on. The living room was filled with more light when the second man entered. It was just enough for Petru to make out the facial features of the bearded man.

Petru relived the moment as he watched the bearded

man yell something to his partner. The video went black moments after that man strode forward towards the camera. With a deft maneuver of his right finger on the phone's screen, Petru rewound the video and paused it just before the bearded man grabbed the camera. He took a screenshot and manipulated the contrast and brightness until he had a reasonably clear image of the man. After saving several copies of the image on his phone and another to the Cloud, Petru sat back and studied the man's facial features.

He guessed he was in his early thirties, but it was hard to tell. With another hand gesture, he zoomed in further on the image. The man appeared to have a small scar on his cheek just below his left eye. He tried further making further adjustments but the image quality was too grainy to be sure.

Petru scratched his chin as he thought about what he should do next. He debated showing the detective the video he had captured and telling him about the break-and-enter. But something deep inside his brain told him to be careful.

He frowned. Who were these men and what did they want? He thought about Luca Razvan again and wondered how far his reach was. There were rumors Razvan had a lot of police in his pocket. He thought about the last time he had been in an interview room reporting his sister's disappearance. Petru frowned as he remembered feeling trapped, like an animal in a cage. The twenty-minute recess while he had waited for the detective's return had rattled him. He couldn't afford to allow himself to be so vulnerable again until he knew for sure who he was dealing with.

Using two fingers on the screen, Petru reset the image to a normal size. He shook his head as he stared at the screen. The guy was huge. It wasn't a natural shape you grew into as you got older. This was a physique you developed with a purpose. Body sculpting, which would have taken years in a gym and probably supplemented by steroids as well. He wondered if he could track him down if he made a careful search of all the gyms in the city. But there were dozens of gyms in Bucharest. It would be like trying to find a needle in a haystack.

Petru grimaced. The picture would likely be a dead end in the hands of most cops. But he was no cop. He had skills in hacking and tracking people online that most people couldn't imagine, let alone emulate. Almost everyone under forty had a digital footprint these days, even criminals. Finding the man's identity on Facebook, or Instagram, or some other social channel would be challenging, but not impossible. Petru mused; first, he would need a computer and access to the internet. And then he would need time. Petru switched off his phone to conserve power. As he crossed his arms to keep out the cold, he began to map out a plan.

Petru did his best to get a few hours' sleep on the bench in the bus terminal, but sleep eluded him. At two in the morning, he gave up and went for a walk inside the facility to stretch his legs. There were only three other people in the terminal now: two travelers and a security guard. He found an unused power outlet between two of the vending machines and wedged himself into the gap to charge his phone. While we waited for his device to power up again, he thought about where he might stay in the future. With only seven hundred euros in his pocket, he needed a place that was preferably free. At least until he found Elena and had another job. He had never been homeless before and wasn't sure where to start.

He had heard about the YMCA, but he wasn't sure if they had a facility in Bucharest. It would be worth checking out. He figured there had to be other homeless shelters as well, run by churches and other organizations where he might stay. He made a mental note to call a few of them later in the day once they were open.

As soon as his phone had sufficient charge to power back on, Petru switched on the device. He kept the power cable plugged in to keep it charging while he started his search to discover the identity of the bearded man. Petru pulled a pen and a small notepad out of his backpack. He decided to start with Facebook.

Petru pictured the man in his mind again. A physique like his was only made and sustained in a gym. He wondered if he had ever competed in any bodybuilding competitions. Most guys his size liked to show off and compete against others from time to time. Petru nodded to himself. This was as good a place to start as any. He made a search of all the gymnasiums in the city that specialized in weightlifting and came up with a list of thirteen. All the gyms had Facebook pages and groups. He started with the biggest gym in the center of the city. There were posts and images of individual members doing personal bests in weightlifting, posts showing groups attending competitions, as well as results. It was going to take hours to go through all the images looking for that one face in the crowd. But he had the time. And as a hacker, he had learned to be patient.

Petru spent the next three hours reviewing the Facebook groups he had on his list. He came across several images of guys with beards who looked similar to the man he had seen in his apartment. But after discovering their identity and searching through their individual Facebook profiles, he had quickly dismissed them as possibilities.

He kept searching, and it was when he got to the seventh gym site that he made the breakthrough. Petru came across a group shot of gym members who had attended a competition. There were seven women and eleven men in the picture. They all had muscular physiques, but unlike the other participants, a bearded man on the far left of the picture wasn't smiling. He almost looked angry, like he didn't want to be in the picture.

Petru's heart raced as he zoomed in on the image. It was difficult to tell if this was the man, but it was worth investigating further. Petru then went back through all Facebook posts for the gym for two years prior and found a second picture of the man. This time, he was on his own and squat lifting. Petru had spent a lot of time in the gym himself, and guessed the man was lifting over four hundred pounds. He didn't have a beard this time, but he was positive he had a match. He read the man's name at the bottom of the screen: Karlos Toma. There was no more information with the post, but that didn't deter him. Now that he knew his name, he could start his search in earnest.

Petru stared at the image and murmured, "Who are you, and what do you want?"

Petru worked through the night trying to track more information on Karlos Toma. But Toma was like a ghost. There were no posts on his Facebook page and no information on his profile. Even his picture was an avatar of a cartoon weight lifter only. It was as if he had set up the page and then forgotten about it. Petru assumed he had another Facebook account, but after two hours of searching, he found nothing.

He had tracked people in the past who didn't use their social media accounts. They were set up with good intentions but never used. Petru didn't think this was the case with Toma. The way he had almost scowled at the camera when his picture was taken with the gym club suggested he did his best to keep off the platform. He continued his search and only came across one other image of Toma on the Internet. It was with two other men. They were sitting at a table in a bar or a restaurant.

Petru frowned. Toma was in the middle and none of the three men were smiling. Perhaps they were too cool for such a facial expression? The guy on the left was maybe ten years older than Toma. He had close cropped gray hair and looked like he had just left the military. The guy on Toma's right was much younger—early twenties, at most. He had a cocky, surly expression, as if he owned the world. They were all wearing tight fitting shirts to accentuate their physiques.

Petru studied the faces of the two other men, hoping one of them had been Toma's partner at his apartment. Neither man looked like the other intruder.

But it was easy enough to find the other two men's social media accounts. The older man had set up his Facebook account six years earlier, but in that time, he had only posted twice. Both posts were photos of his dog, which didn't give him a lot to go on. The younger man's profile was entirely different. He had posted regularly until about twelve months ago, when he had suddenly stopped. He wondered if the man was now dead—it was usually the reason people stopped posting.

He had only one lead, so he decided to run it to ground.

The younger man's profile turned up several friends and associates, all who would need to be checked. He had only been searching for about half an hour when his phone buzzed.

Petru stared down at the screen and saw it was the number for the detective working on Elena's case.

Petru looked up at the wall clock in the bus depot, which showed it was just after eight AM. He pressed answer and said, "Hello."

"Petru, it's Detective Dan Mutu from the Missing Persons Unit."

"I hope you've got some good news for me?"

There was a moment of silence before Mutu responded. "There's been a development. We'd like you to come in."

"Have you found, Elena?" said Petru as he sat forward on the bench.

"We'd rather you come in."

"Either you have found her, or you haven't. Which is it?"

"Petru, we've recovered a body, but we're not sure about the identity. If you could come in and…"

Petru closed his eyes and tilted his head back. He felt sick in his stomach as a wave of emotion flooded over him.

"Petru, are you still there?"

"Yeah… What happened?"

"We found her down by the river. At first, we thought she'd drowned, but…"

"But, what?"

"When the body was recovered, they discovered… she' been shot."

Petru opened his eyes. "Somebody shot Elena?"

"Like I said, we're not sure about the identity."

Petru shook his head as tears filled his eyes. He thought

about Yuri Lebedev as he asked, "Was she shot in the back of the head?"

"Yes…"

Petru gritted his teeth as he thought about Luca Razvan.

Mutu continued, "You almost… don't seem surprised. What are you not telling me?"

Petru ended the call and got up from the bench. His phone buzzed again. He knew it was Mutu calling back, but he wasn't in the mood to talk. After picking up his backpack, he trudged out of the bus station, unsure what he would do next.

Chapter Fourteen

Petru left the bus station immediately after the call from Mutu. The detective had called and texted him repeatedly over the next two hours until Petru finally relented around ten AM and returned his call.

The detective had explained to Petru that he would need to formally identify his sister even though they had found ID on her body.

Despite his protestations, Mutu had insisted. The coroner's office was only about a fifteen minute walk from the bus station. But the trip had taken Petru much longer. He felt numb as he trudged the streets of Bucharest. The gray Friday morning sky threatened rain and matched his mood.

He thought about his relationship with Elena. Until recently, they had been close. A lump rose in his throat as he thought back to memories from their childhood. She had been carefree, popular, and full of life. They had become closer after the death of their father. They had always looked out for each. And even though she had distanced herself from him in recent times, that changed nothing for Petru.

The shock hit him all over again as Mutu's words announcing his sister's death echoed through his head. Petru stopped walking and leaned up against a wall. It was incomprehensible that she was gone. As he grasped the truth, he closed his eyes to shut out the world. How would he tell his mother? He was hoping the body was not his sister. That somehow they had made a mistake. Petru had heard of bodies being recovered with the wrong ID. It was a long shot, but he would cling to it until they proved him wrong.

Petru opened his eyes and glanced up at the clouds as a few spots of rain began to fall. It was too much of a coincidence. This had to be the work of Luca Razvan. He wiped his eyes as he realized Elena had probably been an innocent bystander. A pawn Razvan was using to get to him. Petru paused in front of a cafe and stared in through the glass window. He hadn't had a proper meal in close to twenty-four hours. But he didn't feel hungry.

He stared at his reflection—a young man burdened by grief and anguish. Forty-eight hours ago, he had been doing his best to support his family while he figured out how to go straight. His dreams were now a shattered wreck.

As he breathed in and out to control his emotions, something snapped inside him. He studied his reflection as the rage inside him grew. He watched his reflection morph into anger and fury. In that moment, he decided he wouldn't run, and he wouldn't hide. Razvan had destroyed his family and he knew he was next. He murmured into his reflection, "You're not going to get away with this..."

Petru walked to the next corner and looked up at the street signs. Realizing he was only a hundred yards from the coroner's office, he pulled out his phone. Mutu had told him he would wait for Petru at the coroner's office and to call when he was close. Petru gritted his teeth as he dialed the detective's number. Mutu had promised to escort him through to the viewing room so that he didn't have to wait. He figured it would be only minutes before he knew for sure if Elena had been murdered.

Mutu was waiting out the front of the coroner's office. He had his phone to his ear, deep in conversation, until he saw Petru approaching. Petru heard him bid a hasty goodbye to the caller before putting the phone back in his pocket.

The detective reached out his right hand and shook Petru's hand with a firm grip. "I appreciate you coming so soon, Petru. I can't imagine how difficult this must be for you."

Petru nodded, but said nothing in return. The numb feeling returned as Mutu motioned Petru to follow him inside. "We need to keep this investigation moving, so the sooner we get a positive ID, the better."

They walked through a reception area. It had five chairs arranged in an L fashion around a glass coffee table. The reception desk was made of a heavy dark timber and located on the opposite side of the room. The room was painted a light gray color to complete the depressing decor. A woman sat behind the desk and nodded once at Mutu as he headed down a tiled corridor.

Petru had never been in a morgue before. He found it surreal as he followed Mutu down the dimly lit corridor. The detective got about halfway down and stopped outside a closed door. The door was painted white and simply marked as 'Room 3.' In a low voice, he said, "I'll get you to wait here just a minute, Petru. I have to check with the doctor to make sure the body is ready for viewing."

Petru nodded. He watched Mutu enter the room before he closed the door behind him. After a long breath, he said a prayer; something he didn't do very often. His mother was very devout and had instilled in him since he was a young boy that God wasn't a genie in a bottle that granted your wishes. She had taught him to pray for strength and guidance rather than for good grades or a new soccer ball. In that moment, he prayed for strength.

Petru felt his stomach churn as the door opened again. He could smell a pungent odor wafting out of the room. The smell of death. He closed his eyes for a moment to steel himself as Mutu came up beside him. The detective placed a hand on his shoulder. "I'm going to take you in now, Petru. The body is on a gurney, but under a sheet. We have a chair for you to sit on. Once you're seated and ready, the doctor will pull up the sheet just enough for you to see the face of the body…"

Petru felt his heart race. His mouth was dry, but he managed, "I understand."

Mutu paused a moment. "The body has been in the water a while… there's some bloating… and the three bullet wounds have…" Mutu grimaced. "I'm sorry, but you need to be prepared for that."

"Let's get it over with," declared Petru.

Despite the odor permeating the corridor, he took a deep breath and followed Mutu into the room. He had expected a bigger room. There were no examination tables or stainless steel sinks. Just a doctor wearing a face mask and gown, a chair, and a body covered by a sheet on a stretcher.

Mutu motioned him to sit in the chair. Petru was about

four feet from the gurney and near the victim's head. He felt his heart race as Mutu nodded once to the doctor. He could feel a wave of adrenaline flood through his body as the doctor gently pulled back the sheet. Petru let out a gasp. His crumbling world collapsed around him as he stared at the face of his sister.

Chapter Fifteen

Petru stayed in the shadows of the trees for almost two hours, watching everyone who entered and exited the St. Elias cemetery. It had been five days since he had identified Elena in the morgue. His life since then had been a blur. He had become overwhelmed when he had called his mother to break the news to her. Petru had confessed to her that he suspected Luca Razvan was behind Elena's murder, but he had no proof. His mother had remained stoic, organizing the funeral and insisting he leave the murder investigation to the police.

After explaining the second break-in to his mother, she had agreed it was better for him to remain in hiding until they had captured the offenders, which meant he would miss his sister's funeral. The funeral had been yesterday, and his mother and all his relatives from the village of Băleni had returned home. His mother had begged him to come with them and start a new life in Băleni, but Petru refused. There was unfinished business with Luca Razvan and he had no intention of leaving Bucharest until he had justice for his sister. He also had to pay his respects to his sister.

He had been sleeping rough and was close to exhaustion. A different location each night, and he now only talked to detective Mutu on his phone. All his purchases were made with cash. He hoped that if anyone were looking for him, they would now assume he had fled Bucharest, but he couldn't be certain.

He came to the cemetery each year to lay flowers on his father's grave on the anniversary of his death. His mother had insisted Elena be buried next to her father, so he knew where her grave was. But it was the cemeteries layout that bothered him. St. Elias was located on the outskirts of Bucharest behind a concrete and stone wall that enclosed the entire facility. The wall was about six feet high, making it difficult to see inside. There were several double gates allowing access for hearses and mourners. They were open at present, but provided a limited view into the cemetery itself. St Elias was an eclectic mix of religions, many of whom favored large headstones and monuments for departed family members. It was the headstones and monuments that troubled him. There were thousands of them within the complex making it easy to hide and watch everyone who entered without being detected.

Petru had worn a hooded sweater and sunglasses for the visit. With the hood up, he might be able to hide his identity on the street, but if they were inside and watching Elena's grave, it wouldn't matter what he was wearing. Visiting her grave was a risk. But it was something he needed to do before he could move on. He hadn't seen anyone enter or exit that looked like the two men who had broken into his apartment. He has seen no vans on the street, nor men in parked cars outside the cemetery who looked like they were keeping watch. But was it safe? Petru gritted his teeth as he realized the only way to answer the question was to walk inside.

He had decided on a strategy. He would follow the next group of mourners in. Close enough so that to the casual observer, he looked like one of them. Once inside, he would peel off and head around the interior perimeter of the cemetery. He would approach Elena's grave from the rear. This way, he hoped he would spot anyone who was watching out for him before they spotted him. If it looked safe, he would pay his respects for a few minutes before leaving. The plan sounded good in theory, but that was all it was.

Petru took a deep breath as he watched a family of three—a mother, father, and a young boy—approach the front gates with a large bouquet of flowers. He waited a moment until they were nearing the gate before he stepped from his cover to follow them in.

Petru felt his heart race as he strode across the road. He glanced quickly to his left and right looking for any sign that he was being followed but saw no one. He caught up to the family, but stayed about two yards back as they walked through the gates. The family seemed oblivious to his presence as they stopped a few feet inside to get their bearings. Petru kept walking and veered to the left. He walked for about twenty yards before he stopped in front of a large stone monument. He pretended to read the inscription on the gravestone as he subtly looked to his left and his right. It didn't appear that anyone was following, so he kept moving.

It took Petru five minutes to circle around to the back of the cemetery. He looked over his shoulder every few seconds to make sure he wasn't being followed. When he reached the rear wall, he moved forward through a couple of rows of headstones before stopping behind a large black marble monument.

Petru crouched down to keep himself hidden while he scanned the cemetery. His father and sister were buried in the Orthodox section in the middle. He peered out from behind the headstone, looking for anyone who seemed out of place. He kept up his watch for a good five minutes, but couldn't see anyone suspicious. He rose to his full height but stayed behind the monument for a few moments more, scanning and hoping it was safe.

It was a good seventy yards from his current position to the family grave. Petru was unsure what he would do if he was spotted while he was paying his respects. Escaping through the front entrance might mean he was walking into a trap if Razvan had a team of men after him. He decided he would head for the closest exterior wall. The walls were high, but after years of working out in a gym, he didn't think he would have any problem scrambling over it and disappearing. Petru checked his watch. It was well after five PM. He didn't check the closing time as he walked in, but as the light faded in the late afternoon sun, he figured St. Elias would probably close at six.

He took a deep breath and moved forward, scanning to his left and right as he walked. He stopped about twenty yards from Elena's grave and put his hand over his mouth. The flowers covering the fresh mound of earth suddenly made it real for him. He felt a wave of guilt wash over him as he realized he was the reason his sister was lying there. After taking a moment to compose himself, he looked around again. The graveyard now looked deserted. He moved forward, allowing the grief to overwhelm him as he stopped in front of his sister's grave.

Petru stood for a moment shaking his head as he stared

The Catalin Connection

down at the grave. He bit down on his bottom lip to stop himself from crying as he made the sign of the cross. He glanced left and right to make sure he was alone and then bent down and placed a small bouquet he had brought on top of the grave. After closing his eyes, he said a prayer and then stood up again. He spent a few moments quietly talking to his sister. He told her that he loved her and that this should never have happened. He choked back tears as he told her she would never be forgotten. He concluded by promising her that whoever had killed her wouldn't get away with it. Petru turned and walked to the front of the cemetery. He didn't scan to his left or right on the way out. He was already thinking about what he would do next.

Just as he reached the main entrance way, a familiar voice called out to him, "Petru, is that you?"

Petru spun around to his left as his boss, Andrei Pellea, approached him. Andrei was holding a bunch of dead flowers and said, "Of all the places... what are you doing here?"

Petru scanned to his left and right to make sure his boss was on his own. "I came to visit my sister. Haven't you heard?"

Andrei's eyes widened. "Your sister is dead? I am so sorry. When did this happen?"

Petru ignored the question. "What are you doing here, Andrei? This strikes me as being a bit too convenient."

"I come every two weeks to change the flowers on my mother's grave," declared Andrei, as he held up the dead flowers. "I was just leaving when—"

"I need to go," said Petru.

As Petru strode through the gates, Andrei raced up beside him and said, "Petru, I need to talk to you for a minute. There are some things you need to know."

Petru looked around again. They appeared to be on their own. As he stopped, he said, "You've got one minute."

"I've already told you Luca is furious. So much so that he's got men looking for you right now. If you want my advice... I would leave Bucharest now and never come back."

Petru opened his mouth to tell Andrei he had no intention of leaving Bucharest, but changed his mind. "That's what I'm doing right now. I've paid my respects, and now I'm leaving."

"I think that's wise, Petru." Andrei pointed to his car, a silver Volvo, which was parked about forty yards from the main gate. "You shouldn't be standing here like this. Walk with me to my car. There is one more thing I have to ask you."

"And what's that?"

As they walked, Andrei withdrew a piece of paper from his pocket and held it out for Petru. "Luca says you have something of his that you need to return. I didn't ask what it was, but he told me if I got in contact with you, I should give you his direct phone number..."

They stopped walking when they got to Andrei's car. "I will call Luca in ten minutes and tell him I just met you outside the cemetery. That should give you time to get away..." Andrei looked up and down the street before adding, "It's up to you if you call him or not... I'm just doing my job."

Petru realized something was different about the street as he took the paper. A black van was now parked on the opposite side of the road that hadn't been there an hour ago. Petru swore as two men with guns drawn emerged from behind the vehicle. They both had their weapons pointed at his chest using a double handed grip like he saw cops use in the movies. Both of them advanced across the street.

Andrei sighed as he unlocked his car. "You picked a fight with the wrong man, Petru."

With his gun still pointed at Petru's chest, the taller of the two men stopped six feet from Petru and said, "We're going to walk across the road to the van nice and slow."

As the other man circled around behind him, Petru thought for a moment about running as Andrei drove off. But realized he would be dead before he took five steps. He cursed under his breath, as he wondered how it had all gone so horribly wrong.

Chapter Sixteen

Petru figured he had just a few minutes to live as the two men bustled him into the back of the van. The shorter of the two men pushed him all the way to the rear of the cargo area, while his partner kept his weapon pointed at Petru's chest. Shorter guy got in and sat on a makeshift wooden bench that was bolted to the floor just behind the two seats in the front cabin area. He kept his gun pointed at Petru's chest as taller guy slammed the side door shut. Petru felt his heart skip as he watched taller guy get into the driver's seat and start the engine. The cargo area had no windows, and the air was stale and musty. He knew he was trapped and wondered if this was the same van that Yuri Lebedev took his last trip in.

Taller guy put the van into gear and pulled out into the traffic. Petru guessed shorter guy was about eight feet from him. He had a stubble beard and slightly greasy hair that he wore in a ponytail. His mouth was too big for his face and he had a scar that ran up through his left eyebrow. He sneered at Petru and said mockingly, "Won't be long now…"

Petru ignored the jibe and focused on the gun that was pointed at his chest. He debated rushing shorter guy, but there was no point—he would not miss from that distance.

Petru made no pretense of examining the interior of the van. He ignored shorter guy's jibe, "There's no way out of here, asshole," as his mind raced to find a solution to his dilemma.

Petru had a reasonable view of the front cabin between the driver and passenger seats. He could see the driver waving his fist at other motorists and complaining about the traffic as they moved through the city. He switched his focus to the cargo area. There didn't appear to be any internal latches for either the rear or side cargo doors. Probably removed, he thought, if the van was regularly used for transferring people against their will.

Apart from a rug on the floor, and the wooden bench, the interior was clean. No boxes, no tools, no ropes, nothing that could possibly help him. Taller guy screamed more abuse at another driver as he swerved violently to the left. Shorter guy almost fell off his bench and yelled at his partner, "Keep it steady!"

Petru sensed an opportunity might present itself and readied himself. Shorter guy had been momentarily distracted trying to balance himself and for a fraction of a second, his gun hadn't been aimed at his body. Shorter guy seemed to grow impatient as he yelled over his shoulder, "How much further?"

The driver mumbled, "About five," but said nothing more. Petru didn't know whether he meant five minutes or five blocks or something else. Whatever it was, he didn't think he had much time. He felt bile rise up in the back of his throat as a thousand thoughts raced through his mind. It didn't seem fair that this was the way his life would end. He wondered whether it would be one of these two thugs, or Razvan himself who would deliver the fatal shots.

Petru was shaken from his funk as the driver started yelling again and the van screeched to a halt. Both Petru and shorter guy lurched forward. Shorter guy yelled at his partner as he slammed into the back of the driver's seat and toppled off the bench. Above the squeal of the tires, Petru heard a clunking sound and realized the man had dropped his gun. Rushing forward, Petru shoulder charged shorter guy. He heard the man grunt as he crashed into his chest. Petru felt a wave of nausea flood over his body as the man brought his knee up into his groin.

Petru groaned and collapsed to the floor. Before he could regain his composure, he felt a white-hot pain in his rib cage as the man lashed out with his boot. Petru felt disorientated and close to blacking out. He willed himself to stay conscious as the cabin started to spin. He noticed the man dive to his left as the driver screamed, "Just shoot him! Shoot him!"

Forcing the searing pain to the back of his mind, Petru focused on the man's right arm as he picked up the gun and swung it toward him. He managed to grab the man's wrist just as the weapon discharged somewhere above his head. The boom the gun made in the back of the van was deafening. The man continued to yell for his partner's help as they wrestled for control of the weapon. The man leaned forward and bit down hard on Petru's arm. Petru ignored the pain and swung his left fist at the man's head. The blow found its mark and the gun dropped to the floor as the man collapsed. Petru shoved him aside and dove for the gun. As he gripped the weapon in his right hand, he heard the driver yell, "I'm pulling over!"

Petru tried to get up into a sitting position, but shorter guy recovered and launched himself forward. Petru had never fired a gun in his life. Time seemed to slow down for him as he raised the weapon and pulled the trigger. He barely registered the boom the weapon made, or felt the kickback of the weapon's recoil, as the bullet entered the man's skull just below his left eye. He was conscious of a red mist being sprayed across the left hand wall of the van's cargo area as the man's lifeless body collapsed on top of him. That he had killed a man with the first shot he'd ever fired, was the furthest thought from his mind. He was conscious of the driver yelling, "What's happening? What's happening?" as the van screeched to a halt again.

Petru rolled the man's body away and screamed at the driver, "Don't move!" as he scrambled up onto the wooden bench. After pushing the barrel of the gun hard into the driver's neck, he added, "Your friend's dead and you're about to join him if you don't do exactly what I say!"

The driver raised his arms off the steering wheel and said, "Be cool, man. I'm just the driver. I don't have a beef with you, I'm just doing my—"

"Switch the engine off!"

The driver kept his left hand in the air and lowered his right hand. "Okay, okay! Just relax."

Petru allowed himself to breathe as the motor to the van shut down and the driver raised his right hand again. With the gun still shoved hard into the driver's neck, he said, "If you don't want to wind up dead like your friend here, you're going to do exactly what I say."

The man nodded. "I understand. I understand. I'll do whatever you say."

Petru took a moment to figure out what he wanted the man to do as he scanned through the front window at the street. "Where's your gun? I know you have at least one."

"It's in my jacket pocket."

"Left or right?"

"Right."

"Reach in and remove it with the thumb and forefinger of your left hand and then drop it on the floor. If you so much as breathe, I'm going to shoot you. Do you understand?"

The man nodded. "Perfectly."

Petru pushed the gun harder against the the base of the man's skull and said, "Do it now."

The man soothed, "Easy, easy..." as he slowly removed the weapon.

After taller guy had dropped his gun on the floor, Petru said, "Keep your hands in the air. I'm going to move back a few feet."

The driver kept his hands in the air. "Okay, okay..."

"When I'm in position, I'll instruct you to climb between the two seats and join me in the cargo area... You understand?"

The man nodded. With the gun in his right hand still trained on the man's head, Petru moved back a few feet and then settled into a crouched position with his back pressed up against the van's rear door. He rehearsed the next few steps in his mind and then said, "Keep your hands where I can see them and climb through now."

Petru kept the gun pointed at the taller guy's chest as the

man eased his way between the seats. Taller guy kept his arms up in the air, assuring Petru he wouldn't try anything.

When taller guy had squeezed between the seats he looked down at his colleague who lay in a crumpled heap on the left side of the van and murmured, "God, damn…"

Petru motioned with his gun, "Take the laces out of your friend's boots and do it fast."

"You going to tie me up?" said the man as he squatted alongside his dead partner.

"Only if you're quick. Otherwise I'll shoot you…"

Taller guy seemed to get the message and frantically removed the laces.

"Now remove the man's wallet and phone."

After the man did as instructed, Petru motioned with his gun. "Place them over there where they're out of the blood and then undo your boot laces."

Petru waited until taller guy had completed the two tasks. "Now, tie your boots together—and use double knots."

Petru watched the man tie his two boots together. When he had finished, Petru added, "Now pull on the laces to make the knots tight."

Taller guy pulled hard on his laces and then put his hands in the air again.

"You got any other weapons on you?"

Taller guy shook his head.

"What about your friend?"

"No. We only carry one piece each."

"Remove your phone and wallet and put them on the floor, too. But…" Petru raised the gun from the man's chest to his face and then added, "Be very careful…"

Taller guy's eyes widened with the threat. He nodded

once and removed his phone and wallet with the thumb and forefinger of his left hand while keeping his right in the air.

"Now roll onto your stomach and put your hands behind your back," demanded Petru.

After taller guy had complied, Petru straddled him and jammed the gun into his neck with his right hand while he retrieved the dead man's boot laces with his left. "You ever hear of the hogtie?"

Tall guy let out a muffled, "Yeah. You tie a person's wrists and feet behind their back—makes it hard to escape."

Petru nodded. "That's what I'm going to do to you. I'll have the gun tucked under my arm, but if you give me any grief whatsoever, I'll shoot you dead. You understand?"

"Completely."

Petru moved quickly. First, he bound the man's hands, and then secured them to his feet with the other boot lace. Satisfied the man was now immobile, he rolled off the man and retrieved the two phones and wallets. As he shoved them into a jacket pocket, he reviewed his work. Taller guy was now trussed up like a Christmas turkey, but he figured it wouldn't hold him for long.

Keeping his gun pointed at the man, he wedged himself between the two seats and climbed into the front cabin. He peered out into the street. It was almost fully dark and nobody seemed to pay the van any attention. Petru figured the gunshot must have sounded like a car backfiring and was thankful that he might live to see another day. He gripped the door handle with his coat and opened it just a fraction before glancing back into the cargo area. He debated staying a couple more minutes to interrogate the man, but he needed to keep moving, just in case they weren't working alone.

Petru murmured, "This is your lucky day..." and vanished into the night.

Chapter Seventeen

Petru did his best to blend in with the foot traffic as he strode away from the van. He kept scanning to his left and right for any sign of police and occasionally looked back over his shoulder. He figured it would only take taller guy a couple of minutes to break the restraints and he wanted to be as far away as possible before that happened.

He scanned the street and realized he was in the suburb of Dorobanti. It was early evening, and the streets were busy with people, either heading home from work or out for evening meals at restaurants. He had quickly checked his jacket for any signs of blood from short guy, but he seemed to be mostly clean. He wanted to blend in with the crowd and resisted the urge to run as he walked along the boulevard. He checked the two phones he had stolen from the men. Both of them had password protection, which he didn't have time to break. It was important to discover as much about the men as he could. But the phones would require time he didn't have. He dropped them in a street dustbin without breaking stride and kept walking.

The Catalin Connection

He opened the first wallet as he walked. There was a large wad of cash, but no cards or driver's license. He wasn't overly surprised. If he were a hit-man, he wouldn't be carrying any form of ID while he was working, either. He shoved the wad of cash in his jean's pocket and dropped the wallet in another dustbin before removing the second wallet from his jacket pocket. The second wallet was a replica of the first. A large wad of cash, but no cards or ID. He stuck the cash in his jeans pocket and dropped the wallet in another dustbin as he kept walking. He looked over his shoulder again before disappearing down a side lane. He figured tall guy would be close to getting out of his binds by now and it was important that he got out of the main area of Dorobanti as quickly as possible.

Petru felt the cold steel of the gun in his pocket as he walked. He was tempted to keep it for personal protection. But he knew if he was stopped and searched, the police would be able to link him by the gun to the murder. Petru weighed up what he should do. He tried to think of a safe hiding spot for it, but if he didn't have it on him or close by, it was no use to him. He figured he was better off without it. Hiding out and staying off the grid was his best hope of staying alive.

He shook his head as he walked. Visiting Elena's grave had almost been his undoing. But now that was done, Razvan would have no idea where to search for him. He stopped in the shadows near a dumpster about half-way up the laneway and withdrew the gun. He wiped it clean with the interior of his jacket as best he could. He figured the man's body would likely end up in the river, but getting rid of his fingerprints would further distance him from the crime. Satisfied with his work, he dropped the gun in the bin and headed for the street. He planned to get as far away as possible from the crime scene while he thought about his next move.

Petru walked for over an hour. He kept looking back to make sure he wasn't being followed. Moving at a steady pace, he stuck to the back streets and alleys as he zig-zagged across the city until he reached Piata Romana.

The time spent walking gave him time to think. He had decided he needed a proper bed for the night. Four nights of sleeping rough had left him exhausted. He had heard of homeless people being robbed and murdered for just a few euros. He had found it difficult to find safe places to sleep and had lain awake most nights in the freezing cold, just dozing here and there. A shower and a good night's sleep in a warm bed were what he desperately needed. The money he had taken from the two hit men had swelled his cash reserves to almost one thousand euros. He wasn't about to go crazy with the money, but a night in a proper bed behind a locked door was something he thought he deserved.

Petru emerged from an alley onto Sapte Strada. He knew there were two or three low-cost hotels here. He walked past the first in the group. It was a three story brick construction, but it had a no vacancy sign displayed out front. He stopped twenty yards short of the second hotel, a four-storey beige and orange building, and looked back over his shoulder. He was positive no one was following him, but he checked, anyway. Petru noted the security camera just above the door in the entryway. After adjusting the hood on his jacket to hide his face, he walked in.

The reception area was long and narrow. A night clerk sat half hidden behind a glassed in reception counter. Petru spotted a second security camera and kept his head down as he approached. He noticed a small hole cut into the glass for passing money through like he had seen in banks.

The clerk was a man with a round face who was in his early forties. He was balding with a three-day growth and looked disinterested as he asked, "Can I help you?"

"I'd like a room for the night, please."

"Standard or deluxe. Deluxe, you get a queen bed, Wi-Fi and a free breakfast."

"How much for the standard?"

"Seventy-two euros."

"I'll take a standard, thanks."

Petru went to hand over the cash, but the clerk shook his head. "We need a credit card, its company policy."

"Sorry, I don't have a credit card."

The clerk grimaced. "I could get into a lot of trouble…"

"How about an additional ten to overlook the policy?"

Without batting an eyelid, the clerk said, "That will be eighty-two. Please hand it over all at once as we are being recorded on a security camera."

Petru handed over the cash and tried to look interested while the clerk explained the room policy and checkout times. As the clerk handed him the key, he added, "You're in 204, second floor and down the corridor on the left."

Petru thanked the man as he took the key. He took one last glance at the front door before heading up the stairs. The brown carpet along the corridor on the second floor was threadbare and wrinkled in places through constant foot traffic. But Petru couldn't have cared less. After entering his room, he relaxed for the first time in days as he locked the door and collapsed on the bed.

A shiver ran down his spine as he relived the moment they had captured him at gunpoint. He felt his stomach knot as he relived the struggle in the back of the van. The moment he had shot the bearded guy felt like an out-of-body experience. Petru said a quick prayer of thanks and then opened his eyes.

The room was small—just a double bed, a small wardrobe, and a bedside table. If he were an interior designer, he would have described the entire decor as drab gray. But compared to his previous night's accommodation, it was five star. Petru left his backpack on the bed as he got up and opened the wardrobe. There were three coat hangers and one extra blanket. He noted an electric clothes iron on the top shelf before walking through to the tiny adjoining bathroom. It was just big enough to accommodate a shower, a sink, and a toilet. But that was all lost on him as he focused on his reflection in the mirror above the sink. There were spots of blood on his face and jacket. He decided he would shower and wash the clothes he was wearing before he headed out for dinner. He would pick a quiet cafe, close by, and on a side street. He would get takeout and then return to eat his fill.

As he stripped off his clothes, Petru knew Razvan wouldn't give up easily and it would be dangerous to stay in any one location for more than a night. And that meant he should be planning his next move, but he was too exhausted. Tonight he would sleep the sleep of the dead. Tomorrow would be a new day; a day which he suspected would have enough troubles of its own.

Chapter Eighteen

It was well after eight AM on Thursday before Petru awoke. After a long, hot shower the night before, he'd found a quiet diner on a side street. The diner boasted they served the best authentic Romanian dishes in Bucharest and Petru couldn't resist. He found a corner near the rear exit that was largely hidden from the front of the diner and ordered traditional pork meatballs with cabbage and other assorted vegetables. The food reminded him of his childhood trips to the family's ancestral village of Băleni. After a double serving of Papanași for dessert, he called his mother from the comfort of the diner before returning to his hotel room. He told her he had visited Elena's grave and assured her he was safe. His mother pleaded with him to leave Bucharest and he had been vague in his response and promised to call her again in a few days.

After walking back to the hotel room, Petru went to bed. Despite the fresh sheets and a full stomach, sleep did not come easy for him. He kept thinking about the events of the day. Running into Andrei at the cemetery could not have been a coincidence, despite his ruse with the dead flowers. Razvan had surely used Andrei to lure him close to the van. He wondered how long he'd been there. Petru figured Razvan must have had the cemetery under surveillance since the funeral, knowing that he would show up at some point to pay his respects to his sister. He thought back to his time as a captive in the van. He had gotten lucky, no doubt about it. If it wasn't for the traffic causing the driver to brake suddenly, he was positive he would now be floating in the river. He knew he wouldn't be so lucky a second time.

Checkout time was over an hour away. And he was in no hurry to leave his hotel bed. He picked up a scrap of paper from his bedside table and studied the number Andrei had written down. His boss had assured him it was Razvan's direct number, but he knew that was probably a lie. Petru grimaced and went to screw up the piece of paper, but something inside him told him to stop. It was also possible his boss had been telling him the truth. He decided it was worth keeping, just in case.

He placed the paper back on the table and stared up at the ceiling. After paying for the hotel with the money he had taken from the thugs, he still had over nine hundred euros. But he knew that wouldn't go far. He needed the money to last as long as possible, and he needed somewhere else to live. He had considered cheap hostel accommodation. There were places available for under ten euros per night, but he was worried about being robbed of his cash while he slept. He also figured Razvan might have circulated his picture with a cash reward to proprietors of such establishments to be on the lookout for him. He couldn't afford to take the risk and needed something more private. Something off the grid where nobody would be watching. A place that would give him the time and space he needed to figure out what to do next.

A place came to mind almost immediately. It would give him shelter, but not much more. He nodded to himself. If he was careful, he was confident Razvan would never find him.

After leaving the hotel, Petru headed straight for his new hiding place. He wasn't excited about the squalid conditions he would be living in. He decided he would buy food and other supplies to last him a week. That way, he would only have to leave when necessary to minimize the risk of being spotted. He had gone to a local grocery store to figure out what he needed and realized he would need at least two trips on foot to ferry everything he needed to his temporary home. He had debated getting a taxi or Uber to help him move everything in one trip, but that might leave him exposed. One person would know where he was hiding, and that was one too many.

He opted for two trips to the grocery store—a seventy-minute round trip each time. On the first trip, he had focused on food—everything tinned. He had purchased everything from ham and sardines to baked beans, cabbage, and milk. On the second trip, he had focused on other provisions he would need. Candles, plastic crockery and utensils, a flashlight, bug spray, matches, a new toothbrush, and other household items.

Petru cursed to himself after unpacking his supplies from the second trip. He had assumed his new home had water, but he was wrong. There were taps in both the kitchen and the washroom. But none of them worked. He grimaced as he realized he would need to bring in bottled water and reluctantly made a third trip back to the grocery store. The water was heavy, and it was well after six PM by the time he returned. The three trips had left him weary and hungry. He was looking forward to getting inside and securing himself for the night as best he could.

He looked up at the abandoned warehouse in the evening gloom as he approached for the last time. With the meth lab people in jail, he figured this was as good a hiding place as any. After the run-in with the truck driver, he decided he would only enter and exit the building from the laneway out back. He had seen no one close by during any of his trips and hoped he would be safe for the night. After walking in through the hole in the rear fence and across the rear yard, he put the bottles down on the loading dock.

He looked back at the laneway as he raised the roller door. Satisfied that no one had seen him, he moved the two blister packs of water inside the roller door and then closed it behind him. He located a two-foot-long metal rod that the previous occupants had used to secure the roller door and jammed it in between the door and the frame. He pulled on the chain that lifted the door, but it refused to budge. Satisfied that it was secure, he picked up the water and placed it on an old wooden table he had used to store his other supplies.

Petru opened up a bottle of water and drained about a third of the contents in one gulp. He surveyed his new home as he opened a tin of baked beans. The warehouse was damp and musty and smelled of rats, but it did little to dampen his appetite. The conditions were far from ideal, but it was out of the way and the power was still connected to the ground floor. He had already decided he would sleep in a room in the upstairs mezzanine area. The previous inhabitants had left several dirty mattresses in one of the rooms. Not ideal, but he had found a tarp that he would use as a makeshift cover so that he didn't have to sleep directly on the filth that the previous inhabitants had left there.

He stared up at the mezzanine level as he ate his beans. The building had been designed with two modes of access to the upper level; an electric lift and a wooden ramp that ran along the rear wall. The lift no longer worked, and the ramp looked to be almost rotted completely through in one section. The previous tenants had nailed down a piece of particleboard over the top, but he knew that wouldn't hold for long. He was too tired to do anything about it tonight, but it would be a focus for tomorrow morning. He had found a rope pulley system in an old metal locker that still worked. It would be easy enough to rig up from one of the upper metal support beams in the roof so that he could winch himself up and down safely.

After finishing two cans of beans and a bottle of water, Petru relieved himself in one of the toilets downstairs. They all stank of urine and the plumbing didn't work in any of them. He was not sure how the meth lab people had coped with this problem, but it was one he would address as well tomorrow.

Petru grabbed a fresh bottle of water, two chocolate bars, and a flashlight off the table and trudged up the side ramp. He gingerly stepped across the particle board section and grimaced as the structure groaned under his weight. Once safely on the mezzanine, he shone the flashlight over the railing at the ground floor below. He worried about how safe the facility was for him. He had casually asked Detective Mutu about the meth people and whether they would likely return. Mutu had given him an emphatic 'no.' The building was due to be demolished in three months, and most of the members of the gang would serve prison sentences of between twelve months and five years for their crimes.

Petru moved the beam of the flashlight back to the mezzanine level and walked along the landing to the far end. There was one external door that could be accessed by a set of fire stairs from the outside. He had checked it earlier, and it had been locked tight with a large external padlock, but as he settled in for the night, he figured it couldn't hurt to check again. He had already checked the doors at the front of the building, although they were welded shut. The incident with the two men the day before had spooked him and he wasn't about to take any chances. He pulled on the door and was satisfied that it was secure.

After walking back along the landing, Petru entered a room in the middle section. He could feel the temperature dropping and put on another pullover from his backpack. There were two single mattresses in the room. He had laid them on top of one another and then added a tarp on top to separate him from their filth. He lay down and placed the two chocolate bars and his bottle of water on an old wooden box he was using as a bedside table. It was a far cry from the hotel room he'd had the previous evening, but it was dry and hopefully safe. He opened his phone and checked the battery level. He still had sixty-four percent of battery life remaining, which would be more than ample for his needs tonight before he recharged it downstairs in the morning.

He put the phone down beside him and lay back, using one arm as a pillow, and thought about Luca Razvan again. Petru realized he knew very little about the man. He knew he was the head of an organized crime gang and that he was ruthless and violent. And he knew Razvan had police in his pocket, and that he was arrogant and thought he was smarter than everyone else. But beyond that, he knew little else about him. He did not know where he lived, or where he went after work. It was important that he fill in as many of these gaps as he could so that he knew what Razvan's strengths and weaknesses were. He had no doubt that one of them would not survive. He would either avenge Elena's death or die trying. Petru switched off the flashlight and planned on spending an hour or two mapping out in his mind what he would do tomorrow.

But his body had other ideas, and within minutes he drifted off to sleep. He didn't hear the rats stirring, or the creaks in the building as the wind whipped up outside as a storm brewed. He stirred as his dreams brought him back to the van. The bearded guy demanded that he beg for mercy as he stared down the barrel of the gun. Petru cried out in his sleep, but no one heard him above the pounding of the rain on the warehouse roof.

Chapter Nineteen

After a restless night's sleep, Petru spent Friday morning making repairs to the abandoned warehouse. He started by rigging up the pulley system he'd found to one of the building's roof beams to give him access to the upper level. He then found an old rubber mat which he figured he could use as a sling to sit in. Petru needed something to attach it to the pulley rope and settled on some lengths of wire. With the sling attached, he was able to raise and lower himself by pulling on the ropes. Maneuvering the sling over the mezzanine's balcony to dismount proved more challenging. Petru gave up on trying to perfect the technique and cut out a section of the old wooden safety railing instead.

It took a few adjustments, but eventually, he could raise and lower himself to and from the mezzanine in under two minutes. Petru then turned his attention to the ramp. He had initially thought he would just avoid using it. But the more he thought about it, the more he realized he could use the rotting structure to his advantage. He retrieved a rusty saw from an old wooden trunk he had found in a storeroom

The Catalin Connection

and then winched himself up to the mezzanine again. He peered over the railing at the ramp's rotting framework. With a plan in mind, he inched his way down the ramp until he was positioned just above the area covered by the particle board. Leaning over the side, he used the saw to cut through almost all of the rotting frame.

Job done, he retreated to the safety of the mezzanine, and then lowered himself to the ground level again. Petru took a quick break and wiped the sweat from his brow as he sipped on a bottle of water. Keen to finish the job before he had breakfast, he picked up the saw and walked up the ramp as far as the lower part of the rotted section of planking. Petru repeated the process of sawing almost completely through the timber support frame on the lower side and then retreated to the ground floor again.

Petru nodded to himself, as he stood admiring his work. He was positive the ramp would now give way if anyone heavier than a small child tried to walk across it. He didn't want to leave a permanent booby trap and decided he would collapse the rotted section before he left for good. But for now, it served as an additional safety measure. He didn't trust the wedge in the roller door to keep out anyone who really wanted to get in. The ramp would be an extra safeguard for him, particularly while he was sleeping. Anyone who broke in and attempted to creep up the ramp would be in for a rude and possibly fatal shock as they neared the top.

Petru then turned his attention to the toilet. Without water in the building, it was pointless trying to fix the plumbing, and he opted for a simpler solution. He found an old metal bucket in the washroom that would serve his purposes and added a wooden toilet seat from one of the toilets for comfort. It would require a trip outside each day to empty the contents, but that was a small price to pay.

Petru hadn't eaten breakfast yet and it was now close to ten AM. He walked to the table near the rear roller door where he had stored all his food. He decided on another tin of beans and grimaced as he went to open them. There were fresh rat droppings on the table that he had cleaned yesterday. He had heard of people getting sick and even dying after eating food that had been contaminated by rats and decided he needed to keep his supplies more secure. He figured an old wooden trunk he had seen in the storeroom would be ideal and hauled it out. After transferring his food and most of the water to the trunk, he wiped down his tin of beans before opening them.

Petru checked the time on his phone as he ate his meal. There was nothing left to do in the warehouse. He was already feeling restless and thought about Razvan again. He couldn't let him get away with what he'd done; not to Elena, or to Yuri Lebedev, or the countless others he'd murdered. He debated calling Detective Mutu and telling him everything he knew. But Mutu would have closed Elena's missing person's case when her body had been discovered. And trying to engage with any other police officer investigating her murder might make his situation worse if they were on Razvan's payroll.

He knew he would need to go it alone. But trying to find someone who made their money off scamming people online was next to impossible. Such people knew how vulnerable the average internet user was by having a Facebook profile, purchasing online, and oversharing on social media.

In his first few days of living rough he had tried searching on the internet for more information about Razvan, but it quickly became clear he was looking for a ghost. Like most underworld figures, Razvan favored the dark web, encrypted messages, aliases, and burner phones for communication. These precautions made him almost impossible to track. Almost, but not quite. Petru gritted his teeth as he thought about Elena's murder again. He was safe here, but he wasn't going to avenge her murder by hiding.

Petru knew where Razvan worked and that would have to be his starting point. He would follow him each night after he left work, returning to the warehouse during the day to sleep. He would be patient, confident he would eventually find out where he lived and liked to hang out.

His plan would involve risking his life, that was for sure. But it was worth it to get what he needed. And then the game would change. He would become the hunter and Razvan would be the hunted.

It was just after three PM when Petru caught the subway back into the city. He figured Razvan was unlikely to leave his office before five or six PM, and getting in there much before four PM would mean a long period of trying to conceal himself as he waited for him to emerge from the LEU building.

His train arrived in the city shortly before four PM. Petru figured he had about half an hour to spare before he needed to be in position. Already bored with beans and in desperate need of coffee, he picked a cafe in a side street about six blocks from the LEU building for the wait. Petru stepped in through the front door and ignored the smell of roasting coffee as he studied the layout. The cafe was long and narrow. The serving bar ran down one side of the establishment and a row of tables down the other. The place had been renovated and styled with white tables, contrasting black chairs, and recessed lighting. It was only about half full of patrons, and there was a free table near the rear exit. It was perfect for his needs.

He ordered a burger and a long black coffee. After making his way to his table, he thought about how he would undertake his surveillance while he waited. Petru brought up a picture of the front of the LEU building in his mind. It was three stories high, but narrow and made of white painted brick. It had a laneway running down the right-hand side, which gave access to a rear parking lot and delivery area. Razvan drove a late model black Audi, and he insisted no one else be allowed to park out back but him. There was no exit from the rear of the building. That made the logical place for surveillance to be somewhere on the street where he could watch the front of the building and the laneway. He debated putting the hood up on his jacket and walking up and down the opposite side of the street. But he knew he couldn't do that for two hours without raising suspicion.

After closing his eyes, Petru brought up a picture of the buildings across the street. They were all two or three stories tall and used for commercial purposes. The first building was a pharmacy. He had been inside twice to purchase medication for his mother. There was no access that he could recall to the second floor. And he knew he couldn't hang around inside for more than a few minutes without raising suspicion, so he scratched the pharmacy off his list. The second building was like the LEU building. It was a three-story brick construction but without the laneway. A travel company rented the ground floor, but the upstairs tenants were professional businesses. He had visited the dentist on the second floor a few months back for an emergency filling and recalled the stairwell having windows that faced the street. This building was a possibility. He figured he could hang around on the second-floor landing and watch the LEU building across the street without raising too much suspicion. He would need to be ready to move if he spotted Razvan, particularly if he was using his car. While the streets were congested with late afternoon traffic, he knew tracking Razvan for anything more than a few blocks without raising suspicion would be difficult.

Petru sighed to himself. The best outcome was for Razvan to exit the building on foot. Sometimes he drove in, and sometimes he walked. He was not sure why he had no established pattern but he figured if he stuck to the surveillance for long enough he would figure it out. He contemplated walking around the back of the building to fix a tracking device to Razvan's car. It would make following him much easier, but he knew there were security cameras at the rear of the building. He wasn't sure how regularly they were monitored, but he didn't fancy being spotted and trapped with nowhere to go.

Petru thought about the third building. It was like the second building in size and structure, but it had been closed for months. The building had a for sale sign in the front window, and he figured it would probably be locked. The fourth building was two storeys and rented out to a dry cleaning company. Petru had never been in there but figured, like the pharmacy, he wouldn't be able to spend any time inside without raising suspicion.

He thought about the buildings further up and down the street, as his coffee and burger arrived. He couldn't recall too much about them and he would need to use Street View on Google Maps to investigate them more thoroughly. For now, he had at least one potential option for surveillance.

The smell of his coffee and burger was irresistible. He took a sip of his coffee before savoring the first mouthful of his burger. He was under no illusions about the risks he was taking. He couldn't afford to repeat the mistakes he made at the cemetery and it was sobering to think he might be eating his last meal.

Before taking a second sip of his coffee, he murmured, "You're going to need to be far more careful."

After finishing the coffee and burger, Petru walked the six blocks to the LEU building. He kept the hood up on his jacket as he approached on the opposite side of the street. Mindful of what had happened outside the cemetery, he kept a lookout for anyone associated with LEU or Razvan as he approached. He kept his head down until he entered the building with the dental practice on the second floor. He checked the time on his phone as he walked up to the second floor, it was just before four PM. If Razvan was true to form, he would be in place in plenty of time to watch him exit the building.

Petru paused as he got to the landing on the second floor. He looked along the corridor. All the doors to the professional suites, including the dentist, seemed to be closed. He turned his attention to the window that faced the street. After shuffling two paces to the left, he could see both the front door and the side lane of the LEU building. Petru moved back a little to make sure he was standing in the shadows. He knew it was unlikely that anyone on the street or in the building could see him as he settled in to wait.

The next hour passed uneventfully. A few clients had come and gone from the dental surgery and accountancy practices. When the first client left the dental surgery, Petru walked up the stairs to the third level to wait until they had left. But he found the third floor was mostly unoccupied and decided it would be less distracting to continue his surveillance from this level. It was just after five when a trickle of LEU employees started to leave the building.

Petru found the watching and waiting tedious. And he was anxious for his safety. As nightfall descended, he knew that the lights in the stairwell were now illuminating his face, making him more visible to people on the street. He felt vulnerable and strode along the corridor, trying the doors to each of the vacant office suites. He figured it would be much easier to continue his surveillance from a darkened office, but they were all locked. He returned to the stairwell and looked out the window again. He knew he could easily miss Razvan's exit if he tried to find a more suitable lookout spot. As he contemplated his options, a figure emerged through the front door of the LEU building. At first, he didn't recognize the man. He was dressed in a black tracksuit and was talking on his phone, which concealed most of his face. He headed right at a brisk pace.

Petru felt his heart race. It could be Razvan, but he wasn't sure. He had never seen Razvan in a tracksuit before, but something about his gait looked familiar. His gut told him this was the man to follow. But he knew if he was wrong, he was potentially wasting his first night.

Petru followed his gut and bounded down the stairs three at a time. He emerged onto the street and paused for a moment to get his bearings. The man was still on the opposite side of the street, but walking away quickly as he talked on the phone. Petru was about fifty yards back and set off at a brisk pace. The street was busy with pedestrians leaving work which hampered his progress. He desperately wanted to look back over his shoulder to make sure he wasn't being followed but kept his eyes focused on the man to make sure he didn't lose him.

Chapter Twenty

Petru kept up a brisk pace as he followed the man. With a lengthened stride, he closed the gap to within twenty yards in under a minute. He took a quick glance over his shoulder to check he wasn't being followed and then debated crossing the road. But dodging traffic might draw attention to himself. He muttered to himself to stay calm as he continued his pursuit.

Petru maintained his pace as the man kept talking on his phone. He watched as a man in a business suit brushed by him as he walked in the opposite direction. The man in the tracksuit exploded into a volley of obscenities at the slight bump. He turned and gestured with a pointed finger as the man waved a hand in apology. Petru stopped dead in his tracks. He was unsure what to do as he stared into the face of Luca Razvan.

He was afraid to move just in case he drew attention to himself. He murmured, "That was close," as Razvan put the phone back to his ear and stormed off. He realized if Razvan hadn't been so focused on the man, he could have seen him. He pushed the thought from his mind and started walking again. Petru deliberately dropped back a little, using pedestrians on his side of the street as a partial shield. Razvan walked for another block, talking on his phone before disconnecting. He passed a brown three-story apartment block and then disappeared down a side street.

Petru weaved between the traffic as he sprinted across the street to make sure he didn't lose his quarry. He slowed to a walk as he approached the apartment block and then stopped just short of the corner. He peered around the edge of the building into the side street. The street was little more than a laneway and ended in a dead end. It was about eighty yards long and had a mix of commercial and residential structures. All were two or three levels high and mostly made of either stone or brick.

Petru cursed under his breath. He couldn't see any sign of Razvan. He frowned as he studied the layout, wondering which building Razvan had gone into. His gaze settled on a building at the end of the laneway. Unlike the other buildings in the street, it was painted red. Emblazoned across the building in bold white letters were the words, 'Nero's Gym.'

Petru nodded to himself. The gym made sense, given what Razvan had been wearing. Petru frowned as he counted off three security cameras. He knew modern security cameras would pick him up almost immediately when he entered the street. He stood riveted in his position for nearly two minutes while he weighed up his options. He wasn't one-hundred percent sure Razvan was in the gym. He could always wait it out, hoping he would exit the same way he entered. But most buildings in this part of the city had a rear exit. If he stayed here he might wait for hours for nothing.

"You have to do this," he murmured and set off down the laneway at a steady pace.

Petru stuck to the right hand side of the laneway where cars and vans were parked. They provided him with little protection from the security cameras, but it was better than nothing. As he walked down the street, he kept the hood up on his jacket.

His stomach churned and his heart raced. He tried to look casual and murmured, "Just relax." Out of the corner of his eye, he kept watch on the front doors to the gym. His brain was ready to sound the alert to turn and run at the first sign of trouble. But the gym stayed quiet—nobody came, and nobody went. He got to the end of the lane and paused behind a Kombi van, and studied the building.

The windows on the ground floor of the gym were lit up. To the left of the main doors, he could see people inside running on treadmills and others working out on rowing machines. To the right of the main doors, he could see men lifting weights. From his current angle, he had a limited view and developed a plan in his head.

He would cross the laneway and steal a look through the front glass doors. He figured he should be able to spot Razvan if he was working out somewhere on the ground floor. If he couldn't, he would go inside and take a quick look around. Two minutes max and then he would be out of there. He looked up at the upper level, which was mostly in darkness. He figured they used it as office space, or perhaps for special workout classes. But checking it out would mean more time and more risk.

Petru frowned. He could find himself in the same situation as yesterday if he got this wrong. He could barely feel his legs as he walked the twelve yards that separated him from the front glass doors. He could hear music coming from inside as he stepped up onto the landing. The kind of music that you heard in nightclubs—high energy, with a driving beat.

He peered in through the two front glass doors. To his left, he could see eleven fitness junkies working out on treadmills and rowing machines. There were four men in the group. He studied each male face, but none of them were Razvan. He turned his attention to the right. The space in this section was dedicated to body builders. The layout was like his gym; benches, racks, smith machines, leg machines, multi-function trainers, barbells and dumbbells.

There were six men in this section, but none of them were Razvan. He looked up the staircase, but it was impossible to see anything beyond the landing to the upper level.

He turned his attention back to the ground floor. As he pondered if he should go inside, he spotted an exit sign in the far right hand corner of the weight lifting section. He wasn't sure if it led to a shower and change rooms, or a corridor that gave access to the street behind. It didn't matter, his gut told him he had been here too long anyway.

As he turned to leave, a man descended the stairs. He wasn't dressed for a workout and had his eyes locked on Petru. Petru frowned. He thought he had seen him before, and turned to walk away. Out of the corner of his eye, he could see the man bolting down the stairs.

Petru had seen enough and set off at a sprint. He took a glance over his shoulder and swore as the man withdrew a silenced pistol from his coat pocket as he burst through the doors of the gym. Petru darted between cars as the side window of the Kombi van exploded into a sea of glass.

Crouching down, he darted further to his left, sprinting up the footpath towards the main street. He could hear footsteps behind him and hoped the main street would bring him some safety. But it was still thirty yards ahead.

As he willed his legs to move faster, a man rounded the corner at the top of the laneway. He looked calm and collected as he raised a silenced pistol. Petru tried to dart between two cars as the pistol spat into life. He heard a window in the car behind him shatter before a searing pain exploded in his right hip. He felt his body spin around as another searing pain erupted in his stomach.

Petru felt waves of nausea wash over him as his legs collapsed beneath him. He tried to get up, but his body refused to cooperate. He could hear the sound of a siren as a man stood over him. He looked up into the face of the man who had shot him. The man kept his pistol trained on Petru's head as the man from the gym came and stood alongside him.

The man from the gym said, "Luca will be here in a moment."

Street guy declared, "He's not going anywhere," as Petru's eyes rolled into the back of his head.

Petru momentarily lost focus. When his vision returned, there were three men standing over him. The man in the middle, was a little shorter than the other two and dressed in a black tracksuit.

Razvan leaned down close to Petru and slapped him across the face. "You little piss ant! You're way out of you're league." He straightened up and turned to Gym guy and said, "Give me your gun, I want to finish this now."

Gym guy handed over his gun, and added, "Those sirens are getting louder. The police are close."

Razvan nodded, "You're right," and then leaned down

close to Petru again. He put the gun at his temple and hissed, "This may be your lucky day, if you don't bleed out first…"

Petru's eyes rolled into the back of his head. The sirens were deafening now, almost as if they were inside his head. When he opened his eyes again, all he could see were strobes of red and blue. He could hear frantic voices calling to one another above him as he drifted off to sleep.

Chapter Twenty-One

Petru could hear a muffled beeping sound somewhere above his head. It was rhythmic and coming every two seconds. He tried to open his eyes, but the light was blinding. He tried to call out for help, but no sound escaped his mouth.

He was aware of the woman's voice, who murmured, "I think he's coming around."

There were other hushed voices, but Petru couldn't decipher the words. The beep continued—monotonous, and loud. He blinked several times as his eyes adjusted to the light. He heard the voices again. And then someone taking hold of his right hand. The hand was cool and soft. Petru blinked again, trying to focus on the figure who stood beside him.

The voice said, "Petru, if you can hear me, please squeeze my hand."

Petru took a second to process the instruction before gently squeezing the hand.

The voice said, "He can hear me. Can you please call Dr. Nechita? I think he's in the next ward."

Petru blinked a couple more times. The figure of a matronly woman in her late forties came into focus. She was wearing a light blue uniform with a metal nameplate pinned to her chest. Her dark hair was graying at the temples and pulled back in a bun.

The woman lifted his head gently and said, "I'm going to give you a sip of water. Do you know where you are?"

Petru tried to say the word, "No" but his throat was on fire and he only managed a guttural sound. He took two sips of water and felt exhausted.

The nurse made him take a couple more sips before she laid his head back on the pillow.

He managed, "Where am I?" in a croaky voice.

"You're in Bucharest General Hospital. Do you remember what happened?"

Petru closed his eyes. He remembered visiting Elena's grave and his mother moving back to Băleni. He didn't think he was living in the apartment anymore as he racked his brain. He was sure some things had happened in his life since then… bad things, but he couldn't remember. "No."

"Doctor Nechita will be here shortly," said the nurse in a soothing voice. "I'm sure he'll explain everything to you."

The nurse gently lifted Petru's head again and insisted he drink more water. He managed three sips before he felt nauseous. She laid his head down on the pillow again. As he breathed in and out to settle the nausea, he felt himself relax as he drifted off to sleep.

Petru could hear voices again. He recognized the nurse's voice and another female voice, and then he heard a male voice. The man's voice sounded similar to Luca Razvan. Petru gasped as he felt his heart race.

The nurse hovered above him as he tried to roll off the bed and soothed, "Petru, you're safe. Dr. Nechita is here, and he'd like to talk to you."

Petru swallowed hard as the doctor came and stood by his bed.

Nechita was in his late thirties. He wore a white coat with a stethoscope draped around his neck. The glasses balanced on his forehead looked like they might fall off at any moment. He introduced himself, and said, "Nurse Sandu tells me you don't remember anything?"

Petru shook his head.

"Well, that's not that uncommon. You've suffered a major trauma, and you may never get that part of your memory back."

Petru croaked, "What happened?"

"You were shot. In Cenci Lane. You lost a lot of blood and we had to operate. Three operations, in fact, but you're stable now. And we hope that... in time, you will make a recovery."

Petru closed his eyes and was instantly back in the laneway, trying to escape as he collapsed under a hail of bullets. The doctor continued talking, explaining that he had been shot in the hip and the stomach and that he would probably never be able to walk again, but the words were lost on him.

He tried opening his eyes again, but the nightmare dragged him down deeper. He lay in a pool of his own blood as Razvan stood over him. A wave of panic swept over him as he tried to get up but his legs failed him. Petru wept as he realized he would never walk again.

Chapter Twenty-Two

Nine weeks of rehabilitation in Bucharest General had the doctors and nurses excited about Petru's prospects. But he didn't share their optimism. He had learned to use a wheelchair and control his bowel movements and was almost off all medication. All fantastic achievements in such a short period he had been told.

But coming to grips with the fact he was now a paraplegic was something entirely different. He had no feeling in his body below his navel. He could punch his leg and feel nothing but a sting in his hand. His lower body no longer felt a part of him. In his dreams, he could still walk, but he figured a day was coming when he would be a paraplegic in his sleep as well. He looked up at the wall clock above the door to his ward. It was just after ten AM and he was already back from his morning physiotherapy session, which was now just a few minutes each day, and he was bored.

The other patients from his ward would all be having physiotherapy for the rest of the morning. Most of them had limited or no upper body movement and he couldn't blame the therapy team for giving them more attention.

Petru sighed as he gazed at nothing in particular. Just a curtain separated his bed from the other patients. He had become quite close to several of them and enjoyed the conversation they had each day. They would talk about their lives before the car accident, or the motorcycle accident, or the work accident which wrecked their lives and brought them to the spinal unit in Bucharest General.

But it would be two hours before they would be back in the ward. And then the lunchtime routine would begin. Some of them had to be cradled back into bed before being spoon-fed their lunch, and most of them had to be assisted with their toilet functions. There was no dignity or privacy in the ward and everyone struggled with giving up their independence.

He had only been in the ward a week before he realized how much worse his situation could have been. The doctors had informed him that one of the two bullets had hit the L5 vertebra in his lower spine severely damaging his spinal cord and causing his paralysis. The other bullet had hit him in the hip, but due to the angle of entry, had only grazed the bone.

He still had full use of his upper body and the bullet wounds had largely healed. He had heard murmurings amongst the doctors and nurses that he would be discharged in the coming days and had no idea what would become of him. His mother had all but recovered from her beating and he still called her twice a week. But he was yet to tell her his news. The thought of his relatives descending on the hospital from his home village was more than he could bear. His mother had enough to worry about and his relatives would insist he return to Băleni to live with them—a thought almost as painful as being a paraplegic itself.

Petru rolled his wheelchair out of the ward and along a corridor towards a room that had been set up as an additional exercise room for spinal patients. The nurses and doctors no longer tried to keep him confined to the ward and even encouraged him to develop his own exercise program. He had used his smartphone to search for exercises that paraplegics should be undertaking and was horrified to see how deficient the hospital's rehab program was. He couldn't blame them. This hospital was like most in Romania; overcrowded and under resourced with not enough doctors, nurses or therapists.

Petru wheeled his chair into the room. It was small by comparison to the main therapy room, but it had a few dumbbells and a modified lat pull down machine that could be used by people in a wheelchair.

He started with dumbbells, following a program that he had seen on the internet that had been approved by his therapist. There were a variety of exercises that would help preserve his biceps and upper body strength. The therapist had warned him not to overdo it and to start with just ten or fifteen minutes a day. Petru had been doing the program for ten days now and was already doing half an hour a day or more of exercises. His goal was to be able to lift himself in and out of bed from his wheelchair without assistance. It was Wednesday and he was close. He figured if he kept building up his strength he would be able to manage the task on his own by the weekend.

After completing his bicep curls, he moved on to shoulder presses. Within a few minutes, he had worked up a sweat.

Petru's full memory returned in the days after his hospitalization. He had gone through a range of emotions in the early days. Denial, then depression, and then anger about his paralysis. He had gradually come to accept his situation, but the anger remained as he continually thought about the confrontation in the laneway with Luca Razvan. He knew had it not been for the proximity of the police, Razvan would have finished him. He often wondered whether he would be better off dead? But there had to be a reason why he was spared. His disability changed nothing. He still wanted to bring Razvan down, but he had no idea how he might go about it now.

There had been multiple police interviews, but he gave them nothing. Why was he in the laneway? Did he know who shot him and why? Every question he had met with the same answer, *'I don't remember anything except waking up in the hospital.'*

He was pretty sure the police didn't believe him. But the doctors backed him up, confirming it wasn't uncommon for patients not to remember anything about the events that caused their injuries. He had promised to contact them if he remembered anything, but he couldn't see that ever happening. The police hadn't come across any eyewitnesses. If he pressed charges it would be just his word against Razvan's. And with all Razvan's resources, he would come up with a watertight alibi, making it a fight he would never win.

Petru gritted his teeth. Being a paraplegic changed everything. He would need to learn how to survive on the outside before he contemplated revenge. And that meant finding some place to live and figuring out how he would earn an income. He still had the use of his hands and his brain. Maybe Emil from the computer store would give him his job back? He could still do most of the work, and he was good at what he did. He thought about going back into hacking, but he realized a life of crime was not for him. He grimaced as he continued with bicep curls. He wanted to go straight. Even begging on the streets was preferable to going back to his old life.

Petru put down the dumbbells and wheeled his way under the lat machine. He was now a lather of sweat, but he didn't care. He gripped the machine's handles and began pulling them down, murmuring, "One, two, three…" as he worked his way into a rhythm.

Petru thought about where he might live. His backpack had vanished when he had been admitted to hospital and he had no money. He had heard the nurses say that the government could find him accommodation in a half-way house. Somewhere where he could stay until he found a job. But he had heard horror stories about such places as well. Men in vulnerable positions being raped and worse. Petru shook his head—a halfway house was not for him.

He wondered about going back to Băleni. He knew his family would welcome him and his mother would stop worrying. But the village was small and there would be no work for him there. He would be dependent on family, and that was not the way he wanted to live.

As he pushed on with his exercises, he refused to wallow in self pity. Without a home or friends who would stand by him, things looked grim. A therapist had told him the Romanian government offered a monthly stipend to people in his situation, and although it was modest, it was a start and he wouldn't starve.

Petru sighed as he completed his workout. "What a mess," he murmured. He paused for a moment, sucking in some deep breaths. He didn't want to return to the ward just yet and pulled his phone out of a side pocket in his wheelchair. He had already started looking at private accommodation and jobs on the internet. Both endeavors had proven to be depressing. When he met with his case manager tomorrow, he would ask her how much time he had left in the hospital. He hoped he could stay here at least until his government benefit started and he had some money coming in.

He wondered again how it had all gone so horribly wrong in the laneway? Had Razvan known that he was following him? It occurred to him that maybe he had been spotted across the road in the building and Razvan leaving the LEU building in a tracksuit was a ruse to get him to follow. He wondered if the phone call Razvan had been making while he walked had been to one of his henchman who was following at a safe distance.

Petru looked down at his wheelchair. Trying to tail Razvan to find the information he needed had proven disastrous, and almost fatal. He would need to come up with a different strategy—a different way to make Razvan pay for what he had done. He thought about what he still had that Razvan wanted back. Maybe there was a way? A way where he called the shots and Razvan came to him? He figured he had one last chance. Petru wheeled himself back towards the ward as a plan formed in his mind.

Chapter Twenty-Three

Petru finished the meeting with his case worker earlier than expected. She had informed him the hospital believed he had recovered sufficiently to be released. In hindsight, proving to the nursing staff that he could now get from his bed to his wheelchair without help had been his undoing. He couldn't blame the hospital. Two new patients had arrived in the spinal unit that week and they had moved him out to a single room temporarily. His case worker said he was well enough to leave and was already organizing accommodation in a halfway house for him.

The conversation had become heated. The caseworker insisted he would benefit from the supervision and help, but Petru wasn't so sure. The stories he had heard about such institutions reinforced the feeling he would be better off trying to find somewhere to live on his own. He would be discharged in three days, which didn't give him a lot of time to find something. And with his special needs for accommodation without stairs, it would be no easy task.

Petru checked the time on a wall clock as he wheeled

along a corridor back to his room. It was close to five PM. His evening meal was normally delivered around six PM which gave him time to start his search in earnest now that he had a discharge date.

He paused in his doorway before switching on the light. A man was sitting on a chair in the shadows next to his bed. Petru frowned. The man had his legs crossed and seemed relaxed as he said, "Come on in, Petru. I've been waiting for you."

Petru gasped as he flicked on the light switch and stared into the face of Luca Razvan. He remained in the open doorway and glanced up and down the corridor trying to control his panic. He could see no nurses or doctors, and snapped, "What are you doing here?"

Razvan produced a small knife and used the blade to manicure his fingernails. He said casually, "You and I have unfinished business."

Petru scanned the hallway again. Trying to escape from Razvan in a wheelchair was unrealistic. Apart from calling out for help, he could do nothing except wait for a staff member to show up. As his brain screamed at him not to enter his room, he responded, "I have nothing to say to you."

Razvan looked up from his nails. "On the contrary, we have a lot to talk about. And I have my spies everywhere. I know you will be discharged in three days..." Razvan sneered as he added, "And as soon as you leave this hospital, we are going to have a nice long talk about what you've stolen from me."

Petru thought for a moment. The wrong answer could get him killed. No words came to mind to help his cause and he held Razvan's stare defiantly as he prayed for a staff member to appear.

Razvan seemed in no hurry. As he focused on cleaning his fingernails again, he said, "When I heard that you'd survived the incident in the laneway, I was initially very angry. But then I thought, perhaps it was for the best…" He looked up again and added, "I remember when I was eight or nine and playing in the backyard of our house one morning. There was a small bird hopping around in the garden. It had a broken wing and looked so miserable. Do you know what I did, Petru?"

Petru shook his head.

Razvan laughed. "I picked up a stick and beat it to death. It only took three blows. It was a long time ago, but I still remember it. I justified it to myself at the time that I was doing it a favor." Razvan paused as his face turned into an evil grin. "But the truth is I enjoyed it." He leaned forward and added, "Have you ever played God, Petru? Have you ever decided if something should live or die?"

Petru listened for footsteps in the corridor. When he heard none, he responded, "No."

"I've been thinking about you a lot, Petru. The merciful thing would be for me to kill you after you've told me what I need to know…"

Razvan cocked his head to one side. "But it occurred to me, you're like that little bird with a broken wing. You'll never walk again. You'll be reliant on others for the rest of your life. All your dreams and ambitions have been shattered. I tried to put myself in your shoes. I wouldn't want to live, so perhaps letting you live is the greater punishment?"

Razvan got up from the chair and walked across the room. He pulled Petru's chair into the middle of the room and then grabbed his face. He pressed the knife up against his skin just below his left eye. Petru felt blood trickle down his face as Razvan growled, "I'll decide later if you live or die… but if you live, being in a wheelchair will be the least of your problems."

Petru let out a breath as Razvan pushed him away and walked out of the room. He listened to Razvan's footsteps along the corridor until they faded to nothing. As bile rose from his stomach, he had hoped his nightmare was ending, but maybe this was just the beginning.

Petru tossed and turned for most of the night. He dreamed Razvan had returned in the middle of the night to cut him to pieces. He woke up in a lather of sweat frequently during the night and found it difficult to return to sleep. It was just after seven AM when the hospital attendant woke him as he delivered his breakfast of coffee, scrambled eggs on toast, and an apple. The smell of food made him hungry, but after a few mouthfuls of his scrambled eggs, he became distracted again and pushed his food away.

While sipping on his coffee, he contemplated Razvan's threat. He knew Razvan wasn't bluffing. It was now Friday and he would only have three days to figure out what he was going to do before they discharged him on Monday. He figured wherever he went, Razvan would find him. And he would be dead before the day ended.

Petru let out a long breath. He knew what Razvan was after, but trying to make a deal would be futile. He had been over it again and again in his mind. If he gave him what he wanted, Razvan would kill him. If he didn't, Razvan would torture him until he told him what he needed to know, and then he would kill him.

He recalled Razvan's words from their encounter yesterday; *'I have my spies everywhere.'*

He knew Razvan would have paid off people in the hospital to keep tabs on him. He had to find a way to get out of the building without anyone knowing.

Petru scowled. It would be nearly impossible in his condition. He racked his brain as he tried to figure out what to do next. He contemplated going to the police, but there wasn't enough hard evidence.

Petru reached up his left finger and felt the scab on his face from the knife wound. He shuddered as he realized how much worse his life could get.

He needed to get out of bed. Before becoming a paraplegic, he did his best thinking while walking. As he got used to life in a wheelchair, the motion of wheeling himself around also helped him to think.

As he reached out to grab the handrail on his bed, a male nurse walked into his room. He was about six feet four with short, curly hair and a full beard. Petru guessed the man was in his early thirties. He noticed the man was slightly overweight and that the uniform looked too tight on him.

He stood at the end of the bed and read Petru's chart. "Petru, right?"

"I don't believe we've met."

The man placed the chart back in its holder. "You're right. I'm new.... actually, I don't work here."

Petru reached for his buzzer as a cold shiver ran down his spine.

The man held his hands up. "I'm not here to hurt you. Quite the opposite, in fact. I know all about Razvan, and I know he's gunning for you."

Petru frowned. "Did you say... Razvan?"

"Luca Razvan, in fact," said the man with a nod. "We have a lot in common, and a lot to talk about."

The man moved to the door and said, "Do you mind if I close this?"

"No! Leave it open. I don't know who you are or what you want."

The man said, "Luca Razvan killed my sister as well," and then closed the door.

Chapter Twenty-Four

Silence descended on the hospital room. It hadn't occurred to Petru that there might be others in a similar situation to his. Finally, Petru shook his head. "I don't know what to say."

The man said, "You don't need to say anything for now," as he sat in a chair next to Petru's bed. "First, my name is Nicolai Enescu. My sister's name was Nadia. She knew your sister, Elena. That's how I found out about you…"

Petru frowned. "So, your sister knew my sister?"

"Yes."

"How did Nadia die?"

"They shot her…" choked Nicolai. "And then dumped her in the river. It happened about six months ago."

"I'm sorry."

"Thanks. Let me start from the beginning. I work for the Roma Bank. I have been—"

"Wait," said Petru as he held up a hand. "This sounds like it's going to take a while."

"Yes, we have lots to talk about."

"I don't want to talk here. It will look suspicious if my door stays closed."

"Okay, where shall we go?"

"Head down the corridor. At the end, there's a door on the right that leads into a small gym. We can talk there without attracting too much attention. But you'll have to give me ten minutes. I'm still learning how to get out of bed and dress myself."

"Do you want me to give you a hand?"

Petru shook his head and said he needed to learn to do it himself. He waited until Nicolai had left the room and then pulled out his phone. He would get out of bed and get dressed in a moment. First, he needed to check out Nicolai online to make sure he was telling the truth.

It took Petru close to twenty minutes to get ready. He spent almost half the time checking Nicolai's social media accounts. The man seemed to check out. He posted little on his Facebook account, even though it had been active for six years. He double-checked the information against Nicolai's LinkedIn account and discovered he had a degree in economics and worked at the Roma Bank, just as he had explained.

He had done a quick search for Nadia Enescu but came up with nothing that matched. He wondered if she was a half-sister with a different name, or if they had deleted her accounts. He would quiz Nicolai when the time was right. For now, he had enough. Nicolai probably hadn't been sent to kill him, and it was worth hearing him out.

Petru paused in the doorway to the gym room. He half

expected the room to be empty, but Nicolai was sitting patiently on a stool in the corner.

"Sorry I took so long."

Nicolai waved him off. "It's fine. I've taken the whole day off, so I don't mind the wait."

"I'm going to set up for exercise," said Petru as he wheeled under the lat machine. "That way, if anyone looks in, it won't look so suspicious."

Once he was settled, Nicolai said, "I've been sitting here thinking about where to start. I've decided it's important that you hear about Nadia first."

Petru nodded.

"Nadia was twenty-two. She was studying law at the university. She was intelligent, but not street smart. She liked going to parties and developed a liking for cocaine… that was her downfall."

The story sounded eerily familiar as Nicolai recounted how his sister had fallen into prostitution to feed her drug habit. He wasn't sure exactly how Nadia and Elena had met, but they were friends on Facebook and had probably worked together at some point.

Petru thought it an opportune time to ask his question. "Is Nadia's last name also Enescu?"

"No," said Nicolai with a shake of his head. "It's a long story, but my father didn't treat my mother very well. He used to beat her and Nadia was ashamed to have the same last name as his. She changed her last name to Duca, which was my mother's maiden name, about two years ago."

Petru nodded. The story explained why he hadn't been able to find her immediately on Facebook.

Nicolai continued, "After they found Nadia, the police started a murder investigation but it went nowhere. I got friendly with one of the detectives and he told me off the record it was probably the work of Luca Razvan or one of his associates, but proving it would be almost impossible."

"That sounds familiar," said Petru.

"I started to dig into Razvan's background. I even hired a private detective. He came back to me after just two days and told me Razvan was part of an organized crime syndicate that stretches from here to Canada and the US. Everything from drugs and internet scams to sex slaves."

Petru frowned. "Sex slaves?"

"Yes," said Nicolai with a nod. "The detective told me he sells some of the most desirable prostitutes in Bucharest to overseas buyers for the right price."

"Is that what happened to Nadia?"

"I don't know," said Nicolai with a grimace. "The private detective quit after just two days. When he found out who he was investigating, he told me it wasn't worth his life. Nadia was very head strong. She might have been hooked on drugs, but she would have fought for all she was worth if they tried to abduct her."

Petru thought about Elena and wondered if that was her fate as well. She had done some modeling and was very attractive. The thought of her being sold as a sex slave had never occurred to him. "I worked for Razvan at LEU. I knew about the internet scams, but not about everything else."

"He's pure evil. If you cross him, you'll normally pay with your life." Nicolai pointed at the wheelchair and added, "You got lucky."

Petru frowned. "He came in yesterday. He knows I'm being discharged on Monday. And—"

"He's going to finish the job he didn't finish in the laneway…"

"Yes. How did you know?"

"I've been following your story. I have a few contacts that I've built up over the past six months—people I trust—who have a similar interest in seeing Razvan's downfall." Nicolai shifted on the stool. "Which brings me to why I'm here. If you stay here until Monday, your fate is sealed. You have to get out of here as soon as you can."

"I have nowhere to go. The hospital wants to put me in a half-way house, but I figure Razvan will know about it before I do."

"I have a proposal for you, Petru. That's why I'm here."

"Okay…"

"I'll help you escape from here and I'll find you accommodation if you agree to help me bring down Razvan. I figure with all your hacking experience you can help me get the information I need on Razvan to finally go to the police."

Petru mused, "I want to help, but I can't hack into LEU. I know how it's setup and the data you need can't be accessed via an external network, you have to be inside the building."

"Well, then that's what we'll do."

"No. He has alarms on everything and guards inside twenty-four seven. Even if I was still an employee I couldn't bust in."

Nicolai frowned. "Well… that's disappointing. There must be something you can do?"

Petru chewed on his bottom lip. "There may be, but I can't promise anything."

"I'm all ears," said Nicolai with a raise of an eyebrow.

Petru thought for a moment. What he was about to share he had never shared with anyone else. He knew it was risky giving someone else this information, but he realized he had no choice. "When I first joined LEU, I had a low level job in their call center scamming people out of money. I hated it and knew I had to show them I was more capable. One morning, one of the servers in LEU failed and the guy who normally looks after the equipment was on a day off. They knew I had similar skills—"

"You fix computers too?"

"Before LEU, I worked for a computer company fixing computers and servers. Anyway, they asked me to do the repair. I was escorted to the server room by a security guard—"

"The servers are in a special room?"

"Yes. It's always locked and only a handful of people have a key. The guard was supposed to stay with me, but he was having girlfriend problems and spent most of his time outside on his phone where the reception was better. I replaced a hard drive in the faulty server but had to wait a couple of hours while I restored the data from a backup. While I was waiting, I noticed two servers on their own in a separate rack. I was curious as they were locked behind a Perspex screen."

Nicolai frowned. "No other servers were locked up."

"No. But that's fairly standard in a server room that's already locked. I noticed the cabling to these two servers was a different color, and I figured out it was a separate network."

"So why two networks?"

"That was my question. Curiosity got the better of me. I broke into the cabinet to—"

"You busted the cabinet?"

"No," said Petru with half a smile. "I just unscrewed the perspex door from its hinges."

"So much for security."

"Agreed. Locks only draw attention. They would have been better off without them."

"Okay, so what next?"

"The guard poked his head into the room. When I told him I needed another ninety minutes, he disappeared again."

"He didn't see the doors missing on the special rack?"

"He's not an IT guy. All equipment looks the same to him."

"So they left you alone for an hour and a half?"

Petru nodded. "I thought maybe this was a way to make a name for myself. I found a USB drive in a cupboard and copied the data off the server. It only took—"

"Wait!" said Nicolai, holding up his hand. "How do you make a name for yourself stealing data that LEU already own?"

"I was going to show my boss the security vulnerability."

"That's a ballsy way to get noticed."

Petru grimaced. "I didn't think it through."

"So you made a copy?"

Petru nodded. "It only took fifteen minutes. The data looked like a backup of a single PC or laptop. I had no real interest in the data itself; it was just about proving it could be done."

"So, you think it was Razvan's laptop or computer?"

"That's my guess. But, as I said, I never analyzed it. I screwed the Perspex cover back on and put the USB drive in my pocket. I was almost done restoring the data when the guard returned. He had no idea what I had done. I planned to give the USB drive to my boss and tell him his security sucked, but that never happened."

"Why not?"

"He'd taken the remainder of the day off due to some

family emergency. The following day, rumors were floating around at LEU about Yuri Lebedev. Yuri worked at LEU until—"

"They caught him trying to sell data to a Russian syndicate."

Petru's eyes widened. "You knew about that?"

"Yes," said Nicolai with a nod. "My private investigator in fact. Finding out about Lebedev's murder made him nervous and that was why he quit."

"I got nervous too. I decided to keep what I'd done quiet for a while. I wanted to make sure it didn't blow back in my face. But the more I learned about LEU, the more I realized what I'd done was stupid and could get me killed if it was ever discovered."

"So what happened to the USB? Did you take it home?"

"It's still in the building."

"It's still in LEU?"

Petru nodded. "Taped up inside my locker."

"Do you think it's still there?"

"Probably. The locker door isn't quite full height. There's a space at the top behind the frame that you can't see unless you bend down and deliberately look up. That's where I taped the USB. Unless someone knows where to look, they'd probably never find it."

"You didn't think to bring it home?"

"When I heard about Yuri, I didn't want to endanger my family, so I just left it there."

"And you think it's a backup of Razvan's computer?"

Petru nodded. "It all makes sense now."

"It makes sense now?"

"Razvan knows I've stolen data and wants it back. When he was here yesterday and threatened me, I'm sure that's what it was about."

"How did he find out that you'd stolen the data?"

"I'm not sure. The technique I used bypassed the logging programs on the server, so I'm positive I didn't leave a digital trace. And I couldn't see any cameras anywhere. I'm thinking maybe the guard escorted someone else in at a later date and noticed the difference."

"That the two perspex panels were in place?"

Petru nodded. "That's all I can think of."

Nicolai scratched his chin. "Well, I would still like to get my hands on that device. Having Razvan's personal data might be all we need to sink him."

Petru let out a long breath. "There might be a way… it's risky, but under the circumstances, it's probably worth it."

Chapter Twenty-Five

Petru and Nicolai talked briefly about how to break into LEU. The rest of the time they spent planning how to get him out of the hospital. They had considered Petru simply discharging himself, which he was legally free to do. But that would require paperwork and potentially delays at the front office which might give Razvan's henchman time to get in place to intercept him as he left.

They agreed it was safer to sneak out late at night when there were a smaller number of staff on shift. They had then spent time planning the escape and came up with a route that avoided the nursing stations. Petru was a little uncertain about exiting through the morgue, but Nicolai insisted it would be the easiest place to park close to the building's exit.

After agreeing, they had shaken hands. Nicolai had promised to return sometime after eleven PM. The rest of the day passed slowly for Petru. He did a full workout in his small gym and secretly packed up his meager belongings, including his catheter and medications in an overnight bag in readiness for Nicolai's arrival.

Petru lifted the covers on his bed and checked the time on his phone. It was now four minutes to midnight, and he was getting worried. Nicolai should have been here by now. He wondered if something had gone wrong. He wondered if Nicolai had gotten cold feet. Or if Razvan had used Nicolai as a ruse to find out where the data was kept. But Razvan seemed to prefer threats and violence to get what he wanted. And Nicolai had seemed genuine. The rage that burned within Nicolai when he spoke about Razvan would have been difficult to maintain for the two hours they had spent together if it was fake.

A figure appeared in the doorway as he went to check the time on his phone again.

"Petru?" the figure whispered in a baritone voice.

Petru breathed a sigh of relief. "Come in, Nicolai."

"Sorry I took so long," whispered Nicolai. "I've borrowed a van. That way, you won't be seen. But it took longer than I planned to collect it. Are you ready to go?"

Petru swung his legs off the bed. "Can you help me into my chair? Normally I do this myself, but we don't want to be hanging around here too long."

Nicolai nodded. "I've got a gurney outside. I figure it would be easier to hide you under a sheet on the way out. And I have a wheelchair in the van for you."

Petru noticed Nicolai was wearing the same ill-fitting nurse's uniform he had on earlier in the day. "That makes sense. No one's likely to question an orderly who's taking a body to the morgue."

Nicolai lifted Petru off the bed and carried him into the corridor and placed him on the gurney. After covering him with the sheet, he whispered, "I'll go grab your bag and then we can go."

Petru could see very little from under the sheet as the gurney rumbled along. He could make out lights as they passed underneath them, but not much more. He did his best to lie perfectly still as he acted out his part as the corpse. Nicolai kept him informed of progress every minute or so, whispering the location as they moved along the corridors.

It was only when Nicolai wheeled the gurney into an elevator that Petru realized they had company.

He heard a woman's voice over the grating sound of the door closing. "Thanks for holding the elevator. They're really slow, even at this time of night."

Petru held his breath as Nicolai muttered, "No problem."

The woman asked, "Are you new here? I don't think I've seen you before."

"Yeah, I started last week."

"Where is the patient from?"

"The spinal unit. Gunshot injuries, I believe."

"Gun crime is such a common thing these days."

"Tell me about it."

Petru heard a bell and felt the elevator come to a stop.

The woman said, "This is me. I hope you enjoy your time here."

Nicolai said, "Thanks," as the door opened.

Petru heard the doors close again. Nicolai muttered, "That was close…"

"You handled it well," said Petru from under the sheet as the elevator started its descent again.

"Not long now..." said Nicolai, as the elevator shuddered to a halt.

Petru went quiet as Nicolai wheeled the gurney out into a passageway.

Nicolai whispered, "We have a long corridor in front of us that leads to the morgue. There's one guy there on night shift, but we won't actually be entering the facility. There's a door on the right about halfway down that leads to the car park. When we get there, I'll put you up over my shoulder and carry you out to the van."

"Okay."

Petru could now only see shapes and shadows from beneath the sheet. He figured the lighting was poor in this corridor and felt his body break out into a sweat as the gurney rumbled along. As a paraplegic, he was still learning how to rely on people. He promised himself he would only rely on people he could trust. Was Nicolai one of them? He figured he would know within an hour.

The gurney stopped, and Nicolai ripped back the sheet. Petru blinked several times to allow his eyes to adjust to the light. Nicolai helped him up into a sitting position. Petru breathed a sigh of relief as he scanned to his left and his right. They were about halfway along a dimly lit gray corridor and next to a metal door just as Nicolai had described. His accomplice motioned him to be quiet as he produced a small block of wood from his pocket. Petru watched as Nicolai cracked open the metal door and wedged the block of wood in at the bottom to keep it open.

He felt an icy breeze and figured the door led to the parking lot.

Nicolai returned and motioned Petru to raise his arms.

Petru complied and Nicolai leaned forward, grabbing his left arm as he lifted him up and over his shoulder in a firefighter's carry.

Despite being six-foot-one, Nicolai picked him up with ease. Using Petru's body, he gently pushed open the door and shuffled outside and then across the parking lot. Petru could see puddles of water on the ground below him and realized this was the first time he had been outdoors since the incident.

Nicolai muttered, "I think we're clear," as they reached the back of the van. Half holding Petru, Nicolai opened the rear door and set Petru down on the tailgate. While keeping a firm grip on Petru, Nicolai maneuvered himself inside the van. Petru glanced at the interior as Nicolai dragged him forward. The van was a battered and aging Fiat. It had no side windows, but it did have a wheelchair, just as Nicolai had promised.

Petru breathed a sigh of relief as Nicolai lifted him into the wheelchair.

After getting him settled, Nicolai pushed the chair hard up against the back of the two front seats. "Lock your wheels while I get in front."

Petru complied as Nicolai jumped out of the van. Petru spotted a silhouetted figure through the van's rear windows as Nicolai slammed the doors shut. The man was standing in an open doorway that led into the morgue.

The man yelled, "Hey, what do you think you're doing?"

Petru watched the man sprint toward the van as Nicolai jumped into the driver's seat.

Petru swore as the van roared to life and Nicolai yelled, "Brace yourself!" The van took off with a jerk as Nicolai added, "I'm about to pull a hard left onto the street."

Petru reached up and grabbed hold of part of the van's

frame for stability as the vehicle screeched out of the parking lot. He kept his gaze focused on the man as he stopped at the edge of the parking lot and pulled out a phone.

Petru called out over his shoulder, "He's calling someone."

Nicolai mumbled, "It won't matter. I've covered the plates. The most he'll get is a description of an old white Fiat van."

Petru stared at the figure as he faded into the distance. He wondered who the man was calling. Was it hospital security? Or maybe the police? He felt sick in the stomach as he contemplated the thought that Luca Razvan potentially knew he was now on the run.

Petru kept a close watch on the road through the van's rear windows as Nicolai weaved his way through side streets.

After about ten minutes, he relaxed a little. "I don't think we're being followed."

Without taking his eyes off the road, Nicolai said, "That's good to know, because we're almost there."

"Where are we headed?"

"Rahova. The southern end."

"That's near to where I used to live."

"Then you'll know it's not a great neighborhood."

"I appreciate you doing this... I don't know what to say."

"You can help me bring down Luca Razvan—for the sake of our sisters—that's all I ask."

They were quiet until the van turned into a one-way street. "I have to get the van back before six AM," said

Nicolai. "Once I get you settled, I'll head out. It's about a half-hour drive."

"Do you live alone?"

"Yes, but you're not staying with me…"

Petru felt his gut tighten. This wasn't the news he was expecting. "I thought I'd be staying with you."

Nicolai shook his head as he turned a corner and headed onto a major road again. "I live alone, but I'm setting you up in my uncle's apartment. He went into a nursing home about three weeks ago. His apartment is vacant at present, and it's only two blocks from where I live."

"That's very generous, Nicolai."

Nicolai shrugged and said, "My uncle is disabled. They changed the bathroom for him. It's not much different from the setup you had in the hospital. Also, I've left some groceries there for you and a laptop. You can use the time to do more investigating for us."

"Thanks, Nicolai. This is far more than I expected."

"There's a laneway out the back. I'll pull up there and help you into your chair. The apartment is on the second floor, but the building has an elevator which works most of the time."

"I don't plan on going anywhere, but it's good to know it's there."

"I've told no one that you're coming and I'd like to keep it that way. Razvan will be on the lookout. And a guy in a wheelchair stands out."

"I agree. Staying off the grid was hard enough when I was able-bodied, but now…"

Petru shook his head. He had done his best to prepare himself for life as a paraplegic. But the thought of life on the run in his condition was overwhelming.

Nicolai broke through his thoughts. "We turn up here on the left. That's the laneway. It's after midnight, so hopefully, no one will see us. Once I get you upstairs and settled, I'll be on my way."

Petru watched through the front of the van as Nicolai cautiously maneuvered the van between cars and dumpsters up the laneway. Petru could see that the area was poor, even by Romanian standards. The buildings were all three and four stories high, and looked to have been built in the seventies when brown and beige were trendy colors. Graffiti covered most of the buildings, but he didn't care. This was better than living in the squalor of the abandoned warehouse, particularly in his condition.

Nicolai pulled the van to a halt out back of a four-story apartment block that all the local graffiti artists had tagged.

"This is us," he said as he opened his door.

Nicolai went round back and opened the doors. They went through a similar routine at the morgue, but in reverse, to get Petru out of the van.

Once settled in his chair, Nicolai pushed him up onto a footpath and then in through a metal door at the rear of the building.

"That door's normally locked," he said after opening it. "But it's been broken for two weeks and I'm not sure when it's going to be fixed."

"There are locks on the apartment, right?"

"Yes," responded Nicolai as he wheeled Petru inside. The narrow foyer ran from the front to the rear of the building. There was an elevator on the right and staircase on the left.

Nicolai wheeled the chair to the elevator and said, "Let's hope it's working," as he pressed the button.

To Petru's relief, the elevator door slid open.

The Catalin Connection

Petru wheeled himself inside and said, "Level two, right?" as he pressed the button.

"You got it."

As they rode up, the lift made a grinding sound. Nicolai said, "It's had that noise for over ten years. I don't think it's anything to worry about."

"Good to know..."

After the door opened on the second floor, Nicolai wheeled Petru out into the foyer. "It's down here on the right."

Petru scanned to his left and right as he was wheeled down the corridor. The carpet on the floor was threadbare. And the olive green paint on the walls was missing plaster in places and didn't look like it had been painted anytime in the current century.

But none of that mattered to Petru as they stopped about halfway down the hallway. He was focused on what he would find inside the apartment. Was he walking into a trap? Did Nicolai really have his best interests at heart? He figured he would know soon enough as Nicolai inserted the key into the door.

Chapter Twenty-Six

Petru breathed a sigh of relief as Nicolai opened the door and flicked on the light switch to the apartment. There was no welcoming committee. No sign of Luca Razvan or any of his henchmen. The air smelt of stale cigarettes as Nicolai wheeled him inside. The main living area was painted a creamy-white and was sparsely furnished with just an old leather couch, a small table and two chairs below a window. Petru also noticed a bookshelf that contained mostly paperbacks and a few magazines.

"Sorry, there's no TV," said Nicolai. "I'm hoping to get one for you tomorrow."

"This is great," said Petru as he looked through an archway into a small kitchen. The gray timber cabinets were chipped from years of use. There was an electric kettle and microwave on top of a Formica bench top. A compact refrigerator and stove were nestled against a side wall. He figured all the appliances were modern thirty years ago, but he wasn't about to complain.

Petru wheeled his way back into the living room as

Nicolai pointed at the battered wooden table. "Before retiring, my uncle was a piano tuner and repairer. After he gave up work, he spent hours here each day doing crosswords and listening to the radio. That was his life for nearly fifteen years."

"This is more than I could ask for. It's very generous."

Nicolai shrugged. "Sorry about the cigarette smell. Uncle Aiden smoked Camel cigarettes. I don't think we'll ever get the smell out of here."

Petru explained it was fine and briefly recounted his previous living conditions, assuring his host that the smell of cigarettes was far preferable to that of rats, urine, and mold.

Nicolai pointed to one of two doors on the opposite side of the living room. "That leads to the bathroom. It was altered to help with my uncle's mobility issues."

Petru nodded as he realized he was about to learn how to manage on his own.

Nicolai pointed to the other door. "That leads to your bedroom. There are clean sheets on the bed and extra blankets in the cupboard. I've left the laptop and charger on the side table for you."

"Password?"

"No password," said Nicolai with a shake of the head. "I just reformatted it, so you can put your own on it."

"Got it."

Nicolai explained there was no Wi-Fi and that Petru would have to tether his phone to access the Internet. Petru assured him that wouldn't be a problem.

"If you get stuck, just call."

"Thanks, Nicolai, this is way too generous."

Nicolai grimaced as he placed Petru's bag on the table. "Not really. But after what you've been through, you deserve a break."

Nicolai pointed towards the kitchen and added, "I've stocked the fridge with some microwave meals and the cupboards with some other basic food items. There's a toaster and a coffee pot in the cupboard below the sink."

"Okay, sounds good."

"Is there anything else that you need?"

Petru flushed. "I could do with some more catheters. I only have three and I'm not supposed to reuse them because they're no longer sterile. You can get them from any pharmacy and I'm happy to pay—."

Nicolai waved him off. "I'll pick some up tomorrow night after work."

Two men looked at each other. "I'm so grateful, Nicolai. You have no idea."

"Like I said, you deserve a break."

The two men shook hands. As Nicolai headed for the door, he added, "Make sure you lock this properly. I don't think anyone knows you're here, but we can't be too careful."

Petru called out a goodbye as Nicolai left the apartment. He wheeled to the door and engaged the lock. He sat and stared at nothing as he tried to comprehend what had just happened. Nicolai seemed to be someone he could trust. He wondered what was happening at the hospital. They they would have raised the alarm by now and he wondered if Razvan already realized he'd gotten away. If not tonight, he figured he would certainly know by early tomorrow.

Suddenly, he felt tired as he wheeled himself back to the middle of the living room. He stared up at the ceiling and then closed his eyes. His life as a paraplegic had just begun. He was unsure how long it would last and he would take it day-by-day. For now, he was just grateful to still be alive.

Petru stared up at the ceiling, unable to sleep. The bed was warm and comfortable, but the sudden change in his circumstances was overwhelming. He had been able to relieve himself without too much difficulty, but opted not to take a shower until the morning. After getting into bed, he tossed and turned, finding it hard to settle. The creaks and groans of the building and the traffic on the street below were reminders of his new surroundings. He also feared Razvan's men would burst through the front door to finish the job they started in the laneway. A full night's sleep was not on his radar anytime soon.

He made a mental note to call his mother in the morning. She needed to know about his injuries and he couldn't keep it a secret forever. And now that he was out of hospital, he at least had something positive to tell her. He would be deliberately vague about what he told her. He figured he would keep it low key—that he needed to use a wheelchair for a period of time. She didn't need to know the full extent of his disability, at least not to start with.

Satisfied, he turned his thoughts to Nicolai. Had he been able to return the van without incident? Was he home yet? He still had trouble coming to terms with the man's generosity. Was he on the level? Petru had given this a lot of thought. But the more he interacted with Nicolai, the more he understood and shared the man's hatred for Luca Razvan. He thought it would be a miracle if they both survived this. Razvan was as wily and cunning as he was evil. This couldn't be the first time someone had come after him.

Now that he had a proper laptop, he could start his search on Razvan in earnest. Tomorrow would be spent using the internet and dark web to find as much information as possible. He would figure out a plan of attack with Nicolai after building a profile of Razvan's strengths and weaknesses.

His thoughts were interrupted by his phone as it buzzed on the side table next to his bed. He checked the screen. It was a text from Nicolai asking if he was still awake.

Petru texted back immediately.

A moment later, his phone rang.

Petru pressed answer. "Hey, Nicolai."

"Sorry to bother you. Are you settling in?"

"The bed is very comfortable."

"Good. I forgot to tell you, but if you need to contact me, don't text, okay? I work in an open area at the bank and my text messages display on my phone screen. I don't know who to trust, so it's best just to call. And if I don't answer after three rings, hang up and I'll call back as soon as I can."

"Got it. Do you have my number programmed into your phone? If you do, my name will be displayed—"

"No need to worry. You're in my phone directory as Codos."

"Codos?"

Nicolai chuckled. "Codos was a guerrilla group in Chad back in the eighties. They resisted the domination of their region by the president's army. I figured you were now part of the resistance, so…"

"I like it."

"Also, I'm trying to line up a meeting with a Canadian investigative journalist. He's currently doing research on European money laundering. Are you interested in meeting him?"

"Sure… I guess?"

"It's all off-the-record stuff, and he doesn't know my real name.

"How do you know him?"

"I've read a few of his articles and emailed him once to thank him for an article he did on organized crime. We've exchanged a few emails since and when he told me he was coming to Europe for research, I wanted to tell him what I knew about Luca Razvan. I figured if the police can't get him, at least exposing him through the media would be a start."

"I'm not sure I've got much to add, but... sure."

"We'll talk more about it tomorrow night. No pressure, but I thought you'd be interested."

"Like you said, let's take him down any way we can."

Nicolai said, "See you tomorrow," and the phone went dead.

Petru stared at the ceiling again as he listened to the low rumble of late-night traffic. It hadn't occurred to him that there was another way to bring down Razvan. Petru closed his eyes, but he knew sleep would be hours away.

Chapter Twenty-Seven

After showering, dressing, and eating breakfast, Petru made a large coffee and set up his laptop on the table beneath the window. He spent over an hour trawling the internet and various sections of the dark web for more information on Luca Razvan, but the man was a closed book.

Not deterred, he tried a different tack and turned his attention to Razvan's company, LEU. There, he had more success. The company was officially registered in Bucharest and paid all its taxes. It was listed as a private company that specialized in internet security, which, of course, he knew was a sham. He kept reading and learned that Razvan wasn't the owner, as everyone thought, but just the general manager and part of the company's board of directors.

There were six board members. All were East European, with the exception of the president, Richard Stelovak. Petru was intrigued. Stelovak was born in Romania but now headed up a large construction company in Vancouver, Canada. His company wasn't without controversy and had been the subject of several police inquiries.

This piqued Petru's interest and he found Canadian online newspapers were a wealth of information. Three construction workers had been missing for years and several others had been victims of fatal industrial accidents.

Stelovak's time in Romania before he immigrated also made for interesting reading. He found out through an online public archive of court proceedings in Bucharest that Stelovak had been charged with murder when he was nineteen. The crime was never tried because his lawyer got him off on a technicality. Petru kept searching, but it appeared Stelovak had cut his losses and emigrated to Canada shortly after his release.

By five PM, Petru had built up a decent profile of the LEU board president. Richard Stelovak had very likely started his career in Bucharest as a stand-over man, and after running into trouble with the law, had emigrated to Canada. There wasn't much information about his early years in Canada, but from what Petru could learn, Stelovak appeared to have used every opportunity, both legal and illegal, to build his empire.

Now, as the CEO of a major construction company, he was almost untouchable. He had others do his dirty work and always had an alibi. As his company developed, he went after government contracts to expand his empire. The reports in various media outlets were mixed. Stelovak courted controversy, and many accused him of using bribes and threats to get what he wanted.

Petru rubbed his eyes and wheeled away from the table. As difficult as it was to comprehend, Richard Stelovak made Luca Razvan almost look like a boy scout by comparison.

His thoughts were interrupted by a buzz on his phone. He looked down and saw a reminder that he needed to complete his next bathroom break. He sighed—this was his life as a paraplegic. It was all about routine and pre-empting what your body needed.

After attending to his needs, Petru realized he had forgotten to call his mother. He grimaced as he knew he couldn't put it off any longer. He would never make a harder phone call in his life. His mother no longer had a cell phone, so he called his aunt's home number—she answered on the fifth ring.

After politely chatting with his aunt, Petru swallowed hard when she put the phone down to go and get his mother. He found it ironic that they were both in wheelchairs now, albeit for very different reasons. He knew from her tone when she finally picked up the phone and said, "Hello Petru, how are you?" that she was still sad.

"I'm okay, Mamma. How are you?"

"I'm fine. I still miss Elena terribly, and I also miss you. But I do not miss the city. Moving back here was the best thing for me."

"I'm glad."

"How are you going? Have you found a job yet?"

Petru paused. "Mamma, there's something I need to tell you."

"Are you alright?"

"I've had an accident…"

"What kind of accident?

"I'm not able to walk at present… I need a wheelchair."

There was silence on the phone. He thought he could hear her sobbing before she responded, "Oh, Petru. What has happened to you?"

Petru lied. "I had a scuffle with two men and I fell… When I woke up in the hospital, I didn't have much feeling in my legs. I'm out of the hospital now, but I need to use a wheelchair for the time being."

"Petru, you are so young! Is this permanent?"

"I'm taking it day by day, Mamma."

"Where are you living? Surely it would be better if you returned to Băleni."

"I'm living in a friend's apartment in Rahova," said Petru. He skipped the part about what he had in common with Nicolai, and added, "The government is paying an allowance. It's not a lot, but it's enough, so I'm not on the street."

He could hear his mother weeping in the background again.

"Mamma, you don't need to cry. I'm okay. This is a setback, but nothing more. I'll find a job and start over."

"Oh, Petru..."

"You still have your son, and you know I will always love you," he said firmly.

"I feel so guilty. I should be there to look after you. Promise me that if things get worse, you will call me straight away. We have family here that can help."

"I promise, Mamma. And I appreciate your love. More than you can possibly imagine."

Petru could sense the change in his mother's voice as she responded, "I'm very proud of you, Petru." She had dealt with the shock of the news and was returning to her stoic self as she added, "You're a good boy. I trust you to make the right decisions."

"Thank you, Mamma. That means a lot. I will call you in a couple of days."

Petru wiped tears from his eyes after disconnecting. The call had been much harder than he expected. He felt drained and sat in silence—his mind a whirl of thoughts about his sister, his mother, his disability, and his future. He glanced across at the kitchen. Earlier, he'd found half a bottle of whiskey in a cupboard under the sink and contemplated pouring himself a glass. He grimaced—the staff in the hospital had warned him that it was common for people in his condition to slip into depression when released from hospital. Drugs and alcohol were common ways to ease the pain, but they weren't a long-term solution, he'd been reminded. His phone buzzed—it was a call from Nicolai.

Petru did his best to put on a cheery voice as he pressed answer. "Hey, Nicolai."

"Hi. I've left work and I'm about to head over. How was your day?"

After thinking about the conversation with his mother, he said, "It was productive. I found a lot of interesting background about LEU. It's not what I expected. I'll fill you in when you get here."

"I'm intrigued. Hey, it's Friday night and I normally treat myself to take out. Do you like Turkish food? I thought I'd pick up some on the way over and save you from a microwave meal."

"Sounds great. Thanks."

"Good. I'll be there in about forty minutes. I'll text you when I get to the building. That way, when I knock, you'll know it's me."

"See you then."

Nicolai disconnected, leaving Petru alone with his thoughts again. Petru glanced at the kitchen and then returned to his laptop. He pushed the conversation with his mother to the back of his mind and thought about Richard Stelovak again. He had a lot of information, but there was still more to learn.

The Catalin Connection

Petru had eaten very little during the day and was unaware how hungry he was until Nicolai arrived. The delectable smells of Turkish food emanating from the takeout bag Nicolai carried into the apartment made him ravenous. They agreed to hold over their discussion about Luca Razvan until they had finished their meal.

They made small talk as they dined on lamb and chicken Kebabs, saffron rice, and yogurt Borani dip. Nicolai had purchased a bottle of Italian Chianti as well. He said it would be a long night and the wine would help.

Petru found the food delicious and offered to pay, but Nicolai waved him off, saying, "Consider it a welcome back gift."

After finishing his meal and his first glass of red wine, Nicolai leaned back in his chair. "It doesn't get much better than Turkish!"

"I agree," said Petru, and took another sip of wine.

"Tell me what you discovered today."

"I started my search on Luca Razvan this morning," said Petru as he opened his laptop. "But I got nowhere, so I turned my attention to his company... that's when I made some progress."

"You mentioned Razvan doesn't own the company, right?"

"Yes," said Petru nodding. "There are six board members. Five of them live in Romania, but the board chairman lives in Canada."

"Canada?" said Nicolai with a frown.

"His name is Richard Stelovak. And this is where it gets interesting..." Nicolai remained quiet while Petru explained everything he had found out about Stelovak. He started with his time as a stand-over man in Romania, detailing his career all the way through to his current role with a Canadian construction company. He closed by adding, "If everything that I've read about Stelovak is true, he's as evil as Luca Razvan himself."

Nicolai shook his head. "That hardly seems possible. Razvan is such a lowlife."

"I thought that too. But I did some more research after you called. It all makes sense now."

Nicolai stroked his beard. "How?"

"Richard Stelovak is Luca Razvan's uncle."

"Uncle? Really?"

"Razvan's father and Stelovak were siblings—same mother, but different fathers. Razvan's father is dead now, but the family connection still looks strong."

"That's an interesting piece of the puzzle."

Pointing to his laptop, Petru said, "I'm putting together a summary of the company structure and its board members. It's a work in progress, but from what I can gather, LEU is a front for *multiple* organized crime activities. It goes way beyond what Razvan is doing."

"How so?" asked Nicolai.

"For starters, two of the directors faced charges of money laundering here in Romania."

"Money laundering?"

"They both got off on technicalities."

Nicolai sat up straight. "So it's more than just Razvan's scamming and hacking enterprises?"

Petru nodded. "That's just the tip of the iceberg."

"Our job just got a whole lot harder," declared Nicolai.

"Maybe…"

Nicolai frowned. "Maybe?"

"It gives us a lot more to work with. And as much as they try to cover their tracks, they'll have left something exposed somewhere. We just have to find that exposure point."

"This is really helpful."

"Hopefully, I'm earning my keep," said Petru with a rueful smile. "Also, we need to talk about retrieving that drive from LEU. The information on it might give us a real head start."

"I'm all ears."

"I've been giving it a lot of thought. It is not possible for me to hack into their computer systems. Razvan has deliberately set up their network so that it's not accessible through a firewall. He knows—"

Nicolai held up his hand. "Whoa! Ease up on the tech talk, my friend."

"Sorry. The servers for his business are not connected to the Internet. You can't hack into them from outside. You have to be on-site, and navigate around the guards and alarms."

"It sounds like Fort Knox."

"Exactly. That's why we have to get that USB."

Nicolai held up a hand. "Hold up, didn't you just say they have guards and alarms?"

"Yes. But I think there's a way," said Petru with a grin. "One of us has to pretend we work for LEU. There's only one level of security we have to penetrate to get to the lockers where I've hidden the USB. It's risky, but I think it can work."

Nicolai raised his eyebrows again. "One of us has to walk in? You're in a wheelchair, so that would be... me. Right?"

"Let me tell you how I think we can pull it off."

"I'm going to need another glass of wine," growled Nicolai.

Chapter Twenty-Eight

Petru watched Nicolai pour himself a second glass of wine and didn't protest when his own glass was topped up as well.

"I've given this a lot of thought," said Petru as he picked up his glass. "I think we can get you into the building by posing as an employee."

Nicolai frowned. "How would that work?"

"Let me start with the layout. The front entrance is for visitors only. All employees enter the building through the rear entrance."

"They walk up the side lane?"

Petru nodded.

"And the door is locked, I assume?"

"Correct. You need a security pass. It's one of those systems where you tap your card on the scanner and the door unlocks. Everyone tailgates, particularly when they come back from lunch in groups."

"That happens at our bank. One person unlocks the doors and everyone else just walks in behind."

"Exactly. If you time it right, you should be able to grab the door before it closes on the group in front of you."

"Hang on," said Nicolai with a frown. "People will know I don't work there."

"Not necessarily. I never surrendered my pass, so we can easily stick a photo of you over the top of mine."

"So I just say I'm new?"

"Hopefully it won't come to that. If we pick a group of junior staff who have recently started, they will be unlikely to challenge you."

"You're sure the pass doesn't work?"

"They will have definitely deactivated it."

"What about the guards. Don't they watch the cameras?"

"The guards don't pay much attention to the cameras when people return from lunch. Once you get inside, there's a room on the left. That's where all the lockers are. Razvan won't let us take anything into the office area that we can potentially use to steal his data. So our phones and laptops get stored in the lockers before we go through the scanner to access the main part of the building."

"Got it." Nicolai frowned and then added, "Wait... how did you get the USB out past the scanner in the first place?"

Petru grinned. "I often wore a pair of boots. They have steel caps in the toe that set off the alarms. The guards made me take them off whenever I went through the scanner. I just slipped the USB inside a boot before handing them over."

"They didn't look inside?"

"They did a couple of times when I first started. But then it became routine for them. I carried the boots to the locker, and as I pretended to be putting them back on, I pulled out the USB. It already had the double-sided tape on it, so it was easy enough to stick it up inside my locker when I pulled out my phone to go home."

"So, after I get inside, I just head for your locker?"

"And grab the USB and get out of there as soon as you can."

"What happens if it's been reassigned?" said Nicolai with a frown.

"I've never heard of them re-keying a locker. They will just make a copy of the key and reissue it. Like I said, unless you feel up under the rim you wouldn't know it's there. Kind of like chewing gum under a school desk."

"Hopefully it will be easier to get off than chewing gum," said Nicolai with something approaching a smile. "So, when do we do this?"

"Maybe tomorrow? That will give us time to modify the pass." Petru studied Nicolai for a moment as he stared off into space. "What are you thinking?"

Nicolai frowned. "I like it… apart from one thing."

"And what's that?"

"The security cameras. Right now, I don't think anyone in Razvan's organization knows what I'm doing… this could blow my cover."

Petru and Nicolai talked well into the night. They decided to wait until Monday to execute their plan to retrieve the USB drive. Even though most staff worked on Saturday, Petru reasoned that new starters always started on Monday and a new face would look less suspicious.

At almost eleven PM, Nicolai took a call on his phone. It didn't take long for Petru to figure out he was talking to the investigative journalist from Canada.

They spoke for about five minutes before Nicolai disconnected.

"That was Robbie Mayne," said Nicolai.

"The journalist?"

Nicolai nodded. "He's in Bucharest tomorrow and Sunday and wants to meet. We've agreed to meet tomorrow for lunch at a small restaurant I know in Old Town. There's a closed-off area in the back. We can talk in private."

"Sounds great."

"Would you like to join us? Robbie is giving us all afternoon. I'm sure he would like to hear your story."

"I'm not sure I'm ready to go out in public just yet."

"You won't really be in public. We can take my car. I can park in the laneway out back and get you in through the rear entrance. You won't have to deal with too many people."

Petru mused, "I guess..."

"It's totally up to you. If you would prefer to stay here, we can dial you in and you talk to Robbie by phone. Only..."

"Only what?" said Petru with a frown.

"The restaurant does amazing tapas," said Nicolai with a grin. "And I'm sure Robbie Mayne will be paying."

"Well, when you put it like that..."

They continued their conversation with Nicolai lamenting he should have brought two bottles of wine. They both agreed having Robbie Mayne involved could only help their cause, particularly if they maintained their anonymity.

"Robbie only knows you as Codos," said Nicolai. "He knows nothing of your past besides working for Razvan."

"Does he know about my disability?"

Nicolai shook his head. "I figure you can tell him what you feel comfortable with."

"And what does he know you as?"

"Greg Rio. My middle name is Grigore, so…"

Petru mused, "Easy enough to remember."

"You got it. Its been my online name for years. I saw no reason to change it."

"It's not connected to your real name on social media or anywhere is it?"

"No. Apart from me saying I'm from Bucharest, I haven't divulged any information, not even my age."

"So, what are we going to tell him?"

Nicolai stroked his beard. "I'm thinking everything. I don't see any reason to hold back. He's already told me he has access to several very good analysts who specialize in computer crime and money laundering. He's very interested in anything we can provide on Razvan's organization."

"It's a pity we can't get the USB before Monday."

"I'd like you and me to look at it first, anyway. If we think it has merit and I can send it to him via a secure server for analysis."

Petru nodded. He appreciated Nicolai's caution and agreed that if they could retrieve the USB drive, it would be wise to analyze it first before they made a copy of the data for someone else.

Nicolai glanced at his watch. "I'm tired, so I'm going to head home. Are you good here? Is there anything else you need? Wait…" Nicolai walked across to the table and picked up a second bag he'd brought in with the food earlier. "I got the canulas. The pharmacist said these are the best.

"Thanks, Nicolai, I appreciate it. How much do I owe you?"

Nicolai waived him off. "You've paid for them many times over with what you found out today. Thanks to you, we've got a whole lot more to talk to Robbie Mayne about tomorrow."

After seeing Nicolai out, Petru went through his bedtime ritual and then got into bed. He tried to think up questions to ask Robbie Mayne tomorrow, but he fell asleep before he had the first one panned out in his mind.

Chapter Twenty-Nine

Nicolai and Petru arrived early at the cafe. After being escorted to their table in a back room, Nicolai ordered a jug of water for them. He waited for the waiter to leave and said, "How do you feel about your first trip out since the accident?"

"It feels strange after spending months in the hospital. I'm glad we're in a back room. I'm not ready for all the staring and pity yet."

Nicolai nodded. "I'm sure, in time, you'll get used to it. Getting you down to the car was a lot easier than I imagined."

"It surprised me, too. I'm still struggling with some things, but I feel like I'm getting the hang of the wheelchair."

"You certainly are," said Nicolai with a laugh. "I expected to have to help you get inside from the laneway, but I had trouble keeping up with you."

"Well, at least some things are working out," said Petru, with half a grin.

Nicolai frowned. "If you don't mind me asking, what do you struggle with the most?"

"It's weird. I struggle with the idea that I can't feel anything from my waist down. I can see and touch my legs, but... I feel nothing. That's tough to comprehend."

"I can't imagine how hard that must be."

"I've been doing some research. There are lots of people who lead very productive lives who are in wheelchairs. I read of one guy who climbed a sixty-mile trail through New Guinea."

Nicolai frowned. "In a wheelchair?"

"Actually, no. He literally crawled up the side of a mountain."

"Wow! That's even more impressive than in a wheelchair." Nicolai scratched his chin. "But why on earth would he want to do that?"

"It's called the Kokoda Trail. It was the location of a battle during the second world war. Lots of people climb it for the challenge, but not everyone makes it."

"But a paraplegic made it on his hands?"

Petru nodded. "Yes. The trip took him over a week."

"Well, if that doesn't inspire you, nothing will."

They were silent for a moment while the waiter delivered their water and glasses. When they were alone again, Petru surveyed the ten-by-twelve room they were sitting in. It contained only one scarred wooden table with six chairs. The room was painted in a lilac color and had pictures of flowers on each wall. The room was separated from the main cafe area by one door. Petru pointed to the open door and said, "Are they okay with this being closed when the journalist arrives?"

Nicolai nodded. "I know the owner. We come here sometimes for work meetings when we want to get out of the bank building. He has no problem with the door being closed."

"Good to know. I think it would be—"

A knock on the door brought their conversation to a halt. A man in his early thirties with wavy light brown hair stuck his head through the doorway. "I'm looking for Greg and Codos. Am I in the right place?"

Nicolai got up from the table. He said, "I'm Greg," as he shook hands with the man. Pointing to Petru, he added, "And this is Codos."

The man moved across to where Petru sat and said, "I'm Robbie Mayne. Pleased to meet you."

Petru shook the man's hand with a firm grip and said, "Likewise."

As they sat down, Nicolai said, "I've ordered us Tapas for lunch. The food should start arriving soon."

"Great!" said Mayne as he poured himself water. "I'm starved."

Petru observed the journalist while he and Nicolai made small talk. Mayne explained how he had flown in earlier that day from Naples, where he had been investigating organized crime. The man had a lop-sided grin, which he used frequently and a down-to-earth manner. Mayne stayed away from the primary subject of their meeting while they ate and instead told them about his work as a journalist and his family back home in Canada. Petru was sure this was a tactic he used regularly to gain the trust of those he was interviewing. By the time they had finished their meal, Petru felt relaxed in his presence and began contributing to the small talk.

After their post-lunch coffees had arrived, Nicolai signaled for the door to be closed. Mayne took this as his cue and placed a leather satchel he had brought on the table. "Gentlemen, thanks again for agreeing to meet with me. I'm hoping what you tell me will contribute to my article I'm writing on organized crime in this part of the world."

Mayne paused and pulled a small tape recorder from his satchel. "Everything you say is off the record and in strict confidence. And while recording this is easier for me, I can take notes if you prefer?"

Petru looked at Nicolai. "I have no objection."

Nicolai nodded. "We trust you, Robbie."

Mayne gave a brief background to the article he was writing. He told Nicolai and Petru it would be syndicated across the USA and Canada.

Petru said, "So what's the focus? Organized crime is a big business—drugs, sex slaves, credit fraud, scams, money laundering; the list is almost endless."

"The focus is on the kingpins who control everything," said Mayne. "Most of the crime gang bosses masquerade as legitimate businessmen or even politicians, but they're corrupt to the core. I plan to profile several of them when I have enough evidence."

Nicolai said, "You realize you're going to paint a target on your back."

Mayne nodded. "My work can be dangerous, but I'm more concerned about getting sued than being bumped off. My team fact checks everything and each newspaper's in-house lawyers review the content to ensure they won't face any legal action."

Petru was impressed with Mayne's honesty. "Where would you like to start?"

Mayne said, "From what Greg tells me you're both here because you've had family members murdered by crime gangs…" He paused and pressed a button on his tape recorder before adding, "How about you start at the beginning?"

Nicolai nodded at Petru and said, "Why don't you go first?"

Petru spent the next hour telling his story. He started with his job at LEU and how the security company was a front for credit card fraud and other online scamming ventures. Mayne listened intently and only asked a few questions. Petru then recounted his sister's murder and how he had been abducted after visiting her grave. He concluded by telling him how Razvan had him shot as he tried to follow him down a laneway.

Petru added, "And then I woke up in hospital as a paraplegic."

"I'm so sorry, Codos," said Mayne. "Losing your sister and then winding up in a wheelchair…"

"This doesn't define me!" declared Petru. "If anything defines me now, it's my sister's murder and my wanting to see justice for her."

Mayne held up his hands. "And I'm here to help."

They were all quiet for a moment. Petru sighed and said, "Sorry. It's been a hard road…"

Mayne shook his head. "No need to apologize, Codos. What you've been through would break most people."

Nicolai added, "But Codos is not most people. He is stronger than anyone I know."

Turning the recorder to face Nicolai, Mayne said, "Greg, why don't you tell us your story now? I know you've shared some of it by email, but I'd like you to go back to the beginning, if you don't mind."

It was well after four PM before Nicolai had finished telling his story. Like Petru, he poured out his heart, reliving the agony of his sister's murder, his grief, and his anger.

Petru could tell from Nicolai's demeanor that recounting his story had left him drained. They agreed on a short break and ordered more coffee.

After the coffee arrived and Nicolai had taken a few sips, he seemed refreshed. "The Roma Bank could be the key. I constantly hear rumors within the bank about money laundering. I started secretly collecting evidence when I found out Razvan was on the board." He nodded at Petru and added, "Codos discovered that most of the directors of the bank are also directors at LEU."

Mayne frowned. "So the Roma Bank is a front for the money laundering business?"

Nicolai nodded. "It would seem that way. I've got a bunch of printouts on what we call ghost accounts. There's virtually no information in any of our databases on who owns them or where they operate from. And some transactions are in the millions. I'm happy to provide you with copies of what I have, but without more information on the account holders, I doubt you'll get far."

Mayne said, "Pass it on, Greg. I've got a couple of brilliant analysts who are very good at tracking money trails."

Petru said, "I might be able to help," and then explained how he had stolen information from a server at LEU and stored in on a USB drive.

"So let me get this straight. The USB is still inside LEU? And you have to break in to get it back?" asked Mayne.

"Correct," said Petru.

Mayne raised an eyebrow. "That could be a big risk…"

"Yes, but so could the payoff. I didn't have much of a chance to look at the data," said Petru. "But one file intrigued me."

"What kind of file?" said Mayne as he leaned forward.

"It was a spreadsheet. When I opened it up, it looked

like an old fashioned black book: names, account numbers, companies and dates, but no actual transactions."

Mayne raised an eyebrow. "That could be useful. Particularly if it's a backup of Razvan's laptop."

"We won't know for sure unless we look at it in more detail."

"It's a risky business storing that kind of information on a computer," said Mayne.

"No more risky than keeping a real black book that can get lost or stolen," said Petru. He explained how the server was in a secure room and wasn't connected to any other network.

"I guess it's practical," mused Mayne.

Petru nodded. "Hardly anyone would know about it."

Nicolai detailed their plan to retrieve the USB on Monday. Mayne scratched his chin. "If it really is a digital black book, it could bust this thing wide open."

"It could also get us killed," said Nicolai with a grimace. "But we've come too far to turn back now," he added.

Petru nodded. "One way or another, Razvan is going to pay for what he's done."

Petru's first journey into the outside since his injury left him exhausted. After Nicolai had returned him safely to his apartment, he had opted for a frozen meal, a shower, and an early night. There was a lot to unpack from the meeting with Robbie Mayne, but tonight wasn't the night. He needed to unwind and settled into bed with a Robert Ludlum thriller from Nicolai's uncle's library. He read a few chapters and switched off the light shortly after ten PM.

His mind was a jumble of thoughts. He first thought

about Robbie Mayne as he lay in the darkness. They had promised to keep in touch, and were all hopeful that retrieving the USB would yield some useful data. He then thought about his first day out as a paraplegic. He thought it had been a success and it gave him confidence to do it again. He thought about his family too, and hoped his mother wasn't worrying too much about him. But one thought kept breaking through to the surface. Something that he hadn't come to terms with since leaving the hospital. He appreciated Nicolai's friendship and generosity, but he knew it couldn't last. He didn't think Nicolai would ever turn his back on him now, but there had to be limits to the support he could provide, regardless of what they had in common. At some point, he would need to find a place of his own and be responsible for his expenses. But he had no money, and that left him in a tight spot.

He contemplated contacting the hospital. His case worker had assured him there was a benefit the government paid to people in his condition. But he never finished the application because of his secret departure. Completing it would require a residential address and phone number, something he couldn't risk providing while being targeted by Razvan.

Petru let out a long sigh. The bank account was empty, and the little cash he still had was in the abandoned warehouse with the rest of his things. He didn't feel strong enough to go out there unaccompanied, nor did he feel comfortable using the pulley system to reach the mezzanine level where it was stored. *"What a mess,"* he muttered. Paraplegia was one thing, but being totally reliant on a near-stranger made it worse.

He thought about the possibility of selling off the furniture and contents in the family apartment. But it had been over two months since he'd lived there. He gritted his teeth as he realized somebody would have sold off anything of value by now and dumped the rest. He recalled his last call with his mother. Moving back to the family village was a possibility—at least he wouldn't starve. But he knew the pity would drive him crazy and he would be bored within a week.

"Something will turn up," he muttered.

His thoughts drifted to his father and sister. Were they reunited in an afterlife? His mother was more religious than he was and had assured him they were now together. But he wasn't so sure. He'd never given much thought to it.

But perhaps you should?

He wondered what his father would have done in his situation? He wasn't sure. His mother had always placed his father on a pedestal, but he knew he wasn't perfect. He recalled the conversation he'd had with his mother after the home invasion. He could still see her sitting on the sofa, bloody and bruised as she told him about the small fortune his father had hidden in the apartment. It left him wondering what the thugs had really come for. After finding one of them on the security video and following the trail back to LEU, it was clear they were there for him, not anything his father had hidden away.

It occurred to him that his father may have made up the story about the treasure simply to give his mother hope. Hope that one day they would be starting a new life in a house of their own. Petru frowned. He could never remember his father sugar-coating anything. And he had never lied to anyone in his family to the best of his knowledge. But did he lie to his mother? It didn't feel right.

He asked himself again, '*So what happened to the hidden fortune?*'

It was only a few weeks later that his father had died in the accident. Had he moved whatever it was out of the apartment? Had he exchanged it for cash? His father had been dead for many years and he guessed these were questions he would never find answers to. Petru shook his head as he realized any chance of solving the mystery had vanished when he had abandoned the apartment.

He closed his eyes. Instantly he was six again and playing football with his father as he drifted off to sleep.

Chapter Thirty

Petru had a restless night. He woke early and decided he couldn't accept his current situation any longer. As grateful as he was for Nicolai's help, he had always paid his way and he wasn't about to change his ways just because he was a paraplegic. When he had regained consciousness in the hospital, he realized the two hundred euros he'd had on him when he was shot was missing. None of the nursing staff knew anything about it and he figured it was gone for good.

But he still had over five hundred euros hidden in the abandoned warehouse. He figured if the warehouse hadn't been knocked down yet, there was a good chance his money was still there. A day ago, the idea of returning to the warehouse on his own was unthinkable. But his trip with Nicolai to meet Robbie Mayne had emboldened him. He still had a long way to go in his recovery, but he had proven to himself that he could get around in a wheelchair.

He decided the trip to Sector 4 was a trip he needed to make on his own. There was a train station two blocks from his apartment and even though he didn't have money for a ticket, he'd been able to convince the clerk to let him on for free. After all, who could deny someone in a wheelchair?

The trip to Sector 4 had been uneventful. Nobody took much notice of him, which he was happy about. Several people offered to help him off the train, which he appreciated, but by the time he had wheeled himself to the warehouse, he was exhausted. He was grateful for the rear loading ramp that allowed him access to the warehouse. After getting inside, he had eaten some of his tinned food from the storage box and consumed a bottle of water before dozing off in his wheelchair for an hour.

He checked his watch when he awoke. It was now after eleven AM. He felt strong enough to continue, but wasn't looking forward to using the pulley system to hoist himself up to the mezzanine level. He had scanned the building when he had first entered. As far as he could tell, nobody had been inside in the months since he'd left. The booby trapped ramp up to the mezzanine was still intact, and the pulley system looked exactly as he had left it. Petru looked up at the level above. He had to assume his money was still with his other belongings in the room where he slept.

The ride out on the train had given him time to think about how he would use the pulley system. He figured the sling he'd made would still serve his purposes—it would just need to be lowered completely to the ground to allow him to crawl into it.

He recalled the rope pulley system wasn't too hard to manage. His upper body strength was still reasonable, and he was confident he had enough strength to winch himself up and down. But the real challenge was swinging the pulley across to the mezzanine landing.

Petru focused on the gap he'd cut out of the mezzanine safety railing. The cutout was about eight feet wide and provided an easy landing for him. The pulley system brought him up next to the landing, but there was still about a foot gap he needed to swing across. Petru pictured himself in the sling forty feet above the concrete floor. Without the use of his legs, he would need to improvise. He figured a pole with a hook on the end would suffice. He could use the pole to hook onto the railing to steady himself and then pull himself across.

Petru wheeled into the storeroom. He recalled seeing an old mop handle in there when he had first explored the building and figured it would suffice. Now for something he could fashion as a hook? After scouring several rows of storage racks, he found a box of rusted welding rods. He pulled one out and tested it. It bent easily enough, and he quickly fashioned it into a hook to fit over the mop handle.

Satisfied that he had what he needed, Petru wheeled over to the ropes of the pulley system. He was confident enough that the sling would hold him and that he wouldn't fall out, provided he kept a tight grip on the ropes. But there were no guarantees.

He mumbled, "Nothing ventured, nothing gained," and then used the ropes to lower the sling to the ground. Petru slipped out of his wheelchair and maneuvered his body around until he could slip the sling over his legs. Keeping his left hand on the ground for stability, he leaned over slightly and used his right hand to pull the sling up over his paralyzed legs. Once he had the sling in the correct position, he pulled on the ropes. The sling responded and moved up a couple of inches. After several adjustments, Petru was comfortable he was now secure and attached the hook end of the stick to the sling so that he didn't need to hold it. Petru pulled on the ropes, slowly hoisting himself upward. First five feet, and then ten feet. He looked down and immediately felt dizzy. He mumbled, "Don't pass out," and focused on the landing above as he continued to hoist himself upwards. After five minutes of effort, he was parallel with the landing of the mezzanine.

Petru removed the stick from the sling and hooked it over the safety railing. The sling took on a subtle swinging motion as he pulled on the stick. He pulled a little harder to increase the swing motion. The sling swung a little further toward the center of the warehouse before swinging back over the landing area. Petru let the sling swing through two more complete cycles to get his timing right. As the sling swung over the mezzanine landing again, he allowed the rope to slip in his grasp by almost two feet. He landed with a soft thud on the landing and breathed a sigh of relief. He peered over the edge at the forty-foot drop below and mumbled, "Let's hope getting down is simpler," and then unhooked himself. It took less than a minute to remove himself from the sling.

The room that contained his belongings was about thirty feet further along the corridor. While his wheelchair would have been handy, he was undeterred. Using his arms, he lifted his upper body off the floor and propelled himself forward. By repeating the motion, he was able to crawl forward at a steady pace. Petru figured he would know in less than two minutes if his trip out to Sector 4 had been worth it.

Petru felt his heart race as he crawled to the doorway of the room he had been using as a bedroom. Not because of physical exhaustion, but because of his sense of anticipation. He looked into the room and saw that the bag he had used to store most of his possessions in was still on the bed where he had left it. He took this as a good sign as he continued his crawl into the room.

Without bothering to get himself into an upright position, Petru reached into the bag and thrust his hand into the right interior side pocket. His sigh was audible as he felt the money with his fingertips. After withdrawing the cash, he lay on his back for a moment, staring at the wad of cash as he twirled it between his fingers. Five hundred euros was far from a fortune, but it was enough to give him some independence, at least for the time being.

After shoving the money deep inside an interior pocket of his coat, he propped himself up against a wall and dragged the bag next to him. He was certain he would never return to the warehouse again and needed to decide what possessions he would take with him. All his clothing would stay. Between the hospital and Nicolai, he had everything he needed for now. He pulled out his small portable Sony speaker and Jabra earbuds and placed them next to him—no sense in leaving his two favorite pieces of technology behind. He then pulled out the photos he had brought with him. After capturing images of each one on his phone, he pulled the photos out of their frames. The photos were precious but the frames he could replace. Petru searched the bag for anything else he may want to take. After a few seconds of searching, he found only one item he could not leave behind.

Petru removed his father's ashtray and held it out in front of him. He pictured his father sitting at the cafe table on their balcony, using the tray to catch ash from his cigarette as he read the evening newspaper. Even though he didn't smoke and had no intention starting, he couldn't bear the thought of leaving it behind.

He turned the tray around in his hands as he thought back fondly about his father. It wasn't really an ashtray; more a block of steel with a shallow bowl to catch the ash and an indentation to rest a cigarette on. He remembered as an eleven-year-old asking his father why he needed something so heavy. His father had laughed and told him he was tired of his lightweight aluminum trays blowing off the balcony in strong winds and had made this one to last.

Petru shook his head. The ashtray had remained on the tiny cafe table on the apartment's balcony ever since his death. His mother had insisted it stay there. He recalled her saying, "This was his favorite place to sit, he was happiest here."

He guessed it weighed about four pounds and found himself smiling as he murmured, "Well, this one will never blow away, Papa."

As he continued to turn it over in his hands, he wondered why his father had painted it black. He drew the object close to his nose and smelt its base. Apart from the smell of stale smoke and nicotine, he detected a faint whiff of tar. He remembered his father saying the paint they used on the wharves contained tar to stop the steel from rusting. He assumed this was what he had used on his ashtray to protect it from the elements.

Petru grimaced. The bowl still had traces of ash and grime stuck to it. He would clean it up properly when he got back to his apartment, but for now, it needed a quick wipe-over before he stowed it in his jacket. After rummaging through his bag he found an old t-shirt which would serve his purpose. He started wiping away the built-up ash and grime, but frowned as some of the paint came off too. The base metal below the paint wasn't the silver color of steel he had expected. He wondered if his father had made it out of brass as he continued to rub. After another thirty seconds, Petru frowned again and stopped rubbing. He spat on his thumb and rubbed again at the spot where the paint had come off. He stopped after a few seconds and gasped as he stared down at his work.

"It can't be," he murmured as he placed the ashtray upside down on the floor. Using the corner of one of his discarded picture frames, he scraped more paint away and then exclaimed, "I don't believe it!"

With trembling hands, Petru picked up the ashtray and stared at the gold color of the metal he had exposed. A thousand thoughts swirled through his mind as he contemplated how much this could change his life.

Petru stared out the window as the train rumbled along on its journey back to the city. He barely noticed the changing vista from industrial parks to suburbia as he reflected on his morning. After discovering his father's ashtray was solid gold, he had spent almost another hour on the warehouse balcony. At first, he just stared at it, laughing to himself, as he considered the ingenuity of his father in hiding the treasure in plain sight. And then he contemplated the changes it could make to his family situation.

Feeling well rested and ready to start his journey home again, he had stowed the ashtray along with the other possessions he wanted to keep in his jacket. He then used the pulley system and sling to descend to the ground floor. Wheeling back to the train station had been tiring, but the euphoria of his discovery more than compensated.

He shook his head again as the train stopped in another suburban station. His father's ingenuity gave him a newfound respect for him. He had been gone for many years and yet no one had ever looked twice at the ugly ashtray. Not him, not his mother, and not even his sister, who had also used it herself.

Smiling to himself, he murmured, "Nobody ever guessed, Papa," and then wondered how much it was worth? He dug his phone out of his jacket pocket and searched for a website that gave the price of gold in euros. He guessed the ashtray weighed about four pounds and keyed in the value in the website's calculator. Petru's eyes widened. He had to read the figure twice and let out a long breath as he stared at the number sixty-two-thousand on his screen.

His mind circled back to the story his mother had told him. She was not proud of the fact that her husband had taken a bribe to smuggle something off the wharves without it going through customs. But she understood he was doing this to allow his family to escape from poverty. Whatever it was had to be extremely valuable if the bribe amounted to this much money. He wondered if it was gold bullion that his father had smuggled? It made sense that he would take a share of the spoils as his reward.

As the train pulled out of the station, he figured it was unlikely he would ever know and he pushed the thought to the back of his mind. He needed to focus on the present. Calling his mother had to be his priority. She had to know about his find, and the ashtray really belonged to her and not him. It was right that she should receive the money. He looked around the train carriage. There were at least twenty other people riding into the city. Now was not the time to call. He would wait until he was safely back at his apartment.

Petru pulled up Google on his phone and searched for

gold buyers in Bucharest. There were a few that came up against his search criteria. Most seemed to pay cash for gold, but he wasn't sure if they would buy such a large quantity all at once. He would make some calls later in the day and figure out what to do.

He looked out the window again. For now, he had done all he could. When the train arrived at his scheduled stop, he would get off and head home. He hadn't worked out what he would tell Nicolai yet. Finding the cash was something he would definitely share, but he didn't think it was wise to mention anything about the gold. He thought about where he should hide it in the apartment. The paint being stripped away was a dead giveaway.

But the more he thought about it, the more he relaxed. It had taken him over ten years to discover the ashtray's true value. He figured he could easily cover up the areas he had exposed with boot polish. No one would be any the wiser, not even Nicolai, until he took it to a dealer and had it valued.

Chapter Thirty-One

Despite his euphoria, Petru was exhausted by the time he was safely back at the apartment. After eating his evening meal and completing his nightly routine, he went to bed early. Sleep came easily and he woke early ready for his trip with Nicolai to LEU.

He used the time before Nicolai's arrival to attend to a few things on his to do list. First, he blackened the ashtray with boot polish he had found in a kitchen cupboard to cover up the exposed gold. Satisfied that it looked like an ashtray again, he then made a few calls to local gold dealers about its potential value. Armed with some useful information, he then called his mother. The call had taken close to an hour. She was excited and emotional about his discovery and insisted he keep it, as she had everything she needed.

After the call, Petru had stared out through his apartment window, pondering what he should do. He had weighed the ashtray on some old scales he'd found in the kitchen. The gold dealers he had spoken to all appeared eager to buy the bar, but insisted they would need to test and confirm its purity before they made a formal offer.

While he could definitely use the money, deep down, he believed it belonged to his mother. Her generosity did not surprise him, but the idea of her not being the beneficiary bothered him. He had every intention of making his own way in life if he was still alive after the Razvan thing was over. And a gold bar worth over sixty-thousand euros would not change that.

His thoughts were interrupted as he heard a knock at the door. He knew it was Nicolai because he had texted him minutes earlier to say he was entering the building.

After opening the door and letting his friend in, Petru wheeled back into the living area. "Would you like a coffee?" he asked, as Nicolai sat down on the sofa.

"No," said Nicolai with a shake of his head. "Coffee makes me pee, and I don't want the distraction."

Petru studied him for a moment. "Are you nervous?"

Nicolai nodded. "I hardly slept last night. We need to do this, but a lot could go wrong."

Petru twisted his face as he concurred. "Don't do this if you don't want to. We can—"

"No!" declared Nicolai. "Whatever's on that USB might be just what we need to bring Razvan down. I've thought about it ever since you floated the idea, and we need to get it back."

"Do you want to go over the plan again?"

Nicolai looked at his watch. "We'll have to be quick. It's close to eleven and I need to get into the city and set up before the LEU staff come back from lunch."

"I'm coming with you, of course," said Petru.

Nicolai shook his head. "I don't think that's a good idea."

"Why?" said Petru with a frown.

"I don't think there's any advantage to you being close by in the city. We can still use FaceTime to identify the right group to tail in, but whether you're sitting in a cafe close by, or here in the apartment, I don't think will make any difference."

"Okay. But why the change in plans now?"

Nicolai gritted his teeth. "If I get busted, there's a good chance Razvan will figure out I'm working with you. If he sends out his henchmen to look for you, you're going to find it difficult to disappear in a hurry… I think you're safer here."

Petru found it hard to argue with Nicolai's logic. They were silent for a moment before Petru mused, "If something goes wrong and you need to get out of there quickly, I am going to slow you down. I don't like it, but I think you're right…"

Nicolai nodded. "Let's go over the plan one last time. Then I'll get going."

They spent a few minutes reviewing the extraction plan. When they were both happy they had covered all the possibilities they could think of, Nicolai handed Petru the building pass. "I've stuck my photo over yours and put it back in the plastic sleeve. What do you think?"

Petru examined it for a moment. "Provided no one takes a close look at it, I think it will pass."

Nicolai pursed his lips as he nodded in agreement.

Petru added, "I appreciate you doing this," as he handed the pass back. "I realize you're the one taking all the risks here."

"I'm not gonna lie," said Nicolai as he got up from the sofa, "I'll be glad when this is all over."

After promising he would call as soon as he was in position, Nicolai headed for the door. Petru wished him good luck. He hadn't told him about the money from the warehouse yet, but decided now wasn't the time. Instead, he prayed a silent prayer as he watched his friend leave the apartment. He hoped he would see Nicolai again, but he was realistic enough to know that anything could happen once he got inside the LEU building.

Petru waited for over an hour for Nicolai to contact him. The first contact was a text message.

'I'm in the city. I'll FaceTime you when I'm in position.'

Petru responded with a thumbs up emoji icon and waited. As he stared out the window of his apartment, he thought back over their plan. If the first group of people he tried to tail inside challenged him, the whole exercise was likely a bust. The guards would be notified and they would then be on high alert, possibly even stationing someone at the rear door. But Petru was more worried about what would happen if Nicolai did get inside. There was only one practical exit, and that was the rear door he came in by.

Petru mentally pictured the internal layout of the ground floor. The lockers were in the first room off the hallway and the guards' station and scanner were in an open area about thirty feet further along the hallway. The guards sometimes watched the rear door and sometimes they didn't. If they spotted him, it was possible one of them would come and investigate. They both knew there was every chance Nicolai could be boxed into the locker room and cut off from his exit by a guard with a gun. If that happened, he feared Nicolai could pay with his life.

Petru murmured, "Is it any wonder you're feeling nervous…"

They had both agreed that speed was key. If Nicolai got inside, he would go straight to the locker and use Petru's key. Petru had never heard of them changing the locks in the past, but acknowledged the risk when he had handed Nicolai his key. They had gone over the locker layout. Nicolai would feel up inside the top part of the locker, and if he felt the USB, he would wrench it from its fixture and get out of there as soon as possible.

Petru gritted his teeth—so much could go wrong. Was the risk worth the reward? He and Nicolai had discussed this at length. While we were no guarantees, if the USB did contain a copy of Razvan's personal laptop, it could be the gold that they needed to bring him and his organization down. He nodded to himself. It would definitely be worth it.

A FaceTime call on his smartphone interrupted his thoughts.

He pressed answer and saw a close-up of Nicolai's face as he walked along a city street. Nicolai had an earbud in his right ear and said, "I'm at a bus stop almost out front of the building. Can you see and hear me, okay?"

"Loud and clear," said Petru as he gave a thumbs up for the camera.

"I'm switching the camera from selfie to camera mode…"

Petru watched as the phone's camera switched from the image of his friend to a live image of the concrete pavement. The camera moved and Petru could now see a view of the street.

"I'm holding the camera up to my ear, like I'm making a

normal phone call," Nicolai whispered. "Can you see the video?"

The camera angle was not quite right and showed most people from the waist down. "I can see the street," said Petru. "But the angle is a little low. Can you raise it?"

They experimented with camera angles until Petru was happy. Nicolai's vantage point gave him a view of part of the street and the top of the LEU laneway.

Petru checked his watch. "It's almost one PM. Staff should be heading back now."

"Okay," murmured Nicolai. "If you're happy with this position, we'll just keep the ruse up that I'm on a normal call. You can watch who turns into the laneway…"

It wasn't long before Petru spotted two men he recognized strolling up the street. They were both in their late thirties. Petru recognized one of them as the company's accountant and the other as a software developer who made fake insurance websites. "These are not the guys to follow," he advised. "They've both been with the company too long and they'll likely challenge you to show your ID."

"Got it," said Nicolai.

They waited another two minutes. As Petru kept scanning the pedestrians, another group approached. They were all in their early twenties.

Petru said, "See that group? Three men and one woman? I recognize two of them as LEU staff."

Petru could hear the tension in Nicolai's voice as he responded, "They've turned up the laneway. Should I follow?"

"Yes. They're all new and unlikely to challenge you."

Nicolai whispered, "I'm following now. I'm about fifteen feet back…"

All Petru could see now was the side of the LEU building, bobbing up and down with Nicolai's step. He knew he still had the phone to his ear, pretending to be on a call. "Good luck, Nicolai. Let's keep the line open."

Petru listened to Nicolai's footsteps and the sound of the chatter of the group in front of him. The image of the wall sped by a little more quickly. Petru imagined Nicolai striding hard to get his timing right to tail the group inside. Above the muffled sound of voices and footsteps, he heard a door being opened. He then heard more inaudible conversation, before Nicolai's voice broke through with a muttered, "Thanks."

Suddenly, the camera image on his phone changed. A low-level gloom replaced the well lit image of the side of the LEU building. Petru could barely make out the shadows as Nicolai whispered, "I'm in."

Chapter Thirty-Two

The gloomy FaceTime image turned dark as Nicolai whispered above the sound of footsteps, "The phone's now in my coat pocket."

"I can still hear you," said Petru as he held his breath. He figured he would know in less than a minute if the USB was still there and in under two minutes if the operation was going to be a success. He could hear Nicolai's footsteps, heavy and determined, and pictured him turning left from the hallway and entering the locker room. The locker room was about fifteen feet wide by about twenty feet long. Metal lockers lined the wall on the right-hand side, while the left wall had coat hooks.

Petru heard a jumble of voices. It was typical of a lunchtime return to work. He pictured the group of four hanging up their coats and stowing away their phones while they continued their conversation. Most staff spent under a minute inside the room before they moved on to the guard's screening area. After a few moments, the noise died down.

Nicolai murmured, "They've left. I'm now alone."

The Catalin Connection

Petru wanted to ask him if he had any problems with the group, but didn't want to slow him down, and simply said, "Okay."

He heard Nicolai murmur, "The key works," followed by a metallic clinking as he opened his locker door. Petru held his breath again as Nicolai whispered, "The locker looks empty... just reaching in under—"

A man's voice interrupted Nicolai's hushed whispers, demanding, "Who are you?" Petru swore under his breath as he recognized the voice as belonging to a guard.

Petru could hear an edge in Nicolai's voice as he responded, "I'm Greg."

Although tempted to whisper words of encouragement, Petru realized that any coaching to Nicolai at this point could be distracting. He listened as the guard respond, "I process all the new people here and I don't remember you!"

Above the sound of a locker door being slammed, Petru heard Nicolai say, "There must be some mistake? I got my ID last week, but you weren't the guard."

The guard shouted, "What are you doing in here?"

An enormous thump startled Petru, along with shouting and the sound of someone running.

Nicolai had done his best to remain calm as the guard had challenged him. But when the guard went to unclip the pistol from its halter, he knew there was only one course of action. He was almost six-foot-three and weighed well over two hundred pounds. The guard was four inches shorter and gave away about seventy pounds in weight. While math had always been Nicolai's strongest subject in school, he wasn't thinking about the math or physics of the situation as he shoulder-charged the guard. His focus was on bringing the guard down before he could get the gun out of its holster.

Nine feet had separated him from the guard when he launched himself at his adversary. Turning his body sideways, he allowed the full force of his right shoulder to crash into the guard's chest. He heard a whoosh of air escape from the guard as they crashed to the floor. Nicolai punched the guard with a right cross to keep him down for a moment before standing up. He could hear yelling coming from the guard's station, but ignored it as he sprinted for the rear exit. He feared they might have triggered an automatic door lock. But when he pushed against the door, a cool rush of fresh air greeted him.

Nicolai could hear someone behind him shout, "Stop, or I'll shoot!" as he sprinted up the laneway. He pushed past a trio of LEU staff who had just entered the laneway as they gaped at him in confusion. He heard footsteps at his back and gritted his teeth as he turned right and sprinted down the boulevard. With his bulk, he knew he would tire quickly and needed a place to hide.

'Where do I hide?' his brain screamed as the sound of the footsteps drew closer. Pivoting on his heel, he dashed across the street, with the sound of blaring horns ringing in his ears. Without looking back, Nicolai bolted down a side alley. As he emerged on the adjoining boulevard, he noticed a lot more foot traffic. He rushed forward, weaving between pedestrians as his heart pounded in his ears. Seeing a break in the traffic, he crossed the road and did his best to meld in with the pedestrians. Panting hard, he glanced back but couldn't see any of the guards close behind.

Nicolai realized he needed to get off the street and stepped into a laundromat. He scanned the interior as he sucked in a few deep breaths. Two young women sat side-by-side, staring at clothes spinning in a washing machine. He scanned towards the back and saw a middle-aged man behind a counter texting on his phone. Nicolai glanced back at the front door as he strode toward the rear. He whipped out a ten euro note from his pocket and asked, "Can I use your back exit?"

The startled man stared at the money and then locked eyes with Nicolai. "Are you in some kind of trouble?"

Nicolai nodded. "Yes, but not with the police. Do you want the money?"

The man snatched the note. "Follow me."

Nicolai followed the man through a small storeroom. He sneaked a glance back into the laundromat's main room and was relieved not to see any guards. The man flipped a latch on a steel door at the rear. "This gets you into the laneway. If anyone other than the cops comes looking for you, I'll say I haven't seen you."

"They're security guards, not cops."

The man held up the ten euro note and said, "Then I haven't seen you."

Nicolai thanked the man and disappeared into the laneway. He pulled out his phone as he started walking. The FaceTime connection he'd had with Petru had disconnected. He pressed speed dial as he strode down the alley.

After two rings, Petru answered. "Are you alright? What happened?"

Nicolai said, "I got challenged by a guard." He then relayed a summary of his escape before adding, "I need to keep moving. I'm sure they're still looking for me."

"I understand. And talking to me is a distraction—you need to keep your focus."

Nicolai looked back over his shoulder. "No one's following me, that I can see. So that's a good start."

"I have just one question," said Petru. "Did you get the USB?"

Nicolai grinned as he unclenched his left hand. He'd had it clamped shut ever since charging the guard. He stared down at the USB in his palm and said, "I got it. If they don't catch me before I get out of the city, I'll see you in an hour."

It was well after four pm, before Nicolai knocked on the door to Petru's apartment. He had expected his friend to be buoyant after retrieving the USB, but he seemed subdued as he sat on the couch.

Petru picked up on his mood. "Nicolai, what's wrong?"

"I'm worried. I was hoping I would get in and out of LEU without creating a scene. It's good we got the USB, but..." Nicolai grimaced, "I'm worried about the cameras."

"That they'll have video of you..." mused Petru.

Nicolai nodded. "I figured no one would ever bother reviewing the feed if I had been able to sneak in and out. But after what happened..."

Petru thought back to the incident and nodded in agreement. "They'll certainly be reviewing the video."

Nicolai said, "As it is, I'm sure Luca Razvan has now seen the video. And given it was your locker, he's probably figured out what I stole."

Petru conceded, "This is a setback. I'm sorry, Nicolai."

"Unless, by some miracle, the cameras weren't working, they'll have me cold on video." Nicolai grimaced and added, "And Razvan is on the board of the Roma Bank. It's only a matter of time before they join the dots."

Nicolai let out a long breath and added, "Once that happens, I won't be just some random guy. I'll be a bank employee who's gone rogue."

"How long do you think it will take for them to work out your identity?"

"I don't know. Maybe a day or two." Nicolai's face turned into a wry smile as he added, "And then I'll be on Razvan's hit list just like you."

A somber mood settled on the apartment. No one spoke for two minutes—both lost in their thoughts at the cost Nicolai had paid for retrieving the USB.

"There's one thing I haven't told you about," said Nicolai as he broke the silence. "It's not just me working inside the bank. There's a colleague in the international division who's helping. He and I started at the bank at about the same time, and I've always trusted him. When I told him what happened to my sister, he promised me he would help and he's been getting me a lot of the information we need."

Petru raised a brow. "That's a big risk. Why would he help?"

"I think he's working for Interpol," said Nicolai. "He hasn't said as much, which I understand, but he seems to know a lot about what's happening on the inside."

"Have you told Robbie Mayne about him?"

"Not in so many words. I don't think it's wise for me to be revealing his identity. And things are heating up at the bank."

"How so?" said Petru with a frown.

"My colleague told me last week about a money transfer to an international account."

"Doesn't that happen all the time?"

Nicolai scratched at his chin. "I asked the same question. He told me it was for the sum of three million in US currency. He thinks it's a payoff."

"A payoff?"

"The bank is holding the money in two separate accounts," said Nicolai. "One-and-a-half-million in each. The outgoing transfers have also been setup, but it requires a voice ID to authorize it."

Petru frowned. "Is that usual?"

"Highly unusual. We were going to meet tomorrow night to discuss it in more detail. I tried calling him again today, but he doesn't pick up. I'm really worried about him…"

"Do you think he's met with foul play?"

Nicolai held up his phone. "I've been calling and texting him since last Thursday, but I'm not getting a response. It's as if he's dropped off the face of the earth…"

Nicolai got up and started pacing. "I can't go back to the Roma bank. It's too risky. My fear is they've found out about my friend and they've had him murdered. And I figure that's my fate as well."

Petru said, "Do they know about this apartment?

Nicolai shook his head. "I don't believe so." He stopped pacing and looked around the apartment. "I think we're both safe here… for now at least."

"It goes without saying that that I'll sleep on the couch."

Nicolai shook his head. "No, I'll take the couch." He looked at his watch and added, "I'm going to head back to my apartment. I've got some money there and I need my laptop and the copies I've printed of all the files. I'll also pack a few clothes and head back as soon as I can."

"Do you think it's safe to go there?"

"There are no guarantees," said Nicolai with a shrug. "I've probably got a small window. How long? I'm not sure. I'll go home now and be in and out in under fifteen minutes. We can figure out what we do once I get back."

Petru went to apologize again for all the grief he had caused, but Nicolai held a hand up to stop him. "We both knew what we were getting into. This is a setback and nothing more."

Nicolai sat on the sofa again and opened a plastic bag he had brought in with him. He produced two wireless security cameras and said, "I got these on the way here." He pointed to the main window. "I'm going to install one outside here, and the other I'll install above the rear entrance when I leave. That way, we'll have video surveillance of both entry and exit points to the building."

"Let's hope we don't need it."

Nicolai made a face. "We can't be too careful."

They went over their plans while Nicolai installed the first camera. Once Nicolai had the camera feed setup on Petru's laptop, he gave Petru a thumbs up. "Time for me to go. I'll install the second camera on my way out and text you when it's done. Then you can configure the second feed for the laptop."

Nicolai walked to the door. He turned back as he opened it and said, "If I'm not back in under two hours, something has gone wrong."

Before Petru could say goodbye, Nicolai was gone. He stared at the door and murmured, "Take care, Nicolai."

Chapter Thirty-Three

Petru glanced at his watch. It was after eight PM and Nicolai had still not returned. The sinking feeling in his stomach intensified. He recalled Nicolai's last words; "If I'm not back in two hours, something's gone wrong." It was now close to four hours since his friend had left the apartment. He had called and texted Nicolai at the two-hour mark without getting a response. At first, he had tried to remain positive. There must be a reason, he thought. He had wondered if Nicolai had stopped on the way back to buy beer. Or if his phone was broken. But it didn't take long to buy beer, and a broken phone shouldn't have delayed his return by more than a few minutes. His repeated calls and text messages every half hour had gone unanswered.

The only contact had been an email Nicolai had sent forty-five minutes after leaving his apartment. He opened up the email again and read it again.

The Catalin Connection

From: greg_rio99@proteja.bg To: codos9009@proteja.bg Subject: Account Numbers & RM

Just leaving the apartment after packing and sending a few emails to RM (refer Attachment 1). Also, sending you the two account numbers in Attachment 2 that we talked about that have the $3M for payoffs (might be useful to pass on to RM?). I've shredded anything I've had on paper related to Razvan as I don't think it's safe to leave anything behind.

See you soon. Regards N

Nicolai's apartment was only a fifteen minute walk away. Because of the timing of the message, he knew Nicolai should have been back hours ago. What had happened to him? Had he met with foul play? Had there been an accident? Petru let out a long breath as he stared down at his phone screen again, willing Nicolai to call. He lost patience and pressed speed dial. He held his breath as he waited for his call to connect and then cursed as it went through to voice mail again.

Petru dropped his phone on the table in disgust and stared at the feed from the two security cameras on his laptop. The camera Nicolai had installed at the back of the complex showed no one in the laneway. He switched his focus to the camera out front, which showed people strolling along the street in the early evening. There had been no sign of Nicolai on either camera in the four hours since he'd left the building.

Petru closed his eyes and admonished himself not to panic as he drew in a few deep breaths. Both men agreed that Nicolai's return to his apartment was a risk, but they thought the risk was low. Surely Razvan couldn't have discovered Nicolai's identity that quickly? And to mobilize a team to intercept him at his apartment in such a short space of time seemed almost impossible.

"Stay positive," he murmured, but he didn't really believe his words. Nicolai's return trip should have taken less than an hour. He opened his eyes and gritted his teeth. Something was clearly wrong, and he knew it. He felt helpless as he contemplated the thought of what Razvan may have done to his friend. As he wheeled into the kitchen to get a glass of water, he had a sinking feeling he would never see his friend again.

It was almost one AM before Petru finally gave up and headed to bed. He lay in the darkness, listening to the creaking of the building and the distant sound of traffic. His mind turned over a thousand thoughts. It had been ten hours since Nicolai had left the apartment and he still hadn't heard from him. Petru had made early evening calls to every hospital in Bucharest, but no one matching Nicolai's description had been admitted. Still not prepared to admit defeat, he had then called every police station in the city asking after 'his brother,' who was missing. Nicolai's height, weight, and bushy beard made him easy to identify, but the police had not detained anyone who matched his description. Although he was normally an optimist, tonight his mood was glum. He stared up at the ceiling, resigned to the fact that Nicolai was probably dead, or soon would be.

It occurred to him that staying here any longer could be a huge risk. If they had tortured Nicolai, there was a real possibility he would have told them he wasn't working alone. Petru grimaced as he realized Razvan may now know the address of his apartment. He had no nowhere to go, but he wasn't prepared to walk away—at least not yet. Nicolai would not have wanted that, and Elena still deserved justice. As he continued to listen to the sounds of the city late at night, he started making plans. He would extract the data from the USB tomorrow and email it to Robbie Mayne. If something happened to him, at least Mayne could continue the fight against Razvan. He also needed to figure out what to do about his longer-term accommodation. He was on borrowed time here, and he needed to find somewhere else to stay. There was also the matter of his father's gold ashtray. The more he thought about it, the more he realized he couldn't sell it, no matter how desperate he became for money. The ashtray belonged to his mother, and he had resolved in his mind to return it to her. What she did with it after that was her decision.

Above the drone of the city traffic, Petru heard someone walking up the creaky rear stairs of the apartment block. He froze and wondered if it was a resident, or one of Razvan's hit men coming to take him out. The next thirty seconds felt like an eternity. The sounds on the rear stairs creaking under the weight of someone as they walked up tread by tread sent his mind into overdrive. He pictured a man with a gun stealing up the rear stairs to his floor to look for his apartment. He let out an audible sigh as he heard a man cough at the same time as a key was inserted into a lock. Petru recognized the hacking cough of the two-pack-a-day smoker who lived across the hallway. The man regularly stayed out late drinking and tonight had been no exception. Petru's heart rate and breathing returned to normal. But he knew that staying here, even for just a few days more, could be fatal. He would need to take extra precautions just in case they came after him. He figured he only needed another two days in Bucharest before he could leave forever. For now, he needed sleep. He closed his eyes and prayed a prayer that the end for Nicolai had been swift and merciful.

Chapter Thirty-Four

Petru barely slept and hauled himself out of bed just before seven AM to start the day. After making a cup of coffee, he wheeled over to the living room table to examine the security cameras. The back lane seemed empty, while the front camera showed people heading to work. But there was still no sign of Nicolai. He checked his phone again for messages, but grimaced when he saw no messages from his friend.

As he sipped his coffee, it occurred to him that Nicolai may have spotted Razvan's hit men before they got into position to take him out. The possibility that he had gone into hiding gave him hope. Nicolai wouldn't have returned to the apartment or made contact until he felt it was safe. Petru stared out the window at nothing in particular. Staying here long term to wait was not an option. He believed Razvan would increase his efforts to locate him now that he was certain his data had been stolen.

Petru sipped more coffee. He figured he would stay two more days. If Nicolai was already dead, he would be discovered soon. Razvan never hid his victims—they were usually found floating in the river within several days of their murder. Petru closed his eyes for a moment to stave off a panic attack. Before his accident, he had been confident and cool under pressure. He now realized his confidence had actually been arrogance. Adjusting to his new life was proving more difficult than he could have imagined. Despite their brief acquaintance, he had developed a sense of dependence on Nicolai. That now seemed to be a mistake.

He murmured, "You can't rely on anyone," as he opened his eyes again. Petru glanced at the door. Waiting for news about his friend was going to drive him insane. He needed a distraction and plugged in the LEU USB into his laptop. After downloading the contents to a special folder he had created on his computer, Petru began studying the data.

Within a few minutes, he was convinced he had what they wanted—a backup of Razvan's laptop. Like most hackers, Razvan was meticulous in the setup of his laptop. The folders were laid out like a tree directory structure, which made his job easier. Razvan appeared to keep meticulous records of nearly everything in his life. There were folders for medical records, his property portfolio, and even a security assessment of his penthouse. Petru smiled to himself as he scanned the data. Information was gold. Knowing Razvan's personal information, including his residence, made his nemesis more vulnerable.

Petru spent the next hour opening individual folders and scanning their contents. It wasn't until he accessed a Clients sub-folder that he felt he was getting close to finding what he was after. Petru clicked on a spreadsheet entitled 'Transactions' and was prompted to enter a password in Microsoft Excel. Password protecting a document was like putting a neon sign on it to show its importance. Petru nodded to himself—this file would be worth investigating.

After an hour of unsuccessfully trying to guess the spreadsheet password, Petru pushed back from the table in frustration. He had tried combinations of Razvan's name, date of birth and address without success. He was grateful for the spreadsheet's simple password security that allowed him unlimited access attempts. Petru debated setting up a copy of the file with one of his own software programs for cracking files. He knew from experience that his program could take days to generate the correct combination. He knew the most efficient way to hack a file was by stealing the owner's password. He often achieved this by tricking a victim into using their password on a fake website or by impersonating someone they trusted. But that wouldn't work with Razvan. Luca Razvan had written the hacker's manual and wouldn't fall for one of his own tricks. Petru knew he would have to go 'old school' and figure it out himself.

Petru heard footsteps on the back stairs and glanced at the front door to his apartment. He had to admit that focusing his energy on the task at hand was therapeutic. It eased the stress of waiting for news on Nicolai. He would pause every time he heard someone walking up the back stairs—hoping against hope that Nicolai would knock on his front door. When the footsteps faded away, he wheeled back to his table and scratched his chin as he thought about different approaches. He had searched Razvan's emails for password clues, but found nothing obvious.. He had tried various combinations of the LEU company name and its year of incorporation, with no luck. He had tried street names where Razvan lived as well as the name of the boulevard where LEU operated from. All with no luck. But he was patient—and cracking personal passwords was a challenge he always relished.

Petru decided he would try a different angle. Sometimes people used a family member's name or a pet's name as a password. But as far as he knew, Razvan was single and had no children. Petru scanned Razvan's folder structure again and clicked on photographs. Like everything else on Razvan's laptop, the folder was organized into sub-folders. It was the one labeled 'Personal' that he clicked on first. Petru breathed a sigh of relief. The folder contained only fifty-seven photographs and wouldn't take long to explore.

He began double-clicking on each photograph to open up a preview. Most of the photographs seemed to be mementos from Razvan's childhood. There were photos of him with an older couple and one other boy. Petru assumed these were family shots with his mother and father, and perhaps a brother. Petru continued to click through the photos. He recognized the same family faces in several pictures. There were also several class photos taken of Razvan when he was only about seven or eight. Razvan smiled in every photo, just like the other kids. Petru shook his head. Razvan as a boy looked young and pure. He wondered how such an innocent-looking child could grow up into a monster.

Petru kept clicking through the photos. There were several photos of Razvan in later years. One showed him working out in a gym and another showed him graduating from university. The graduation photo intrigued him. The woman he saw in the early family pictures was standing with him. Petru could see the facial resemblance and was certain this was Razvan's mother. There was no sign of the father in the picture, and he wondered if he had died during his childhood. He found a photo of a gravestone while searching through the photographs. Petru checked the metadata for the picture and discovered it had been taken in Bucharest three years ago. He zoomed in on the gravestone and read the words chiseled into the marble fascia. Petru murmured, "Aurelia Razvan," as he read the inscription. He continued reading until he came to the words, 'Beloved mother of Luca and Emil.'

A smile spread across his face. He now had the name of Razvan's mother, as well as her maiden name, year of birth, and year of death. Using shortcut keys, he switched to the Excel spreadsheet and rapidly keyed in combinations of Razvan's mother's name. The program unlocked with his fourteenth attempt—Razvan's mother's maiden name and year of birth.

Petru spent the next two hours studying the content of Razvan's Excel spreadsheet. The file contained twenty-six tabs. It appeared to be meticulously ordered. He wished Nicolai could have been here to help with the analysis. While he was good at computer hacking, financial data was not his forte. He surveyed each sheet. The first sheet was a list of companies, both Romanian and international. Each company entry had a bank account and a reference number. Nothing too sinister in that, he thought, but the second sheet appeared more promising. This sheet had a list of payments to bank accounts and dates. The company reference numbers from sheet one reappeared on other tabs. Even though Petru was an amateur in this form of analysis, even he could recognize the pattern. Large sums of money were being moved between entities. Each entry had a single word cryptic description. 'Loan,' 'Bonus,' 'Payment,' and 'Transfer' were common. Petru nodded to himself. There was no doubt in his mind he was looking at Razvan's money laundering journal.

Petru scanned the other tabs within the spreadsheet. They all contained further information on companies and journals of payments. He had seen enough. This information would be vital to Mayne's investigation. Petru's fingers hovered over the keyboard. Even though he had Mayne's email address, Petru had never communicated with Mayne by email. He was cautious and never sent sensitive information to any address he had not verified. He needed an introductory email first.

To: catalin1989@cybamail.com   From: codos9009@proteja.bg
Subject: Introduction

R, I'm writing to you because Nicolai is missing. We have retrieved the data we talked about, which looks promising. Before I send it I need to confirm I have the right email address. Can you confirm what my mode of transport is? C

Petru pressed send and let out a long breath as the lump in his throat returned. Admitting in writing that Nicolai was missing gave it an air of finality. He glanced at his phone for messages out of habit and then cursed at the blank screen. With every passing hour the chances of Nicolai still being alive diminished. He debated calling the hospitals and police again, but figured it was pointless. They had his contact details and promised to call if Nicolai turned up. As he went to push away from the table to make a cup of coffee a new email message appeared in his Inbox. It was from Robbie Mayne.

To: codos9009@proteja.bg From: catalin1989@cybamail.com
Subject: re: Introduction

C, I'm really sorry to hear about Nicolai. Let's hope we can all get through this alive. Your mode of transport is a wheelchair and your sister's name is Elena. I know you're doing it tough. Do you need money? If so, send me your bank details. R

Petru nodded to himself as read the message. He was confident he was communicating with Robbie Mayne. He attached a copy of the spreadsheet to the email and then prepared a message to go with it. He started by thanking Robbie for the generous offer of money. He paused as he went to decline the offer. His goal was simply to bring Razvan down. Nothing else mattered. But he knew his money wouldn't last long either. In his condition, finding somewhere else to stay and getting out of the city would cost him more than his savings. He was sure Robbie Mayne understood this, and his offer was genuine. Petru changed his message. He thanked Robbie for his generous offer and included his bank account details. After pressing send, he glanced at the clock on his computer screen before pushing back from the table. It was now after midday. He decided tonight would be his last night in the apartment. It was too risky to stay any longer. If Nicolai hadn't showed up by this time tomorrow, he would assume the worst and make his escape.

Chapter Thirty-Five

Petru rubbed his eyes and looked up from his laptop screen. It was just after ten PM and he had spent too much time in front of his computer. Leaning back in his wheelchair, he massaged his neck muscles as he thought about what he would do next. He had decided tonight would be his last night in the apartment and had already packed his bags. He stared at the handwritten note he had written for Nicolai. Petru didn't think he was still alive. But if he had somehow survived and returned in the coming days, at least he would have his contact details.

Petru rolled his head around in a circular motion to ease the tension in his neck. Once his muscles had stopped cramping, he glanced down at his laptop screen again. He focused on the two images from the security cameras. He couldn't see anyone in the rear laneway and out front there were just a few people on the street. Using shortcut keys on his keyboard, he opened up his email application. His eyes widened as he reread the message Robbie Mayne had sent to him less than an hour ago.

The Catalin Connection

To: codos9009@proteja.bg   From: catalin1989@cybamail.com
Subject: Introduction

C, I have wired $1,000 US to your bank account (it may take a day or two to clear). Let me know if you need more (I'm happy to help). I've passed the file you sent on to my analyst. The information looks solid. We are confident we can use it to build a case against Razvan for money laundering. Have you heard from Nicolai yet? Please be careful. One of my colleagues here has been killed in a hit-and-run two nights ago. It appears as though I'm the next target, so I'm going to ground for a few days until we have all our evidence collated. Be careful, these guys are playing for keeps! Best, R

Petru blew out a long breath. He was thankful for the money that Mayne was sending and had already begun his search for a place to stay. He re-read the sentence about Mayne's colleague being killed in a hit-and-run. Alarm bells rang in his head. Mayne had been right—the crime syndicate had spread as far as Canada and the USA. The news of a death on the other side of the world only strengthened that view.

He was tempted to call a cab now. He checked the security cameras again. The street out front still looked quiet. Could he risk one more night? He didn't fancy spending a night on the streets or trying to find a hotel at this late hour. He had bolstered his security as best he could to the apartment.

"Just ten more hours," he murmured.

His phone buzzed, breaking his train of thought. He looked down at the number. It was a fixed landline from somewhere in Romania. Since escaping from his apartment, he had picked up a new SIM for his phone. Only a few people knew the number. He debated letting it go through to voicemail, but then realized it might be Nicolai.

"Hello."

Petru's heart sank as a man's voice he did not recognize responded, "Am I speaking with Petru?"

"Yes."

"I'm Detective Marin. You lodged a missing person's complaint about your brother yesterday?"

"Yes. Have you found him?"

There was a pause on the line before the man said, "We'd like you to come down to the police station. We may have found your brother."

Petru felt his mouth go dry. "Dead or alive?"

"It's a little complicated. Could you come in?"

Petru grimaced. "I can't. I'm in a wheelchair."

There was a pause before Marin said, "Is there someone else from your family who could come in?"

"He's dead, isn't he?"

More silence. "I'm sorry, but we can't discuss this over the phone. Is there someone—"

"Just answer me this. Was he shot and dumped in the river?"

"How did you…"

Petru gritted his teeth. "Nicolai has a distinctive mole on his left wrist."

He held his breath as he heard two men conferring in the background. After almost a minute, Marin picked up the phone again. "We really need someone to come in for a formal… meeting."

"Does he have a mole on his left wrist?"

More silence followed before the detective answered, "Yes."

Petru closed his eyes. He sucked in deep breaths as the shock of his friend's death sunk in. Marin suggested they could send a police car around to pick him up, but Petru was no longer listening.

Chapter Thirty-Six

Petru glanced at his laptop's digital clock. It was 1:47 AM, but he was still wide awake. Although the news of Nicolai's death had rocked him, he now had other things to focus on and felt sick to his stomach as he returned his gaze to the images from the security cameras.

He watched the feed from the camera concealed just above the entrance to his apartment block, as the grainy image of a man walked into the building. He grimaced. The same man had walked past his apartment block six times in the last hour.

He knew he was next on the list and if his plan did not work, he would probably be dead within the hour. After taking several deep breaths, he switched off the camera feeds and opened another program on his laptop. He spent a few seconds adjusting the laptop until the device's webcam captured most of the left-hand side of his apartment. He then pulled out his smartphone and opened an app that connected to his laptop webcam. Petru adjusted the contrast on his phone until he was happy with the live feed he had of his apartment and then he pushed back from the desk in his wheelchair.

As he wheeled across the darkened living room, he told himself now was not the time to panic. He had made all the preparations he could and hoped the planning would pay off. Petru estimated he had about two minutes before the man would be at his front door. The elevators were slow and unreliable and he knew the man would take the stairs. Watching his second-floor neighbors as they came in the building on his security camera, he had timed how long it had taken those who preferred the stairs to reach the fourth floor.

The fourteen-year-old boy who lived with his mother in the apartment next door had set the best time at one minute fifty-two seconds. The average time had been well over two minutes. He figured whoever they sent would climb the stairs cautiously, careful of who might be awake and watching, even at this late hour. Petru maneuvered his wheelchair into the only bedroom of his apartment to check everything one last time.

He had decided it would be safer dozing in his wheelchair until morning rather than getting into bed. At least in his wheelchair he had a slim chance of escaping if they came after him. The mound he had fashioned in the bed from spare blankets to represent his body did not need any final adjustments. Petru pulled a small digital voice recorder from his pocket, which he had used to record himself while sleeping. The recording went for close to twenty minutes, which he figured would be more than adequate for his purposes. He pressed the play button on the recorder and adjusted the volume to a level he thought was equivalent to that of someone in a deep sleep. He gently slid the device under the pillow and pulled up the top sheet to cover most of a dark-brown blanket he had fashioned into the shape of his head. Petru studied the ruse, hoping that whoever they sent wouldn't bother to switch the light on first.

To increase his odds of survival he had pulled two springs out of the lumpy old sofa in the living room earlier in the day. He had then fastened them with screws to the internal side of the bedroom door. With some trial and error, he had tested how far the door needed to be opened before the springs compressed tightly up against the bedroom wall. The optimum gap to snap the door shut when it was let go seemed to be about four inches. Petru had then made a latching mechanism from a wire coat-hanger he had twisted and fashioned into shape. Once fitted, the latch successfully held the door in the open position until it was tugged on by a piece of string. He then removed the inside doorknob and was satisfied that, provided his attacker was fully in the bedroom when he released the latch, it would lock him inside. Petru never really thought he would need to use the trap as he studied his handiwork one last time. It would only buy him a minute or two before his assailant broke down the door, but he hoped it would be enough. Conscious that valuable seconds were now ticking away, he wheeled out of the bedroom and then reversed his wheelchair into the small bathroom.

As he sat in the darkness, Petru gently closed the door to wait. He could feel his heart beating loudly in his chest. He breathed deeply and admonished himself to stay calm. He had practiced the routine a few times and was reasonably comfortable with it. Now was the moment of truth. Petru picked up his phone and studied the video feed from his laptop. The screen showed his living room, but the image was grainy and lacked sufficient contrast. He made a few adjustments on his phone until the living room furniture appeared as silhouettes on the screen. He nodded to himself. He was confident he could now see the outline of anyone who entered his apartment.

Petru transferred the phone to his right hand and then gingerly lifted a metal ring off a hook with his left. He delicately slid the ring onto his index finger. The metal ring was attached to a piece of string that went through a tiny hole in the bathroom through to his bedroom. The other end of the string attached to the release latch for his bedroom door. If the latch mechanism worked properly, only a slight tug on the string would snap the door shut. It sounded good in theory, but it would only work if his adversary was fully inside the room. If the man only went as far as the doorway before he started firing, he knew his life expectancy could be measured in seconds..

After waiting half a minute, Petru heard a soft but distinctive clinking metallic sound. He knew someone had picked the lock to his front door as his phone screen showed the front door slowly swing open. At first, the doorway appeared empty. Then, the silhouette of a man carrying a silenced pistol appeared on the screen. The man appeared to be in no hurry and stood in the doorway with his gun raised—watching and listening. Cautiously, the man took two steps into the apartment and scanned for signs of danger. Satisfied there were no imminent threats, the man silently closed the door behind him.

Petru watched as the silhouette walked several steps forward before stopping directly outside the bathroom door and tilting his head slightly as if listening for sounds that would point to the location of his quarry. The apartment was silent except for the sound of Petru's rhythmic breathing emanating softly from the recorder in the bedroom. Petru had not stepped foot inside a church since he was a young boy, but prayed with the fervor of a monk that the man would go to the bedroom first. The facts were simple. If the man checked the bathroom first, he was as good as dead.

The man stood still and turned his head slowly from side to side. Although it was difficult to tell from the camera angle, he did not appear to be wearing any night vision goggles. Petru figured he was probably waiting while his eyes adjusted to the darkness before moving any further into the apartment. The stress of waiting made his hands sweat and he feared losing even a slight grip on the metal ring.

After what seemed like an eternity, the man took one step forward and then another toward the bedroom. The man moved forward again and stood at the entrance to the bedroom with the gun raised in a firing position. Without warning, he disappeared into the bedroom and, almost simultaneously, Petru heard the muffled sound of the silenced pistol as it discharged three times in quick succession.

Petru pulled hard on the ring for the release latch. He felt the string go taught before the bathroom reverberated to the sound of the bedroom door slamming shut. Before Petru could register what was happening, he heard the unmistakable sound of several more muffled gunshots being fired at the bedroom door.

Petru grabbed a length of piano wire and his travel bag from a shelf in the bathroom. After opening the door, he quickly maneuvered his wheelchair to the front door. The noise coming from the bedroom was loud and persistent. The man was obviously throwing his entire weight at the door in an effort to break the lock. Petru estimated he needed two minutes to be ready for what he needed to do next. Judging by the amount of force the man was using, he was not sure the lock would hold that long.

He opened the front door and quickly wheeled down the hallway to the building elevators. Petru pressed the call button for the elevator before sliding out of his wheelchair. The stairwell for the apartment block was located next to the elevators, and in preparation, Petru had screwed two small unobtrusive steel hooks into the banister support posts just below shin height. He used his hands to slide from one post to the other to quickly fasten the wire between the two hooks before pulling it taught and tying it off. Petru barely heard the bell that signaled his elevator had arrived over the din coming from his apartment. Just a few seconds more, he prayed, as he got back into his wheelchair and wheeled to the open elevator doors.

Petru reached in and pressed the ground floor button and then the close button, before reversing his wheelchair back several steps. The sound coming from his apartment had changed subtly in the last twenty seconds. Petru knew the lock on his bedroom door had almost broken and his time was up. As he wheeled down the corridor towards a small alcove where he planned to hide, he heard a crashing sound from his apartment as the lock finally gave way and the bedroom door burst open.

He barely reached the alcove before he heard his front door burst open and then the sound of running footsteps. Petru did not have time to turn his wheelchair around to see what was happening. As he sat in the alcove's darkness, catching his breath, he listened to the sound of the man's running footsteps and pictured him running past the elevator to the stairs. The footsteps were replaced almost immediately by the muffled thumping sound of a body tumbling down the stairs before the apartment block once again became quiet.

There was no time to celebrate as he pulled a two-feet wooden stick from his carry bag and wheeled quickly back to the stairwell. Petru looked down. He could see the man sent to kill him lying on his side in the gloom on the landing below. He was not unconscious as he had hoped, but he was nursing his left wrist, which was pointing out at an odd angle. Petru locked his wheels before easing out of his wheelchair and on to the floor in front of the stairs. The man did not seem to notice as Petru released the trip wire. Petru knew he needed to move quickly and twisted his body around and pulled himself down the stairs headfirst.

The man writhed in pain and did not notice his presence until he was only three stairs above him. As the man reached down for his gun with his good hand, Petru clubbed the man across the head with his wooden stick. He used measured force; enough to disable him, but hopefully not enough to cause permanent injury.

The man instantly let go of the gun with a groan and collapsed on the floor. Petru slid down the remaining steps and retrieved the weapon. Before climbing the stairs again, he studied the man's face. His assailant was in his early thirties with short, almost crew cut blonde hair. He had sharp features and a familiar cruel look, even though he was unconscious. Petru was positive he had never seen him before. The man groaned and his eyelids fluttered as he tried to turn his head. Petru knew he would not be unconscious for long and quickly searched the man's pockets for some form of ID, but found nothing.

Even though Petru had worked for the syndicate, he had never used a gun. Turning the gun over in his hands now, he found what looked like the safety catch. Next to the safety slide was a small red dot, which he presumed meant the safety lock was off and the gun was ready to fire. As Petru gripped the gun in the firing position, he thought about what the syndicate had done to Elena.

Petru pointed the gun at the man's head and put his finger around the trigger. He paused as a numb feeling spread over him. Despite his hatred for the man and the organization he represented, something inside prevented him from pulling the trigger. He frowned. Clearly, the man came to kill him. He sighed as he re-engaged the gun's safety switch. He was not a killer and never would be. The man stirred again and Petru knew it was time to leave the apartment block for good. Using his hands, he crawled back up the stairs.

After clambering back into his wheelchair, he placed the gun and his travel bag in his lap. Petru hoped not to meet anyone at this hour of the night, but he did not want to take any chances. He wheeled back to the elevator and pressed the call button, conscious that the man would recover shortly. While he waited for the elevator to arrive, he thought about what had just happened and contemplated his future. He was lucky to be alive. With little money and being confined to a wheelchair, he knew he was still an easy target, even with a gun.

The elevator doors opened and Petru wheeled himself inside. He felt no euphoria as he pressed the button for the ground floor. As the elevator doors closed, he knew the odds were still stacked against him and it would be a miracle if he were still alive in a week's time.

Chapter Thirty-Seven

The elevator seemed to take forever to reach the ground floor. Petru used the time to think about his escape. Front or rear exit? If the hit man had a partner, he would probably wait out front in a car. Razvan wouldn't be expecting to chase a guy in a wheelchair and covering the rear exit seemed an overkill. He decided his escape would be through the rear doors. The laneway would allow him to get well away from the building under the cover of darkness. He was hopeful he could find a spot to hide before they gave chase.

Gritting his teeth, Petru awaited the ding of the elevator bell as it reached the ground floor. It was possible there was a second man stationed in the lobby to cover the elevator and the stairs. If that were the case, he figured this could almost be his last breath. He raised the gun into a firing position as the elevator door slid open. Petru could see no one in the shadows of the lobby. After dropping the gun back in his lap, he rolled forward two feet. Far enough to see out into the full lobby, but not far enough that he couldn't back into the elevator if needed.

He couldn't see anyone lurking in the shadows and rolled forward another two feet. He glanced through the glass panels of the front door of the building. No one seemed to be lurking outside on the street. He had seen enough and spun his wheelchair to the left and headed for the rear exit. Unlike the front door, the rear door was solid. There was no way that he could see out into the laneway and if someone was waiting out there, they would have him cold.

Petru took a deep breath as he reached up and opened the door with his left hand. He backed up his wheelchair with his right hand, stopping when he had the door open about three feet. He wheeled forward and felt the chill of the night air as he emerged into the laneway. He gave his eyes a moment to adjust to the darkness. As he heard the click of the door as it closed behind him, he was conscious of a second sound—footsteps. They were deliberate but not hurried. Petru let out a gasp as he spun his wheelchair around and stared at a man in a dark overcoat. The man was about six-two. Petru realized he had seen him before as he pulled a gun from his coat pocket and pointed it at his chest.

They stood staring at each other for several seconds. The man in the coat asked, "Is my partner dead?"

Petru shook his head and said, "No," as he racked his brain to figure a way out of his dilemma. He frowned and added, "I've seen you before. You were the driver in the van."

The man gave a subtle nod. The gun remained rock steady in his hand as he asked, "If he's not dead, then where is he?"

A lump formed in Petru's throat. "He's currently unconscious in the stairwell. I think I broke his wrist."

"How on earth did you do that?" said the man with a slight shake of his head.

"I'm just trying to survive."

They stared at each other for a few more seconds. Petru debated picking up the gun from his lap. But he realized the man would shoot him long before he got the gun into a firing position. "So, what are you going to do? Kill a cripple in a wheelchair?"

The man nodded. "Razvan wants you dead."

"Even though I spared you your life in the van?"

The man shrugged. "Life is complicated."

"I saved your life twice that night."

The man stepped forward until there were only about eight feet separating them. He cocked his head to one side and barked, "And how do you figure that?"

Petru stared him down. "First, it would have been far easier for me just to put a bullet in your brain. Spreading your brains across the windshield would have been a lot less effort than tying you up."

"That I get," said the man with a nod. "But what's the second way?"

"I left you with your gun. Remember? I told you to drop the gun on the floor in the front before I got you to climb in the back."

The man nodded again but said nothing.

"After I had you tied up, I just wanted to get away. I didn't need a second gun…"

Petru did his best to control his breathing as he added, "I used to work for Razvan and I know how he operates. It occurred to me later that if you had your gun, you could tell Razvan whatever you wanted to save yourself. You were just the driver. A scuffle broke out in the back, and there was a gunshot. By the time you had the van pulled over, I had escaped and your partner was dead."

Petru paused and then murmured, "That story would be a lot harder to sell if you couldn't produce your weapon."

The man glared at Petru.

Petru asked, "Am I right?"

The man kept the gun trained on Petru's chest. "If I let you go, I'm signing my death warrant."

Petru nodded. "But if you shoot me, you're going to have to live with the fact that you shot someone who spared your life. Someone who now lives permanently in a wheelchair. Can you live with that?"

Before the man could answer, a crackly voice said, "Kostos should've been in and out by now. Have you seen him?"

Without breaking eye contact, the man produced a small two-way radio from his pocket. "It's all quiet here. I haven't seen him."

The voice said, "Hold your position. I'm going in through the front to check on him. I'll let you know what I find."

The man responded, "Okay," and then put the two-way back in his jacket pocket. He stared at Petru for a second and then said, "I'm not sure why I said that. But I did, and it's done."

He lowered the weapon, and added, "We're even. If I see you again, I won't hesitate to put a bullet in you."

Chapter Thirty-Eight

Petru wheeled his chair up the ramp and positioned it next to the roller door. Despite the cold, he was hot and sweaty. After reaching up a hand to wipe his brow, he closed his eyes and slumped forward in his chair for a moment to catch his breath. It was close to ten AM, and he desperately needed sleep. He had been on the run ever since encountering the second hit man in the laneway. After escaping the apartment, he had immediately sought another hiding place. In a nearby laneway, he found an unlocked rear door to another apartment block. Petru had wheeled inside and then hid in a ground floor alcove while he planned his next move. He recognized the danger of staying in the city while Razvan tried to hunt him down.

He considered holing up in a secluded, cash-only hotel. But that was still a risk. A guy in a wheelchair was an easy target for Razvan to track down. He considered going back to Băleni, but that could endanger his mother. He had settled on returning to the abandoned warehouse for now. The seclusion made up for the lack of running water and freezing nights. He figured he would be safe enough here until he figured out his next move. He had waited until morning before leaving his hiding spot to join the morning rush to the train station. The trip to Sector 4 was uneventful, and the train ride gave him thinking time.

He groaned as he pulled up the roller door. As a paraplegic, he knew this was another easy task for most that he would struggle with for the rest of his life. After getting the door up about five feet, he rolled inside. He did a quick scan of the interior to make sure he was alone. Once satisfied, he lowered the door and wedged in a bar to prevent it being opened from the outside. He needed sleep, but he was also hungry. Petru wheeled himself over to his food locker and removed a tin of beans and a bottle of water. While he ate and drank, he gazed up at the pulley system that he would need to use to get to his sleeping quarters. He decided he would wait a few more minutes for his strength to return before he attempted to hoist himself up.

Petru let out a sigh as he thought about the last twenty-four hours. His friend was dead and Razvan had closed the net on him far quicker than he expected. He figured they must have beaten the apartment's location out of Nicolai before they had killed him. Petru shivered as he thought about how much Nicolai must have suffered. He looked down at his phone out of habit and realized he had a missed call from Robbie Mayne. He was grateful for the distraction and called his answering service.

"Hi Codos, it's Robbie. I'm sending you a digital voice file by email in about twenty minutes. It's a recording of Richard Stelovak's voice command to authorize the release of funds from two secret banks accounts. It's a long story how I came across this, but a former business partner double crossed Stelovak by planting a bug in his office to record his conversations. These two accounts have three million dollars of bribe money in them. If you know the account numbers, and I believe you do, the money is yours. The two associates who the money was meant for are both dead. I'll explain it all later, but you need to act fast. When Stelovak and Razvan find out these guys are dead, they'll move the money and the opportunity will be gone. I'll call you tomorrow. Take care."

Petru shook his head. He couldn't believe what he had just heard. He played the message back twice to make sure he had heard it correctly. He wondered what kind of deal Razvan and Stelovak had going if it required millions in bribe money. Petru hoped Robbie was safe. People were dying on both sides of the world and he had a feeling the body count was going to continue to mount. He pulled his laptop out of his carry bag and powered it up as he thought about the money. He was trying to go straight and planned never to steal from anyone ever again. But taking money from Razvan and Stelovak seemed like a reasonable payback for the injuries he had suffered. He frowned as he recalled the last email he had received from Nicolai. He was sure it had included the numbers for the two accounts Robbie had referred to, but not the passwords. Petru grimaced. If Nicolai had them, he had never passed them on.

He gritted his teeth and then murmured, "So close and yet, so far." The account numbers were of no use to him without a password for access. The skills he had gained in his fraud career were no match for a bank. They typically gave you five or six access attempts before the account was suspended for an incorrect password.

Petru clicked on his email's Inbox to check for new

messages anyway. The most recent one on his list was from Robbie Mayne, as he expected.

C, I hope this email finds you still alive, and that you got my earlier voice mail message. I have attached a file which has a recording of Richard Stelovak's voice on it. The recording is a voice authorization to release funds from two bank accounts. I don't know the account numbers, but I'm told you do? If that's the case, please withdraw the money and use it for yourself (no one deserves it more than you). I'll call you in a day or so once I'm safe. Take care! R BTW - here are the passwords as well. They were secretly recorded as well, but I don't know which account they go with, but I'm sure you can figure it out: Account 1 Password: xc82kdH6A9c8 Account 2 Password: f8eU39Mcs2l9

Petru stared at the message in disbelief. In theory, he had everything he needed to withdraw the money.

Petru knew there was no time to spare. He copied Stelovak's voice file to his phone and then switched to the Internet browser on his laptop. With his hands shaking and his heart racing, he brought up the online banking portal for the Roma bank. He clicked through the welcome screen and then keyed in the first account number. He took a deep breath when the browser prompted him for a password. Petru keyed in the first password provided by Robbie Mayne. He double checked his keystrokes and murmured, "Please, God," as he pressed enter. He cursed out loud as the browser returned a message he had seen a million times before.

Incorrect User ID, account number or password.

Undeterred, Petru re-keyed the account number, and

then clicked on the password field again. Carefully, he keyed in the second password, checking each letter and number as he went. When satisfied that it was correct, he pressed enter again. The screen refreshed. But rather than an error message, Petru was presented with an account information screen. His mouth fell open as he read the balance of the account; one-and-a-half-million. Petru shook his head as he re-read the number, unable to believe he was this close to so much money.

Petru felt a rush of adrenaline through his body. He noticed the transfer button on the top menu of the screen was grayed out. He saw a red button labeled 'Voice Authorization' beside it. Petru clicked on it and a microphone icon appeared. Petru had seen this extra layer of security before and held up his phone near the computer. He clicked the microphone button on the Internet banking application and then play on his phone. He found it hard to stop shaking as he heard Richard Stelovak's voice for the first time:

'Richard Stelovak, funds transfer approved.'

Petru's eyes widened as the Internet banking screen on his laptop refreshed again. A lump formed in his throat as the screen now prompted him to enter the bank account details for his funds' transfer.

Petru awoke to the sound of his phone alarm. He rubbed sleep from eyes as he checked the time on his phone. It was just after one PM. He had been asleep for just on two hours. He figured that was enough to keep him functioning while he planned his escape from the city. He realized now that even staying at the warehouse was too dangerous. People could have spotted him at the train station or while he was making his way to the warehouse. Razvan had a broad network, making it possible that even this location could now be compromised.

He propped up on one elbow and stared across at his wheelchair. He had worried about leaving it on the ground floor while he slept. The chair would be a dead giveaway to his presence if someone broke in while he slept. He decided he needed to hoist it up to the mezzanine and hide it in his room while he slept. He had found a length of rope in the shelving units and tied it to one end of it to his chair. After using the pulley system to lift himself safely up on the mezzanine, he had hauled the chair up after him. It had been a struggle, but he figured it was worth the peace of mind it brought him.

Petru sat up and leaned back against the wall. He made himself comfortable on the mattress and contemplated what he had to do. He needed a safe place to stay far from the city. He figured he would target a large regional town. Somewhere big enough that it had a hospital, doctors, and the medical facilities he would need. He would target somewhere at least two hours' drive from Bucharest. He hoped that would be far enough away from Razvan's clutches. Second, he would need transport. He would have to hire a wheelchair taxi and a driver willing to accept a large fare for a long out-of-town trip. Petru yawned—he would have liked more sleep, but that would need to wait. He would sleep the sleep of the dead when he was settled in his new location.

After opening up his laptop, he launched his Firefox browser. He had just keyed in his search terms for suitable towns when his phone buzzed. He stared down at the screen —it was Robbie Mayne.

Petru pressed answer and said, "Hi Robbie."

"Hi, Codos. It's good to hear your voice."

"And you. Are you safe?"

"Yeah. I'm holed up in a farmhouse out of Vancouver until this is over. It's been crazy here."

As he looked around the filthy room he had just slept in, Petru responded, "It's crazy here, too, Robbie."

"Are you safe?"

"I'm hiding out in an old warehouse," said Petru with a frown. "But I don't think anywhere in Bucharest is safe anymore. I'm making plans to get out of the city. Today is my last day, in fact."

"I think that's wise."

"So, from your last email, it looks like you're taking some serious heat over there?"

"The body count is mounting up. Another three people associated with Stelovak and Razvan died yesterday. It's a long story, but if you're making plans to get out of the city, that needs to be your focus. We'll talk about this more when you're settled."

They were silent for a moment before Robbie added, "Did you get the money?"

Petru let out a short laugh. "It's in my bank account. I can't believe it, Robbie. I'm richer than I could ever imagine. And I can't thank you enough."

"No need to thank me. It was dirty money, and after what you've been through, you deserve it more than anyone. Can I help you with anything?"

"You've already done more than enough, Robbie. I don't know how I can ever repay you. Thank you just doesn't seem enough."

"You already have repaid me, Codos. My analyst is busy going through all the information you gave us and joining up a lot of the dots. Razvan and Stelovak's crime syndicate is now on Interpol's radar, thanks to you."

Petru thought of Nicolai as he responded, "I'm glad we could help."

"If you're making plans to get out of the city, I don't want to hold you up. Call me when you get settled and you have more time to talk."

"Okay, sounds good. Before I go, there's one more thing you should know…"

"What's that?"

"My real name is Petru. We've come a long way and I don't need to talk in code anymore."

"Thanks for trusting me, Petru. Stay safe and call me if you need anything."

"Thanks, Robbie."

Petru disconnected and then rummaged around in his bag. He pulled out the gun he'd taken from the hit man in the stairwell. He turned it over in his hands and thought about how much more useful it would be now with live ammunition. He figured the man who had broken into his apartment must have used all his bullets trying to blast his way out of the locked bedroom door. He sighed as he put the gun to one side and searched through his bag again. He found his battery power-pack and plugged it in to his phone to keep it fully charged. He then picked up his laptop again and returned to his search for out-of-the-way hotels in country towns. As he scrolled through the list, he decided he wouldn't be too choosy, at least not to start with. The main objective was to get out of the city as soon as he could. He would allow himself a maximum of twenty minutes to find something suitable and then he would order his wheelchair cab. Petru glanced at the clock on his laptop again. He hoped to be on his way out of the city within the hour.

Chapter Thirty-Nine

The next thirty minutes were a blur for Petru. After finding a suitable country hotel to stay in, he had packed his bag and ordered a wheelchair taxi to pick him up. Out of habit, he had checked the rear laneway before lowering himself to the ground floor. Petru stared in disbelief as he saw a black Mercedes cruising up the rear laneway. He knew before the vehicle stopped that Razvan had found him.

A bloodbath had followed as three men stormed the building. One of them fell through the ramp as it collapsed and now lay splattered on the ground floor. The second man, the Mercedes driver, still had his arm hooked through a broken window next to the upstairs fire exit. He hung limp and hadn't moved in five minutes. Petru suspected he was dead as well. The third man, whose body lay just four feet in front of him, was unconscious. It was difficult to tell whether the blow he had delivered to the man's skull had killed him or not, but he wasn't moving.

But Petru wasn't concerned about the man's health. His focus was on the gun the third man had dropped. It lay on the floor next to the man's body. Petru let go of the crowbar and slid out of his wheelchair. As he dragged his body forward, he became aware of another presence in the building. He looked up and saw a figure standing in the shadows next to the fire exit. The figure showed no urgency as he studied the driver's body which was still caught in the broken window frame.

Petru knew it was Razvan before he emerged from the shadows. The man raised his gun and pointed it at Petru's head as he walked forward. A cruel grin spread across the face of his nemesis as he moved along the corridor. Razvan stopped about halfway along the mezzanine and leaned over the balustrade. He let out a low whistle as his gaze settled on the man who lay on the concrete below. Razvan shook his head. "Unbelievable."

He returned his gaze to Petru and nodded toward the man who lay in front of him. "Is he dead too?"

Petru pretended to study the man for a moment. Razvan hadn't seen the man's gun yet because his body hid it from view. He figured if Razvan took a few more steps forward, the gun would become visible. The gun was six inches from Petru's fingertips. Before becoming a paraplegic, it would have taken him a fraction of a second to reach forward and pick it up. But as a paraplegic, dragging his body forward enough would take him much longer. He admonished himself to stop Razvan from coming any closer until he had picked up the weapon.

To keep the conversation going, Petru responded, "I don't know."

Keeping the gun trained on Petru, Razvan stared at the pulley system. "Is this how you get up and down?"

Petru nodded.

Razvan shook his head as his focus switched to the

collapsed ramp. "I've gotta hand it to you. For someone in a wheelchair, you're proving to be hard to kill."

Razvan's gaze returned to Petru as he added, "But your luck has run out."

"So it would seem."

Razvan leaned back against the balustrade. "We can do this the easy way or the hard way. The easy way is you give me what I want, and I'll make it quick and clean. One bullet to the head. It will be painless and over in a second…"

He let his words sink in before he added, "The alternative is I shoot you in the stomach and let you bleed out slowly. You may not be able to feel your legs, but you'll scream like a pig. It's your choice…"

Petru had a good idea what Razvan was angling for, but asked anyway. "What do you want?"

"I've had some communication with my uncle in Vancouver. It appears three million has gone missing from two of our accounts. We both think you stole it."

A lump formed in Petru's throat. "Why do you think I have the money?"

"Your friend, Nicolai, became very talkative…" said Razvan with a sneer. "Before the end, we learned a lot of information about you and the money. We've checked the two accounts and they're both empty. We've got the bank tracing the money trail, but I don't care to wait."

Petru thought about his answer as he tried to buy time. "Let's say I know where the money is. How do I know you'll live up to your end of the deal?"

Razvan sneered. "You don't. But let me put it to you this way; there are a lot of bodies here and I don't intend to be around when the police arrive and start asking questions."

Petru nodded.

"I want to finish this as soon as possible. And I don't plan on leaving any witnesses for the police to interrogate."

Petru glanced down at the gun again and noticed the unconscious man's phone had slipped out of his pocket. He had an idea and said, "The information is on my phone," as he dragged his body forward.

Razvan shouted, "What are you doing?"

Razvan started shouting as he strode forward. Petru responded, "I'm just retrieving my phone—I dropped it on the floor." As he used the man's body for cover, Petru gripped the gun in his right hand and the phone in his left.

Razvan continued to scream at him as Petru lobbed the phone in Razvan's direction. Razvan stopped and stuck out his left hand to catch the device as it spiraled through the air.

Petru ducked his head and fired blindly at his nemesis. The gun bucked in his hand and made a booming sound that echoed throughout the building with each shot he fired. He knew little about guns or the capacity of their magazines. The gun he was firing was a standard Glock 40 with a fifteen-bullet magazine. He kept pulling the trigger until the magazine was empty.

Petru only stopped firing the weapon when the booming discharge of the gun was replaced by clicks signaling the magazine was empty. He kept his head down, expecting to hear Razvan's footsteps striding forward to finish him. But he heard nothing. Slowly, he raised his head above the man's body. He looked along the mezzanine walkway. Razvan lay in a crumpled heap on the floor. He wasn't moving and didn't make a sound.

Petru wondered if he was dead until he saw the fingers of his right hand twitch. Using his arms and hands, Petru raised himself up as much as he could. He scanned the floor for any sign of Razvan's gun and spotted it about ten feet in front of him. Getting hold of the gun was the key to his survival. Petru started dragging himself forward. He heard Razvan let out a groan and gritted his teeth as he saw Razvan lift his head. He was still six feet from the gun, and Razvan appeared to be recovering quicker than he expected.

Petru inched forward as Razvan rolled onto his side. He heard Razvan mutter, "Son of a bitch." He lifted his head again and watched as Razvan examined the left leg of his jeans, which were covered in blood. Petru kept pulling himself forward, his focus now solely on the gun, as Razvan tried to get to his feet. He got to within three feet of the gun, when Razvan let out a bloodcurdling cry. He looked up to see Razvan now standing unsteadily on his feet. His nemesis stepped forward, but his leg collapsed beneath him.

Razvan crashed to the floor beside him. They both reached for the gun, but Razvan was a fraction quicker. After grabbing the weapon, Razvan swung it around towards Petru's head. The gun discharged as Petru grabbed a hold of Razvan's right hand. The shot went wide but left a ringing sound in Petru's ear. Both men struggled as Razvan tried to swing the weapon towards Petru's face again. Petru kept his two hands wrapped tightly around Razvan's right hand. The gun discharged twice in quick succession, but both shots hit the wall high above them. The men fought for control of the weapon for almost a minute. Petru ended up on his back, staring up into Razvan's face, but maintained his vice grip on the gun. Razvan grew impatient and started screaming obscenities as he fired the weapon again in frustration. But Petru matched his opponent's strength and held the weapon wide of his head as it discharged.

When the magazine was empty, Razvan let go of the weapon and hit Petru flush on the jaw with a vicious left across. The blow momentarily dazed him as Razvan murmured, "I'll strangle you with my bare hands."

Petru was conscious of Razvan's hands wrapping around his neck. Without the use of his legs, he found it impossible to roll Razvan off him. He knew his only hope was to fight fire with fire as Razvan's vice-like grip started to crush his larynx. Reaching up, he clamped his hands around Razvan's neck. Petru gritted his teeth as Razvan thrashed about trying to break free. Petru felt his brain fogging through lack of oxygen as Razvan maintained his hold. He willed himself to stay conscious, knowing it would soon be over for whomever passed out first. Razvan's grip held firm as he looked into Petru's eyes. Petru larynx burned like fire as he tried to break his captive's grip. The pair struggled for close to a minute as each man refused to yield. Petru was buoyed by the sight of his nemesis' face turning red as his eyes began to bulge. Petru's lungs were now on fire, screaming for oxygen. He maintained his grip on Razvan's neck as he sensed his opponent's strength beginning to wane. Razvan's face turned into swaying images of yellow, blue and green as the room began to spin. Petru felt an urge to vomit before his world faded to black.

Petru opened his eyes, but found it hard to breathe. He became aware of his surroundings as the roof of the warehouse came into focus. His throat was on fire, but he was still alive. He looked down at his chest and realized Luca Razvan was slumped across his body. Petru shoved hard and rolled Razvan off him. They were both covered in blood—Razvan's blood. He kept a wary eye on his nemesis while he recovered. When the warehouse stopped spinning, he glanced at his phone and realized he'd been unconscious for about ten minutes. Razvan hadn't moved. Petru reached out a hand and placed it on the carotid artery on Razvan's neck. He couldn't feel a pulse and assumed Razvan had died of blood loss from the bullet wound to his leg. Petru felt no remorse. But nor did he feel any sense of justice or triumph. All he felt was relief. Relief that this nightmare was over… hopefully.

Petru waited for his strength to return and then rolled over onto his stomach. Using his arms, he dragged his body forward towards the pulley system. His taxi would be here in fifteen minutes and he had no intention of missing it.

Epilogue

Petru asked the driver to slow down as he approached the village of Băleni. Little had changed in the ten years since his last visit. The open fields and farmland looked unchanged since his childhood. He felt a lump form in his throat as they drove through a small forest. He was close to the village, but still unsure about what to tell his mother. She would find his wheelchair confronting and he felt uneasy about telling her he was still on the run.

As they emerged from the forest, he found the sight of the first stucco houses in the village reassuring. They were a uniform blend of colors from off-white to terracotta. He figured most of them had changed very little in the decades since their construction. It was a reminder that not everything in the world was changing. He nodded to himself. Perhaps this was part of the reason his mother had wanted to return.

He closed his eyes and breathed in to ease his tension. The last forty-eight hours had been a nightmare, and he didn't want his mother seeing him on edge. After his encounter with Razvan and his men, he had lowered himself to the ground floor. Covered in blood, he had used most of his bottles of water to clean up before changing his clothes. He packed very few of his remaining belongings for the trip. Now that he was a multi-millionaire, he figured he would treat himself to some new clothes. He made it out to the front of the warehouse with just minutes to spare before the wheelchair taxi arrived.

He had planned to drive out of the city immediately. But after his ordeal, he needed food and sleep. He instructed his driver to take him to an out-of-the-way hotel on the city's outskirts. They agreed on a price for the trip out of the city the next day, which included a bonus for the detour via Băleni. The driver had picked him up at nine that morning and the trip had been uneventful.

He opened his eyes again as the taxi went over a pothole in the village's main street. It would not be long before he would see his mother again. Although he looked forward to seeing her, he knew the conversation would be difficult. She would insist he stay in the village and would be heartbroken to learn he had come to say goodbye.

The taxi drove on at a rambling pace. They passed the bank and court house which both looked unchanged since his last visit. They continued on past his uncle's bakery. It, too, looked unchanged. It was like stepping back in time; he thought. The streets were quiet. Nobody, not even the dogs, seemed to be in a hurry.

The taxi turned left into a side street and drove one more block to Aruk Street. His aunt and uncle's houses were side-by-side, about half-way down on the right-hand side. After the taxi pulled up out front, Petru waited patiently while the driver opened up the taxi's cargo door and lowered the wheelchair ramp. His aunt's house was hidden

The Catalin Connection

behind a five-foot-high brick fence. It was still unpainted, a task his aunt had planned to do for longer than he could remember. The two-storey stucco house with a terracotta tile roof was in dire need of painting. Despite its drab appearance, it had a homely feel.

As the driver helped him back his chair down the ramp, he asked Petru if he needed his help to get to the front door. Petru noticed a new sturdy wooden ramp on the footpath leading to the front door and declined the driver's offer. After agreeing on a return time, Petru waited until the taxi had driven off before he looked up at the house again. He took a deep breath and then wheeled forward up the ramp.

Feeling a mix of emotions, Petru knocked on the front door. He was eager to see his mother, yet anxious about the news he had to disclose. He heard a woman's voice inside before the door opened. His aunt, a stout woman in her early sixties, initially wore a cheery look on her face. But that quickly turned to a frown as she recognized her nephew.

She managed, "Petru, this is a surprise," as she stared at his wheelchair.

Petru managed half a smile. "Hello, Ana. How are you?"

His aunt recovered and said, "I'm fine. You have come to see your mother?"

Petru nodded. "I can't stay long. In fact, I'm just passing through."

His aunt opened the door wider and said, "Come, come. Your mother is in the back near the fire. I will go get her."

She led Petru through to a sitting room at the front of the house, and said, "I'm sure you and your mother have much to talk about. You can talk in here without being distracted."

Petru rehearsed what he would say while he waited. He heard muffled voices from somewhere else in the house and then a cry, which he recognized as his mother's voice.

Petru admonished himself to hold it together as the door to the sitting room opened again. He said, "Hello, Mamma," as his aunt pushed his mother's wheelchair into the room.

Petru's mother dissolved into tears as he wheeled forward. He did his best to control his emotions as he leaned across and hugged her. They both wept as they embraced.

Finally, his mother let go and said, "I thought I had lost you."

Petru shook his head. "I'm fine, Mamma."

"But you are in a wheelchair."

"It was the price I had to pay, Mamma," conceded Petru. "But the man who killed Elena will never hurt anyone again."

His mother pointed at his wheelchair. "Is this permanent?"

"For now. But I'm not dwelling on it. There are worse things in life than being in a wheelchair. You have said so yourself."

"But you are so young," said his mother with a shake of her head.

Petru didn't want to dwell on the subject and reached into a bag he had on his lap. "I have something for you."

His mother's protest that she needed nothing turned into a gasp as Petru withdrew the ashtray. She held a hand over her mouth. "Oh, Petru, you need this more than I do."

The Catalin Connection

"No, Mamma. This is rightfully yours," said Petru as he handed it to her.

His mother gazed at the object and then shook her head. "I spent hundreds of hours searching for this. How did you discover it was more than an ashtray?"

"I had to move around for my safety and needed to travel light. I was considering not taking it with me and noticed a scratch on the bottom. The metal color underneath was gold and not steel, as I expected…"

His mother shook her head. "I have everything I need here. I'm sure your father would approve of you melting it down and using the money to support yourself."

"I have had some good fortune, Mamma."

"Living in a wheelchair is not good fortune," said his mother with a frown.

Peru reached out and held her hand. "I need to tell you what has happened," he said, and then explained selected parts of his story. He glossed over the confrontations and the fact that he had killed five men. He focused on the investigation and the money he now had in his bank account.

His mother's eyes widened as he told her the amount. "Are you wanted by the police? Surely they are looking for the money?"

Petru hesitated. He knew the police would mount a full investigation into what had happened at the warehouse. But he didn't think they would suspect a guy in a wheelchair of being capable of that much carnage. And he knew an organized crime boss was not going report his bribe money as stolen.

He answered as truthfully as he could. "I'm not a suspect in any crime that I know of, Mamma. And that's not likely to change."

"Are you still in hiding?"

"It's safer this way," said Petru with a nod. "I'm not worried about the police, but a man in Vancouver with Romanian links concerns me. It is better that I stay in hiding until I know it's safe."

His mother's bottom lip quivered. "So, you are not staying?"

Petru felt a lump in his throat. "I can't, Mamma. If I stay here too long, I might put you in danger, and our family has been through enough."

"When will I see you again?"

"I'm not sure. I'll contact you when I can, but it might be a while before we see each other."

Petru reached across and hugged his mother.

She gripped him tight and refused to let go. "Promise me you will stay safe, Petru."

"I promise, Mamma."

Thirty minutes later, Petru was back in the taxi. Saying goodbye to his mother proved to be his greatest challenge. She seemed to understand that he needed to stay in hiding and he had promised to call her every other day. He took comfort knowing that she was happy with her new life.

Petru looked out the window as the taxi cruised towards Târgoviște. As they passed fields that were now fallow and ready for next year's crop, he saw a farmer working on his tractor. He appreciated the simple life of a farming village. But he wasn't sure it was the life for him as he contemplated his future. While he detested the smog and the traffic, the energy of the city had its attractions.

Petru smiled as he thought about the ashtray again. His

mother had been adamant she would not melt it down, as it had too much sentimental value. She had declared, "It will be yours one day, Petru. When I pass…"

He had insisted that he share some of his wealth with her. His mother initially refused. But she had then wavered when he suggested using the money for some home improvements to his aunt's house. Finally, she conceded a new heater and gas stove would make life more comfortable. He had transferred fifty thousand euros to her account as soon as he got back in the taxi. He knew she would spend only a fraction of that amount, but he felt better knowing it would improve her life.

Petru made a mental note of the things he needed to do when he got to Târgoviște. There were medical supplies, which he figured he would get while he still had the taxi. Next, he would check in to his hotel and enjoy a late lunch. He salivated at the thought of what he might order. With his wealth, he could now order anything on the menu. A medium-rare porterhouse steak with boiled potatoes was at the top of his list.

Afterward, he would take a nice, long bath in his suite. He frowned as he pondered the challenge of how he would get in and out of the tub. But the frown quickly turned to a smile. After what he had accomplished in his wheelchair, getting in and out of a bath was going to be like child's play.

Next in The Catalin Series

vinci-books.com/catalin-code

In a world of organized crime, trust is scarce, and survival is never guaranteed.

When Robbie Mayne's best friend dies under suspicious circumstances, he embarks on a perilous quest for the truth. As he navigates a treacherous web of deceit, Robbie finds himself entangled with a ruthless crime syndicate. With betrayal lurking around every corner and time running out, Robbie must risk everything to unravel the mystery before he becomes the next target.

Turn the page for a free preview…

The Catalin Code: Chapter One

The Priest made the sign of the cross and started the final part of the funeral service as they lowered the casket into the ground. Frustrated by a flight delay, Robbie had arrived a few minutes after the service had begun and had been forced to stand at the back of the assembled group of mourners. As he surveyed the gathered crowd, he saw a number of faces he recognized—some he had not seen since high school. Today, like Robbie, they all wore a look of shock and grief as they paid their respects and said a last goodbye.

Jet lagged from a non-stop flight home from London, the last twenty-four hours had been a giant blur. No sooner had he got off the plane than his phone had started to ring. As a freelance journalist, he was used to wading through dozens of messages while he waited for his baggage after a long-haul flight. The second message this time had been from his mother, asking him to call her as soon as he could. He knew from the tone of her voice that something was wrong. When he returned the call, he could barely believe his mother's words.

"I'm so sorry, Robbie. Aaron has been killed in an accident."

His mother explained that his childhood friend, Aaron MacDonald, had died three nights earlier in a hit-and-run accident near to his apartment in Vancouver. His mother didn't know the details, other than the police believed it was most likely a drunk driver. She apologized for not being able to get the message through sooner and explained the funeral arrangements, but by then, Robbie was no longer listening.

Robbie felt guilty that he had not seen 'Mac' for some time. After collecting his bags, he had sat in an airport lounge for almost two hours, finding it difficult to accept that his oldest and most trusted friend was gone. As Robbie listened to the priest's words, he recalled the day their lives changed forever while they were still in high school.

They had been through a lot together. As he stood with his head bowed, Robbie remembered how much he had relied on Mac in later years following the car accident that had killed his wife Annie and left him requiring months of rehabilitation. Mac had been his rock through his recovery. The doctors healed him physically, but Mac was the one who got him out of his funk and helped him start again.

It didn't seem fair that the anchor in his life since Annie's death was now gone as well. He listened intently to the rest of the service and then said his own prayer at the end. As the mourners dispersed, Robbie worked his way through the crowd to speak to Mac's sister, Laura.

Although he hadn't seen Laura for nearly three years, he knew Mac and his sister had remained close. Robbie knew Laura would be doing it tough.

As he moved through the crowd, a deep gravelly voice called out, "Robbie?"

Turning around, Robbie looked into the face of a tall man who was dressed in a dark suit and wearing sunglasses. Although he was now slightly heavier and had a full head of graying hair, Robbie would have recognized Nick Carney anywhere. Slightly taken aback at seeing Nick amongst the mourners, Robbie reached out and shook Nick's hand.

"It's been a while, Nick."

Nick nodded and replied, "Twenty-five years, Robbie."

Robbie tried to hide his surprise as he thought about what to say in response. He had not seen Nick since the end of high school. He remembered Nick had left their hometown of Cypress Falls on a sporting scholarship to study for a degree in criminology.

After graduating, he had joined the Vancouver Metropolitan Police as a base grade police officer before transferring to the newly formed state Organized Crime Task Force. Robbie had followed Nick's career through the newspapers, as he featured regularly as part of a successful team breaking up crime gangs. He had risen steadily through the ranks and had made Deputy Director of the OCTF in his late thirties.

As tactfully as he could put it, Robbie asked, "I didn't know you and Mac kept in contact after school?"

Nick lowered his voice just slightly and replied, "Let's just say I'm here because one of the four of us honored the promise we made and took what we knew to the grave."

Nick waited for a response and when none was forthcoming, he took off his sunglasses and studied Robbie with a slight look of amusement. "You'd have to be suffering from brain damage, not to remember, Robbie?"

"I remember, Nick. Even though it was at the end of

high school, not a single day goes by that I don't think about it."

Nick nodded and began scanning the crowd as he replied, "You see Jerry here today?"

"My connecting flight into Vancouver was delayed and I arrived late. You're the first person I've spoken to."

"You'd think if the Director General of the OCTF could make the funeral of a former school friend, so could the Mayor?"

Robbie remembered reading about Nick's recent promotion to the Director General role when the incumbent had retired after a protracted battle with Parkinson's disease. It had surprised him that Nick had made it to the top job after surviving a corruption incident several years ago. Several of his senior colleagues were still serving jail time after being found guilty and he wondered whether Nick got the job because of his ability, or because he was the last man standing?

Ignoring Nick's big noting of himself, Robbie replied, "I guess Jerry's schedule keeps him busy."

Nick replied flatly, "I wouldn't know."

Robbie knew Jerry and Nick's friendship had soured in recent years. After high school, they had remained close friends as they built their careers until Jerry had made a run for Mayor. Jerry's electoral campaigning happened at the same time Nick was making the newspapers as one of those allegedly involved in the OCTF scandal. Jerry had been a prominent Vancouver lawyer at the time and had publicly distanced himself from Nick to avoid any collateral damage to his campaign for the Mayor's Office.

Their relationship never recovered after they exonerated Nick, and the two continued to trade the occasional insult at one another when the opportunity arose in the media.

Robbie had no interest in pursuing the conversation and felt the feeling was mutual as he watched Nick put on his sunglasses and scan the crowd.

"Hey, Nick, I'm going to head over and catch up with Laura."

Nick nodded as he kept scanning the crowd. "You do that, Robbie, and if you see the good mayor of Vancouver, remind him that Mac's untimely demise changes nothing."

Before Robbie responded, Nick moved off into the crowd of mourners. Robbie shook his head. Nick had been arrogant and self-serving in high school, and nothing appeared to have changed in the years following.

While monitoring the crowd for Jerry, Robbie waded through the sea of mourners to pass on his condolences to Laura. Mac had never married and most people who attended the funeral seemed to be aware of how close Laura had been to her brother. Robbie waited to see her, almost as if he was in a queue as other groups gathered to offer their condolences as well.

He watched Laura as she spoke to the couple ahead of him. Even though she was close to forty, she had lost none of her beauty. He was worried about how she would cope now that her brother was gone. Laura had worked for many years as a police officer and was serving with the OCTF when the corruption incident broke in the newspapers.

Unlike Nick, who knew how to play the political games, Laura had resigned because of the stress from being hounded by the media, even though she was totally innocent. He recalled how Mac had helped her get back on her feet again as she struggled with a drinking problem and a difficult divorce in the aftermath.

As he watched her say a last farewell to the couple ahead

of him, he made a mental note to check on her regularly in the months ahead to make sure she didn't sink into a long-term depression again. Still seated, Laura turned towards Robbie and as soon as she recognized who it was, she rose and came forward. Unable to hide her grief, she wept uncontrollably as Robbie held her tightly. They held each other for a long time, neither embarrassed nor feeling the need to speak.

Finally, Robbie said, "I'm so sorry, Laura."

"I'm sorry for you too, Robbie. I know he meant as much to you as he did to me."

Laura sobbed again, and Robbie squeezed her tighter.

After recovering slightly, Laura let go of Robbie and said, "I'm glad you could make the service, Robbie. Your mother told me you've been in Europe and I was worried you might have missed today."

"Mac was my best friend, Laura. I would never miss this."

"It means a lot to me that you're here. Mac has idolized you since you were teenagers, and I'm glad you got to say goodbye."

Robbie frowned. "It's such a shock, Laura. I'm still having trouble believing he's gone. I spoke to him a few days ago when I was in Europe, but I never expected it would be the last time I would ever talk to him."

"I feel the same way, Robbie. I'm numb all over and just can't believe it's really happened."

"Have the police arrested anyone yet?"

Laura shook her head. "Robbie, I need to talk to you about Mac. But not here and not now. Are you in town for a day or two?"

Robbie had made no plans beyond today. He had to complete a story on white-collar crime syndicates he had been working on, but he had planned to fly back home to the east coast to do that.

"I don't have any actual plans so, sure, I'll fit in with you."

"It might be nothing, but I'd like to talk, anyway. Mac hadn't been himself for the last few weeks and some things don't add up. It's probably nothing, but you know him better than anyone else, Robbie, so if you don't mind?"

Robbie wasn't sure how to respond. He remembered how stressed Mac has seemed on the phone when they had last spoken. It was totally out of character for his friend, who was usually very laid back. Robbie had promised to call as soon as he returned, and he now wondered if it was somehow connected?

He knew now was not the time to talk about it and replied, "Sure, it would be nice to catch up, Laura."

They said their goodbyes and agreed to meet after Robbie had recovered from his jet lag. Robbie looked around the crowd at several familiar faces he knew he should catch up with, but he wasn't in the mood to talk. Instead, he went back to his rental car and sat thinking about the accident.

He watched as the mourners slowly dissipated and the cemetery grounds men came and filled in Mac's grave. When they had finished, Robbie got out of the car and walked back to the graveside. Now alone, he stared down at the fresh mound of earth and still found it difficult to believe his friend was gone.

He did his best to remember some of the good times they had together, but his mood darkened as he thought back to nineteen eighty-nine and what Nick had said earlier. One of the four of them had taken what they knew to the grave as they had all promised.

He wondered whether Jerry ever thought about what had happened? He was disappointed he hadn't come to the funeral. He knew Mac and Jerry had stayed in touch and got together for the occasional meal. Surely nobody was that busy that they couldn't find time to say goodbye to someone they had shared so much with?

He thought about Laura again and wondered again what she meant when she said, 'some things didn't add up.' The more he thought about it, the more uneasy he felt. He pulled his smartphone from his pocket and opened up his email application. Using his finger, he quickly scrolled back to the last message he had received from Mac.

To: robert.mayne@promail.com From: <Mac/>
Subject: Call ASAP

Robbie,

Please call me as soon as you get off the plane. It doesn't matter what time of day or night. A lot has happened while you've been away, and we need to talk.
Mac

Robbie looked down again at the fresh mound of earth. Hit and runs were normally an accident, but he knew he couldn't leave it at that. He would need to make sure.

Robbie wanted to say a few last words out loud to his friend, but knew he wasn't strong enough to get them out coherently. Instead, he silently thanked Mac for his friendship and murmured, "It's not over, Mac", before he turned and walked away.

The Catalin Code: Chapter Two

Dressed in a charcoal gray Italian designer suit, Richard Stelovak sat at the defense table and cautiously watched the jury file back into the stately wood paneled courtroom. He ignored the murmurings of the sizable crowd in the visitors' gallery and glanced down discretely at his watch. They had only been out for a little over an hour, which he took to be a good sign.

With slim, angular features, manicured nails and a two-hundred-dollar haircut, Stelovak looked every bit the accomplished, middle-aged business executive. He had been attentive throughout the trial, polite to the judge and opposing council attorneys, and had carefully followed the script prepared by his defense team.

His legal team's attention to detail impressed Stelovak, and he was confident the seven-figure sum he had paid to retain them and buy off the judge would be worth it. He had followed their instructions to the letter; no guarded whispers at any point to lawyers during the trial unless scripted, no doodling on notepads, looking at the ceiling, staring at jury members, or anyone else for that matter. He would be judged as much on his demeanor as his testimony as he sat on show in front of the jury.

The contacts had been a nice touch as well. His penetrating blue eyes gave him an aloof, if not cold and calculating look. To the jury, his eyes appeared a warm hazel color that was in keeping with the compassionate, law-abiding image the defense team had been cultivating for him throughout the trial.

Stelovak was as annoyed as he was anxious about the trial. In the middle of finalizing a development deal that would provide Stelecom with over two billion dollars in development and construction revenue over the next five years, the trial was something he did not need. He was glad the trial would be over today and satisfied that everything that could be done had been done to get the right verdict.

Arriving as a seventeen-year-old Romanian immigrant and speaking little English, Stelovak had quickly found his way into the gang culture in Vancouver but was smart enough to realize he would be dead before he was thirty if he didn't get out and make it on his own. Carefully using and exploiting every legal and illegal option at his disposal, he had left nothing to chance as he built Stelecom Industries from a modest earth moving business into a multi-million-dollar construction and development company. Today was no exception.

Besides Randolph Keaton, his twenty-nine-year-old in-house legal counsel, who, for an annual retainer of four hundred thousand dollars was on call twenty-four hours a day, Stelovak had engaged three of the finest from the law firm, Phipps, Babb and Associates, including Michael Phipps, one of their two senior partners.

Stelovak had hired Phipps and his firm not only for their

exceptional legal skills but also for the unique association they had with several judges on the bench who, for a fee, could discretely engineer court room outcomes. Bribes and payoffs were commonplace for Stelovak in his construction business and were always handled by highly trusted associates, using company entities completely separate to Stelecom. He had been careful about the bribe to be paid to the presiding judge, Simpson Hanley, and insisted they covered it under the single flat fee for legal services he paid to Phipps's law firm to make it impossible to trace.

The verdict in favor of Stelovak's company in a lawsuit brought by the widow of a subcontractor who had been crushed to death by a hydraulic lift on a Stelecom construction site had been negotiated weeks earlier. Intermediaries for both Phipps and the judge had brokered the deal by phone without ever meeting. Hanley had a string of gambling debts and found himself in need of money to stop his problem from going public. A discrete one hundred and seventy-five-thousand-dollar cash bonus would be paid if he could deliver a favorable outcome for the defendant. As promised, he made life in his courtroom hell for the plaintiff's team throughout the trial.

Stelovak looked across at their table. The confidence and swagger the lawyers had shown at the beginning of the trial was gone. They had not handled the trial or Judge Hanley at all well. They had given Phipps a lot of latitude and he was able to twist the facts and make a convincing argument that the hydraulic lift collapse had been accidental and the result of a design flaw, that the manufacturer had never reported to Stelecom.

Grab your copy...
vinci-books.com/catalin-code

About the Author

Trevor Douglas is a multi-award winning author and the recipient of the gold medal for the Best Crime Fiction Novel, and the gold medal for the Best Overall Novel in the 2024 Global Book Awards.

Trevor is married with two adult sons and when he is not writing, enjoys bushwalking, watching AFL and discovering the best coffee shops in Brisbane with his wife.

After a long and successful career as an IT consultant, Trevor now writes full time.

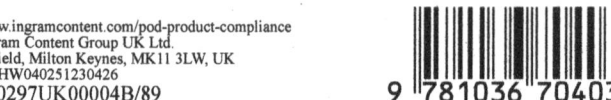

www.ingramcontent.com/pod-product-compliance
Ingram Content Group UK Ltd.
Pitfield, Milton Keynes, MK11 3LW, UK
UKHW040251230426
470297UK00004B/89